S0-BFD-078

My Name is Mata Hari

Remy Sylado

**English rendition by
Dewi Anggraeni**

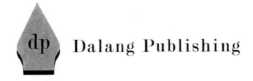 Dalang Publishing

My Name is Mata Hari
Originally published as *Namaku Mata Hari* in 2010 by Penerbit PT
Gramedia Pustaka Utama, Jakarta, Indonesia
(ISBN: 978-979-22-6281-0)
Copyright © 2010 Remy Sylado
English rendition copyright © 2012 Dewi Anggraeni

Cover design by Robert Kato
Book design by Son Do

All rights reserved. No part of this book may be reproduced or transmitted
in any form or by any means now known or to be invented, electronic or
mechanical, including photocopying, recording, or by any information
storage and retrieval system without written permission from the author
or publisher, except for the inclusion of brief quotations in a review.

Dalang Publishing LLC
San Mateo, CA
www.dalangpublishing.com
dalangpublishing@gmail.com

ISBN: 978-0-9836273-0-2
Library of Congress number: 2012938382

My Name is
Mata Hari

On the Rendition of
My Name is Mata Hari

Being a writer of fiction and nonfiction, I always maintain that you use the right side of your brain (intuitive) for fiction, and the left side (rational) for nonfiction. Producing novels, short stories, and plays is distinct from essays, articles, academic papers, reviews, and discussion papers. And translating or rendering fiction and non-fiction works into another language is not very different in terms of which side of the brain is used.

I know which side of my brain was active when I was rendering *Namaku Mata Hari* into *My Name is Mata Hari*. After working through one-third of the manuscript I had to drop other tasks related to writing because I was falling deeper into the story. It probably helped, I suspect, that I was familiar to a varying degree with the places where the main character, Mata Hari, is depicted as having visited and lived. The fact that the story is set in a much earlier era added to my curiosity and fascination with the ambiance of each place. As I followed Mata Hari in this historically dramatic context, I was drawn almost involuntarily further into her life. At some stage I actually moved into her psyche, and felt what she felt—confusion, despair, anger, frustration, vengeful, and powerless—followed by the discovery she had considerable power albeit not without the accompanying dilemma in exercising it. Throughout the story, I lived her pride at her own achievements. As a character, Mata Hari is a complex entity, and her life is remarkably possible and impossible all at once.

The work, while emotionally absorbing, was not without problems. Historical inaccuracies occur in any story of this scope and complexity, and the most glaring of these have been corrected. As the book was first published weekly in serial form, there was also inevitable repetition. For the English rendition, I reduced this repetition. This fortunately did not weaken the strong ties I had developed with the main character. In fact, toward the end I shed more than a few tears walking in her path. Even weeks after I finished the work, I was still a little dizzy and occasionally disoriented.

Yes, it's that kind of story.

Dewi Anggraeni
May 2012

My Name is
Mata Hari

Prologue

Mata Hari did not fear death.

Waiting in her cell at Saint-Lazare prison for execution by the military court, she raged at Père Arbaux in his black soutane and the nun in her blue habit she called Soeur. She bitterly complained that in her last hours she was not allowed to see the two people she loved.

Père and Soeur gave solace to Mata Hari and she understood the meaning of peace when the three were together. She asked them to convey to her daughter, Non, and her lover, Vadim Maslov, how pure and selfless her love had always been. In fact, it was this love that gave her the strength and courage to face death.

When she looked back at her life, Mata Hari was struck with extreme disappointment and alienation. While Western civilization promoted slogans of universal humanity, it also encouraged nationalism, and the poverty of meaning in nationalism generated the First World War.

She found it hard to identify with any particular nationality or race. Mata Hari was Dutch and claimed some Javanese ancestry. She was also an exotic dancer and a courtesan.

Now she sat in prison because of another part of her identity, her work as a double agent for Germany and France, two nations with their own strong sense of nationalism that were fighting one other in the theater of war.

She had become involved in spying while performing as a dancer throughout Europe and the Middle East. Mata Hari had agreed to this because of what she saw as the superficial discourse of democracy in the West. She had discovered that what Western people saw as universal humanity only stretched as far as the spirit of the Renaissance and the *Aufklärung* in European history. Beyond Western civilization, humanity was perceived as local, not universal.

Her opposition to nationalism had begun when she lived in Ambarawa, before moving to Batavia (now known as Jakarta) during the last years of the nineteenth century.

In the Dutch East Indies (now known as Indonesia) she had seen the discrepancy clearly. The Dutch beguiled the native people by manipulating their kings, regents, sub-regents, and local leaders into becoming protectors of the status quo.

Mata Hari rebelled against her position as a woman. Her husband, Rudolph MacLeod, a Scot and Dutch military officer in the Dutch East Indies, was a womanizer whose frequenting of brothels led to their son being infected with syphilis at birth. Norman John was born in Amsterdam and died in Batavia, and their daughter, Jeanne Louisa, born in Batavia, probably died on the island of Banda in the Moluccas.

Her anger and frustration galvanized her resolve to become a freethinker; to Mata Hari a freethinker was never far from being an atheist. This anger drove her to take revenge on her husband by reckless dalliances with a number of men for amusement, in particular high-ranking military and state officials. Eventually she became a courtesan as well as an exotic dancer. It was while carrying out her two occupations that she did her spying, playing one officer against another, which finally ended in arrest.

Her dramatic life captivated Père and Soeur. They regularly visited her in prison, their official brief being to guide her back to God's path while waiting for execution.

This is Mata Hari's story to Père and Soeur.

Chapter One

I am Mata Hari.

I implore you, Père and Soeur, while you have sworn to a life of celibacy, do not dismiss peremptorily the skills and character of a courtesan.

I am a genuine courtesan.

And I am a dancer in the true sense.

I am a Dutch woman with Javanese blood flowing in my veins.

After reading Adolf Bastian's *Indonesien: Oder die Inseln des Malayischen archipel*, and agreeing with his theory on the unity of mankind, I took to referring to the Dutch East Indies as Indonesia, in protest of Dutch colonialism. According to Bastian, the country includes Soematera, Java, Bali, Borneo, Celebes, the Moluccas, and all the other islands.

The name "Mata Hari" is Malay for sun, *sonne* in German, *soleil* in French, or *zon* in Dutch, and so forth.

People have also called me Lady MacLeod, after the name of my husband Rudolph John Campbell MacLeod, a Scot who was a Dutch military officer in Indonesia. I swear on my mother's grave, I hate Ruud MacLeod. He is the most dishonest man in the world.

At the same time, my conscience tells me I cannot deny that there is something in my character that drove me to become a courtesan.

Don't be scandalized. This is truly what I think. The skills of a courtesan are a gift from God, not only Satan. It is hard to set the realm of God apart from Satan in a human being if what is regarded as the receptacle of goodness and the hotbed of evil is none other than the human heart, and the human heart is not an independent agent.

Let me explain. It would be wrong to blame Satan when we know that behind Satan's power, God gives him the freedom to rule people. At least that is the conclusion I have after reading the story of Job.

Maybe I should not discuss this problem with either of you, Père and Soeur. I am not here to give an academic discourse for people who regard themselves as clever but not smart, or those who are smart but not intelligent. Intelligence is needed to understand talent or character.

I must emphasize that I am proud of being me, because I have participated in everything that makes me who I am.

While the French authorities set the date for my execution after being convicted of spying for Germany, let me tell you the story from the beginning, why I have done what I have done, and how I became who I am.

I start my story from when I was in the Dutch East Indies, the country I call Indonesia, on the island of Java, the origin of my mother, Antje van der Meulen. It was there that my longings and vengeful sentiments reverberated. I grew to be the person I am because of my husband, MacLeod. It was he who morally corrupted me.

After what he did, I proved to the world that no man is so strong as to withstand a woman's temptations, and there is no beauty as wholesome as a man's desire for a woman's vagina. Many high-ranking officials and military officers address the public about morals yet harbor in their hearts indecent thoughts and images of the boudoir.

I am now in Saint-Lazare prison, charged and convicted of betraying France to Germany. The truth is I don't give a damn about nations. What I did was follow my heart, something completely and naturally human.

When I speak of humanity, I mean the inherent good in the human being rather than quibbling about national borders and the people of the nations, and what is called nationality and nationalism. It is obvious that nationality and nationalism have been used as an excuse to wage wars. I have absorbed the beauty of the performing arts and incorporated peace in me without making an issue of national borders.

For that reason, I believe that my or anyone's endeavors in the name of humanity should not be regarded as treason, but as human deeds. I am therefore very angry that the French authorities called me a traitor. I curse Pierre Bouchardon, that gangling, emaciated French captain. His bulging eyes are like shiny, glittery buttons. He is too dumb to understand my beliefs about the essence of humanity.

Every time he interrogated me, it was in the context of he and I being of different nationalities. He forced me to confess that I was a German spy with the code H-21. Whenever I said no, he said yes.

Even more irritating, he would ask the questions I had answered, over and over again until I fumed, my head pounding. Meanwhile he smiled nauseatingly and dumbly bit his index finger.

The biggest torment for me, a Dutch woman with Javanese ancestry, is going without the two showers daily, as is custom in the Indonesia. In this prison there is no bathroom. They only give me a bowl of water once a week to wash myself. I worry that this depravation will make me old before my time.

I was arrested on the train from Spain to France on February 13, 1917. Outside the earth was covered with snow. At first I was brought to the Elysées Palace Hotel, then transferred to Saint-Denis Detention Center. I now reside in the Saint-Lazare prison. Two months I have been here, months that feel like two centuries in hell.

The problem began at the onset of World War I. I was in Berlin to perform exotic dances. I had drawn inspiration from the *natya* reliefs on Boroboedoer Temple, where I tried to find the ancestral spirit of my mother. In Berlin, German intelligence officers approached me and introduced me to their senior officer, Fräulein Dr. Elsbeth Schragmüller. I was offered payment far bigger than any honorarium I normally received for one performance. They also tried to invoke my nationalist fervor by reminding me that I was Dutch, and that the Dutch national anthem began with an admission that the Dutch are of German stock:

Wilhelmus van Nassouwe ben ick van Duitschen bloet. (Wilhelmus of Nassouwe, the blood in my veins is German.)

I was then given a brief to spy on the French for Germany.

After my time in this prison, I am beginning to wonder: was I mistaken? Maybe I was disappointed instead. The question I am unable or unwilling to answer is, why was I so in love with my own body, and why did I make my body an idol for sexual encounters with so many men?

In the end I am convinced that I only loved one, a twenty-one-year-old Russian, Flight Captain Vadim Maslov.

Sooner or later most everyone will be forgotten, erased from historical memory. But I am convinced that I, Mata Hari, will never disappear from the people's collective memory.

Pondering over my past, I know for sure that my current destiny cannot be separated from the path I had trod since marrying Rudolph MacLeod and started a life with its own notes in Java. In fact, it is karma.

By the way, don't forget that I refer to the archipelago as Indonesia, despite the fact that the Dutch government calls it the Dutch East Indies. I also remind myself that my mother was of Dutch and Javanese parentage.

I am proud that my name is Malay. I can translate the words into seven languages, because as a dancer I performed across the European continent into Turkey and Egypt, where I was also a courtesan and spoke the local languages.

When people found out that I could speak seven languages, they called me the polyglot harlot. I had no reason to feel insulted. Instead, I was flattered.

Death is the one certainty in life. When I die, I want to die as a person of no particular nationality, or a speaker of any national language. I want to die as an exotic dancer who has danced naked. For that reason, I want to die naked too, absorbing the essential beauty of the verse I read in Job: *Naked I came from my mother's womb, and naked I will depart.*

Chapter Two

That is the year I was born from the womb of Antje van der Meulen, who had Javanese blood in her veins.

My father, Adam Zelle, gave me the name Margaretha Geertruida. My mother said that my father had chosen that name from a booklet of Catholic saints' names. I thought that was a little odd. In Leewarden, Friesland, the northernmost province of the Netherlands, the population mostly consisted of Protestants of the rigid Calvinist tradition and the daily language was not Dutch but Fresian, an offshoot of the Anglo-Saxon language.

I don't care about any saint's name. My father called me Margriet, the name of a flower; my mother called me Rietje, an endearing abbreviation of my name.

Everyone, including myself, will forget these names. Sometime in the future I will be remembered as Mata Hari, a name of my own creation to go with my career, without the reinforcement of the Javanese birth ritual that calls for eating red and white rice porridge.

After my first menstruation at the age of fourteen, something strange happened with my vagina. All of a sudden I found pleasure in fingering myself. I fantasized about my finger enlarging to the size of a carrot or a potato that moved in and out rhythmically. The pleasure was one that humans have always sought. Its discovery pushed me to leave behind my childhood days and launch into puberty. At eighteen years of age I married, eager for the continuous enjoyment of what I imagined to derive from a carrot or a potato.

A man twice my age advertised for a wife in the 's Gravenhage newspaper. The wording of the advertisement drew my attention: Scot officer working for the Royal Netherlands Indies Army is looking for a wife to accompany him to the Dutch East Indies.

Two things attracted me to the advertisement.

First, marriage made a girl into a complete woman and eventually a mother. But before being a mother, she fulfilled her position as a wife. So she needed a man to be her husband. I knew that to be a real woman I must have a man in my life. It would be impossible to test my womanhood without a man entering my body. To test myself as a woman I had to accept that the vagina was designed by the Creator to be matched with the penis in peaceful copulation. This was a law of nature, the basis of human knowledge throughout the ages. Through the vagina and the penis, men and women are attracted to and find one another. I will believe in this law of nature until the end of my life.

The second point was that if I became the wife of an officer posted in Indonesia, I would find the spirits of my mother's ancestors. I could commune with them in the cradle of Javanese culture, Boroboedoer, absorbing into my psyche the mystery carried in the sounds of *gamelan* music played in *slendro* and *pelog* scales.

I aspired to draw on the Javanese mystical beauty by allowing myself to be the medium for the spirits of my mother's ancestors deep in the ambience of *gamelan* music. I was rocked into semi-consciousness in this fantasy. Images of me dancing, liberated from the constraints of Western aesthetics with inflexible techniques in their dances, flashed through my consciousness. I would let myself go, dancing to tunes that would guide my body naturally into its raw but pure, wild, new movement.

Even after marrying and traveling to Java to live in Ambarawa and Batavia, I had not considered that dancing and liberating my body from Western aesthetic limitations would also result in remuneration.

Somewhere along the way I changed my mind. A Latin proverb I have remembered since the age of ten, *Tempora mutantur nos et mutamur in illis,* says how easily life changes with time. Who knew that I would change even before the times?

With my husband, Rudolph John MacLeod, I experienced real life, not a childhood dream. Let me explain that in brief and simple sentences. Taking care of a family, being a parent of our two children, was difficult. Within three weeks into my married life, I already worried about my ability to continue.

Maybe that is what I meant by following my moods. I changed faster than the times. Just imagine. At the time of my wedding, I felt so proud. I believed I was at the gates of heaven and being welcomed by the angels. I saw Rudolph John MacLeod as a greater hero than Robin Hood. His formidable moustache, curled upward at both ends, was just like that of Gatotkaca, a character from the epic *Mahabharata.*

We first met after I answered his advertisement in the newspaper. When he came to see me, I was very impressed by his moustache. The way he spoke was also rather attractive. He spoke proper Dutch and gained my father's respect with his speech.

When I told my father that I wanted to marry this officer, he looked angry at first, but after some time he winked and yawned, saying to me in Fresian, "I am the head of this household, but I go along with whatever my wife says."

I wondered why he said that. Had he hallucinated that my mother was still alive? Maybe deep down he had regrets. Did he realize that his bad behavior had driven his wife to an early death? The Western concept based on the teachings of the Church about woman being inferior to man had resulted in men feeling justified in being inconsiderate.

My mother passed away when I was fourteen years old, as I began having my first stirrings of physical longing for a man and started to fantasize about carrots and potatoes.

She could no longer take the beatings she received from my father, who directed his anger and frustrations at her. My father was angry because his hat manufacturing business was going bankrupt. He was unable to compete with the mass-produced hats imported from Germany, France, and even America, which were more stylish. As he turned to drink to escape his failure, my mother was the target of his anger and his fists. She was too accepting, a trait she inherited from her Javanese ancestors who called this *nrimo.*

I wish my mother had had the courage to stand up to my father, who treated her with complete disrespect and did not know what to do with his own life. In my opinion, men who drink to escape their misery are damned weak. They have no courage to face what life gives them. What happens in life is not immutable. We have to be creative in addressing the bad turns. As for my mother, she was certainly wrong in accepting what happened to her as if it were her fate. I was frustrated to see how my mother cowered. If I had a husband like my father, I would challenge him to a fight in a boxing ring. Before the official start, I would launch into an attack, kick him in the groin and crush his carrot or potato until he learned his lesson.

I am telling you this because I want you to know I don't give a damn about how the West treats women as inferior and, according to one of St. Paul's letters in the Bible, regard men as master of the household: "But I want you to realize that the head of every man is Christ, and the head of the woman is man."

For centuries, Church dogma has caused women to be regarded as mere complements to men. They are caricatures in the theatre, music, and the other arts. I am angry at the Church for not taking St Paul's other letter seriously, the one that says in God's presence, men and women are equal: "Nevertheless, in the Lord woman is not independent of man, nor is man independent of woman. For as woman came from man, so also man is born of woman."

On behalf of my mother, I swore to bash that bully. However, before I matured into a strong and courageous woman, my mother left this life.

I grieved and grieved, but soon realized that tears would not get me anywhere. They would not wash me free of hatred or love. This later reminded me to be strong and brave. Whatever the future brought, I had to confront it. I had to be swifter and craftier than a squirrel leaping from one branch to another.

Chapter Three

An educated middle-aged man tried to court me before I married Rudolph John MacLeod. He had such embarrassing and irritating manners that I was repulsed. I won't mention his name.

I didn't like him from the start because he had no moustache. In those days, near the end of the nineteenth century, no matter how good-looking a man, even if he had the body of Hercules, without a moustache he couldn't aspire to be the mate of a girl as pretty as I was.

Regardless of how many volumes of poetry he wrote to express his love, only the titillating tickles a moustache made when he kissed a girl gave him any chance of winning her.

Therefore, the man with the embarrassing and irritating manners was bound for the dustbin even before we began. I never chose anyone like him, even to kill time or test my sexual appetite.

This is a typical girl's ranting, not a promise, let alone a pledge.

Human nature being what it is, what is said is not necessarily what is done. There is an expression in Dutch, good Dutch, which says, *In het hart des mans zijn veel gedachten, maar de raad des Heeren die zal bestaan,* which in essence means that man proposes and God disposes.

I learned the expression in seven languages, not by rote as I did biblical verses in Sunday school, but because I liked the sound. The contents were free of any moral weight, and did not undermine my freethinking stance.

I accepted my elders' stories that there was God above yet I also knew Satan was always vigilant around me.

The man with the embarrassing and irritating manners was actually my teacher. How to confront amorous advances from one's teacher? I couldn't very well stand still like the statue "Shiva, King of the Dancers" in the Rijksmuseum in Amsterdam. To what extent was I able to ignore him? He was my teacher.

While attending school, I wanted to complete my education in order to work as a primary school teacher. At least I would be financially independent since my father's income or its lack could not be relied on. He rarely cared about the future. It made no difference to him whether or not a deluge swallowed the Earth.

I went to school in Leiden, a city with many scholars on Indonesia in a number of disciplines: anthropology, law, culture, and language. The teacher in question told me about an uncle of his, a scholar who had written books about the people or ethnic group with yellow skin and slanted eyes that lived in north Celebes.

I paid little attention to his stories because I disliked him. Regardless of how enticing the stories he told to lure me into his trap, I remained uninterested.

One Sunday he cajoled me into a walk with him to the west of 's Gravenhage, along the Scheveningen beach. It was late in the afternoon and I wanted to go home but he pleaded with me to sit on the sand to watch the sunset.

I was restless and angry because it was summer and the sun would not set until nine o'clock. That meant that we had to sit there with a bag of *speculaas* and not even a cup of coffee for three more hours. It was an unproductive way of spending time. Even the prophet Abraham would have run out of patience waiting to see how the sun set in that part of the world. I tried to talk him out of it by saying that I was tired and sleepy.

Instead of listening to me, he sung a lullaby. I was in absolute despair because he sounded like a squealing pig.

The wretched joker sang the song three bloody times. I was expected to pretend I enjoyed his singing. Because I didn't want to listen to the biblical lyrics of the song again, I said, "You are a good singer."

Heavens, he believed my lie. If he only knew how he had hurt my ears and made me want to vomit.

Beaming, he said, "I studied music several years ago with van 't Kruys, the well known Dutch musician."

"Did you?" I pretended to be impressed. "How interesting."

To my horror, he grabbed my hand and brought it to his lips. "Oh, I knew you'd say that."

"What?" I pulled my hand back, quietly panicking. "Did I say something wrong?"

"Not at all, my sweet." He quickly took my hand again and brought it to his chest.

My panic intensified. Now he called me "my sweet." I felt heady and uncertain. Something stirred in me. Was I falling under his spell?

What happened afterward was nothing unusual when a man and a woman are isolated from the crowd. We were alone on the expanse of beach, showered with the occasional spray from the sea. When he took me in his arms and kissed me passionately my mood turned from bewilderment to inexplicable physical desire. I let myself go and enjoyed what was happening. I was only jolted awake when I felt my hymen tear.

After that I knew that I was no longer a virgin, and that I had allowed it to happen.

What was I to do next?

He disappeared.

I was miserable.

However I learned to accept that life would not always give me what I wanted. I learned that in life I had to be prepared to wear two masks, one for tragedy, and another for comedy. Eventually I learned I had much more to address ahead of me, including happiness and sadness, and I had no choice but to go through it all.

Firstly, I felt that creature called man had abused me. After taking my virginity he disappeared. But more than that, I was convinced that to fulfill my womanhood I needed a man, a penis to mate with my vagina. Carrots and potatoes were poor substitutes.

Chapter Four

I married Rudolph John MacLeod on a beautiful day in 1895.

From that day on I expected my friends and relatives to address me in the English way as Mrs. MacLeod. As for me, I called my husband Ruud, the way one would say his name in Dutch.

Ruud and I were married in an official military ceremony. If, for one reason or another, the marriage went bad and we wanted a divorce, it would have to be conducted in a similar official ceremony.

Immediately after the wedding we made preparations for our move to Indonesia. Though Ruud's skills were needed in military engineering work in East Java, our departure was delayed because of unfavorable political situations in the archipelago. The governor general of Batavia, Sir Carel Herman Aart van Wijck, had to address serious problems in Atjeh, and there were also rumors that the Dutch were suspicious of the intentions of the British stationed there.

We had to wait until I gave birth. In Amsterdam we lived with Ruud's sister, not far from the Rijksmuseum where I often went to gaze mystified at the brass statue of the god Shiva.

It was in the house of my husband's sister that I began to harbor malicious thoughts about men. From my perspective they seemed fair. In matters of the mind, the value of an idea depends very much on who is making the evaluation. In Malay, the only language I love, I have made a truism, *kebenaran bisa direka melaloei pembenaran*: you can justify anything and turn it into the truth.

If there were an objective truth about malice, it would be possible to turn malice on its head with such a convincing argument that people would start doubting it. Suppose I did something that was seen as malicious by other people; I would turn their views around by offering another set of values, which they could accept as an alternative truth. Anything people do for survival can be justified.

My problems stemmed from my anger at Ruud's suspicions about me. They were so exaggerated that I swore on my mother's grave to one day teach him a lesson.

Ruud offended me on the first day of our marriage. Aside from being extremely fastidious, he was very old-fashioned.

The first time we had sex was like torture. He behaved like a lion that had been starved for weeks, and that was an indication of what followed. It was the same each time we had sex.

I never had a chance to reach orgasm because I was in pain, especially when he bit my nipples before ejaculating. He might as well have been masturbating since he never gave any thought to my pleasure.

During the few moments of post-coital rest that first time, he sat up and scowled. Hell, I should have scowled after the pain and frustration he caused me. Even so I tried to humor him. I hugged him from behind and kissed his ear but he didn't respond. He pushed my arms away and leaned back looking as if he had been treated unfairly.

I asked, "What's the matter?"

He kept scowling.

I was confused, but quickly regained my composure. Trying to make light of the situation, I said, "You look like a general when you scowl."

His face went crimson and his eyes nearly popped from his head. He yelled, "You think that's funny?"

I didn't know what else to say.

He looked at me disdainfully and tossed his head toward the nearby chair. "Sit," he ordered.

Beginning to feel angry myself, I took a seat. "What?" I asked, hugging my legs.

"What," he repeated.

This infuriated me. He had insulted me by his disrespect. I was his wife for heaven's sake. I was not going to tolerate his abuse.

"What's the matter?" I asked, defiant.

"I have a question," he said.

"I'm listening," I replied.

Instead of asking the question, he stared at me and made me angrier.

"You are not a virgin," he said.

I was confused, but still angry. I didn't answer.

"When did you lose your virginity?"

I refused to respond.

He pressed on, "Well?"

"Well what?" I said.

"Why didn't you tell me you were not a virgin?"

"Did you ask?"

"I am asking now."

"Is my being a virgin or not a problem with you?"

He glowered. "Of course it is. I adhere to the Anglican Church norms. I was born in 1855, four years before Charles Darwin published his *On the Origin of Species by Means of Natural Selection.*"

"What does that have to do with my virginity?"

"You don't understand?"

"No."

"Then I will explain," He rose and pointed at me. "For forty years we human beings have been able to differentiate between monkeys and ourselves. We are different because our women have hymens. Monkeys don't. We have history, monkeys don't. For that reason, a woman without a hymen is equal to a monkey."

"So?" I was furious.

"I am disappointed that I married an eighteen-year-old girl who is not a virgin," he shouted.

"What are you going to do now?" I stood and faced him. "Do you want to divorce? Say it, Uncle Ruud."

He was surprised when I called him "uncle." He didn't expect me to react with such ferocity. I was capable of arguing in a strident voice, more than those ineffective actresses in Joost van den Vondel's plays at the Schouwburg, the main theater in Amsterdam.

His mouth slackened and his thick moustache drooped at both ends like that of a drenched mouse.

My shouting brought Ruud's sister to our room. She wanted to mediate, but I was too upset to notice her intention.

"Say it with your sister as a witness, that you want to divorce the eighteen-year-old girl because she is like a monkey for not being a virgin," I screamed. "When you have done so, I will leave her house."

His sister hugged me and tried to calm me down. "Take it easy, Margaretha."

I shook myself free. "No, Uncle Ruud insulted me."

"Go to hell." Ruud's voice was raspy. "I asked because it is my right."

"It was a rude question," I said angrily. "You equated me with a monkey. When did you last look in a mirror? You are the real monkey. You are an old monkey, Uncle Ruud."

Suddenly I was struck and hurled across the room. My head spinning, I hit the wall before slumping to the floor unconscious.

Alas, alas
Who are the guards
Able to release the chronicles of my name
Charged with guiding me to freedom?
Perhaps I was wrong to devote myself
Not to faith but to ire.

Chapter Five

Sudden calamity can result in planned pleasures.

When I regained consciousness, I found myself in bed, wracked with pain from my jaw and one side of my face. I remembered Ruud slapping me hard, but I didn't know who was so kind as to carry me to bed.

When I opened my eyes, two people were beside me. Ruud sat on the bed and glared while his sister stood behind him and looked at me full of pity.

I began to hope that something good might come out of this dreadful event.

When he saw me open my eyes, Ruud took my right hand and held it tight. He swallowed and said gently, "Darling."

I hoped he regretted his actions.

However I can't remember him saying anything that meant an apology for what happened. He could have said, "sorry," expressing remorse in his own language. He could have apologized for slapping me so hard he knocked me out. But he did not. And I had to accept the situation. People are different. Maybe for Ruud it was more important to show his feelings in deeds rather than using words. Not being an expert in human behavior I didn't know. I only knew that Ruud no longer wanted to hurt me. Maybe when I was unconscious, he feared that I might die. And he, a middle-aged man, would have lost a pretty young wife. It would not be easy for him to find another wife; he had to advertise in the newspaper for me.

On the other hand, if I were to become a divorcee, I would be very desirable and surrounded by candidates eager to take his place.

When I was honest with myself, I suspected his change of behavior was the result of a serious talking-to by his sister, who cared for me.

One day during the third month of my pregnancy, I had just walked in from a shopping trip in the Kalverstraat shopping center, I overheard a conversation between them. "Be thankful that a man your age found a girl as pretty as Margaretha willing to be your wife. Don't be so demanding."

"I only wanted to know who was with her first."

"That is selfish and self-centered."

"Why?"

"She never asked how many women you raped since you joined the military, nor how many Zeedijk prostitutes you screwed."

"In any case, I'm disappointed."

This made me respect my sister-in-law. She was like a substitute mother. She occasionally joined me for walks to the Dam, bringing bread crusts to feed the seagulls. We would stroll hand in hand at the square in front of the royal palace where Dutch kings ascended to the throne. These walks were part of the physical exercise necessary during my pregnancy, so that my muscles would be flexible enough for a problem-free childbirth when the time came.

Whenever I felt tired, she held my hand and taught me to inhale and exhale. I breathed as she instructed, looking at the seagulls hovering over our heads, willing us to throw crusts for them.

One morning at the square, we saw a man dressed in colorful gypsy clothes, propped on a footstool, and playing a flamenco guitar. He accompanied a dancer who also wore a bright costume.

I placed a coin inside the upturned hat at the feet of the guitarist, requesting them to play and dance another number or two. I was fascinated by such dance. It was more enchanting than classical dance like ballet, which was choreographed to the music of well-known composers. I enjoyed every moment of the gypsy dances, their humorous movements called *bulerias*, and wild movements called *farruca*. There were parts specifically for legs and feet, *zapateado*, and turns for arms and hands, *filigrano*.

While I watched, I knew I could perform those movements. I told Ruud's sister and she looked at me incredulously. "You can dance?"

"I've been dancing since I was a toddler."

I often fantasized about being a dancer who could transport her audience. To do so I would dance with my mind, body, and spirit merged together. I had visions of performing a number where my two arms would move in such a mystifying way that the audience would think they saw four arms, just like the haunting statue of the god Shiva.

Chapter Six

Where was Ruud during my pregnancy?

Only he and God knew where he was when I needed him so badly. He never came with me on my walks to the square. I was worried about my body and anxious about our future. Sometimes I wanted to beat him up, pinch him hard, pull and twist his ears, yet I also craved his presence, being caressed or rocked in his arms.

But he was never home. I heard ugly rumors spread by those who were jealous or envious of us, or plain bored. I told myself not to take notice, but I have to admit that I was disturbed, especially as my sister-in-law, his own sister, paid attention to the rumors. She suggested that I should address the situation.

I had no idea where Ruud went in the mornings, afternoons, and evenings, when he left me alone with my insecurity about my pregnancy and life in general. He reeked of alcohol when he staggered into the house late at night. In his awful state he demanded sex, behaving as usual like a starved lion.

When my pregnancy advanced beyond three months, his sister told him forcing sex on me was dangerous in my condition. This made him go out more often. Sometimes he stayed away all night.

I kept hearing about his going to the red light district. If it were true, I would have been very disappointed because I had persuaded myself that

Ruud really loved me and feared losing me, his young wife, especially with him being old and bald. What if I was wrong?

He invariably became irritated each time I asked where he went. Scowling, he said that it was a man's business and none of mine. I had to thank my luck he didn't tell me to shut my mouth.

One evening, as my pregnancy entered its seventh month, Ruud was leaving when his sister repeated the question I had asked earlier, "Where are you going?

To my surprise, he answered, "I want to have fun. I'm tired of waiting for the ship to leave for the Dutch East Indies."

"You want to have fun?" His sister walked to the dining table and poured water from the jug to a cup.

"Yes," said Ruud. "You remember my old mate, Charles Pears? His ship is moored in the North Sea canal."

His sister cleared her throat before drinking the water from her cup. I saw that she didn't believe her brother. Ruud walked out after a peck on my cheek, and my sister-in-law said gravely, "Don't believe him. He is lying."

"What do you mean?" I asked.

"He knows how to tell stories," his sister replied. "He should have been an actor. Actors are good at telling stories."

"But he is my husband," I said, not understanding what my sister-in-law had implied. "I trust my husband, as I should."

"Yes, very good, Margaretha," she said. "It is good for a wife not to have suspicions about her husband. Suspicions only limit your own scope of movement. However, you don't know my brother. His mind has always been as filthy as a sewer."

"I don't understand," I said.

"I know him well," she said. "He was my brother when he was a child, and still is my brother now that he is older."

"I don't know what you're talking about," I said. "He told you he was going to the port."

"Yes, Margaretha, that was what he said. And we know, don't we, a port is near the sea. What he meant was the red light district."

"The red light district?"

"Yes, Margaretha, that's where my brother has been going. You must believe me. He goes there often."

"No, please don't tell me those lies."

"Margaretha, this is what people are saying. He often goes to Walletje, Rode Lamp, or Zeedijk."

"I don't believe you."

"At first I thought he had stopped his disgusting habit. I believed that after marrying you, he'd be cured of it."

"I will not believe what you're saying until I see it with my own eyes."

"Oh my God. You're like Doubting Thomas."

"I have to trust my husband."

My sister-in-law hugged me. I sensed she was at once proud and sad. Doubt began to swell in me, and I became angry. Was there something wrong with me? Why did Ruud still seek the services of prostitutes? Was it because I complained about him biting my nipples? Or was it because his sister had told him not to have sex with me in the advanced state of my pregnancy? Did that make him think he had to go elsewhere?

I thought about the situation. I remembered him saying to his sister when I eavesdropped behind the door, "In any case, I am disappointed."

What did he mean? Was it also because he was disappointed that he had so far refused to apologize for hitting me?

I resorted to the easiest option, accepted the situation, and moved on. Still I promised myself that if the situation turned bad and I was the one to suffer, I would fight back. I would follow the maxim: one must be ready to adjust appropriately to any given situation.

If dishonesty is part of men's character, women should address this fact by adopting the same. More straightforward, if a husband is allowed to be unfaithful, a wife should be given the same entitlement.

> *From Adam's rib, I read,*
> *Eve was created.*
> *For a husband's fling, I say,*
> *A wife redresses the score.*

Chapter Seven

At the end of my pregnancy I was continuously rocked between periods of self-doubt and moments of anger and jealousy, interspersed with an occasional moment of happiness. I gave birth to a son. It is extremely difficult to describe how I felt when I realized I had become a mother.

Disoriented like a kitten that manages to climb and reach the top branch of a tree but is stumped at the realization of having to come down, I was hit by the fact that Mrs. MacLeod had given birth.

The boy was duly given two names. One, Ruud's choice, on which he hysterically insisted: Norman; the other, my choice presented without the possibility of argument, was John. The child was registered as Norman John MacLeod.

In terms of sounds, I liked those English names for my son. Norman reminded me of the name of the Scandinavian who conquered Normandy in the tenth century, and his descendants who conquered England in 1066. John was the name of one of Jesus' disciples.

I was proud of myself for having safely given birth to a healthy baby. I had fulfilled the first task of being a woman, to become a mother and breastfeed a baby. However I was also unhappy. People whispered to each other that my baby was not healthy because of his father's reckless behavior.

I ignored the rumors. I saw nothing particularly different that set my son apart from other babies. He had eyes, ears, a nose, and the right number of fingers and toes.

The official document posting Ruud to the Dutch East Indies had been issued. I was excited about our imminent departure. We were going to Central Java, Ambarawa.

I was thrilled about going to Java. I couldn't wait to immerse myself in the ancestral spirit of my mother, which I hoped would be a rich source of inspiration to achieve the ambitions I had only dared to tell to the statue of Shiva.

According to those who had worked there, Ambarawa had a cool climate. Situated between two cities, Semarang to the north on the coast of the Java Sea, and Magelang to the south, Ambarawa was flanked by Mount Soembing on the west and Mount Merbaboe-Merapi on the east.

Railway lines connected Ambarawa to Semarang and Magelang, so visiting those two cities would not be a problem. The trains, I heard, had gear wheels in the middle between the left and right rails. To climb to Magelang, the locomotives pushed the carriages instead of pulling them from behind, relying on the hard work of the gear wheels.

I was on my way to realizing my dreams. Nothing would stop me. I knew this was only a wish, several degrees below a vow but still more binding than any contract. It was a desire I had kindled in my heart while Ruud became increasingly uninterested and I resorted to dreams for solace. I now had something tangible to look forward to. This was better than the earlier situation that had me trapped in uncertainty.

Ruud was going to work in a tropical land, and not have the opportunity to visit red light districts like in Amsterdam. Yet I still suspected that all was not well. There were incidents, seemingly small in scale that grew in significance when pondered.

My sister-in-law could be right. I didn't know my husband very well.

We said no prayers when we left Holland.

Following the official opening of the Suez Canal in 1869, trips to the East Indies began with a train journey and continued by ship. We headed south to Genoa, the only deep-sea harbor in the Ligurian Sea. There we boarded a ship and voyaged southeast through the Tyrrhenian Sea to

Egypt where we entered the Suez Canal. From the Red Sea we continued to the Indian Ocean.

The train journey was extremely exhausting. We were unable to do anything to break the boredom of sitting and occasionally nodded off to sleep like a couple of sick cats on their way to the veterinarian. In our tilted cabin on the voyage through the Mediterranean Sea before entering Port Said, Ruud wanted sex while I was breastfeeding Norman John. There was no refusing him, and again he behaved like a starved lion. I realized that where sex was concerned, he was deranged.

As we entered the 190-kilometer Suez Canal, a disagreement between us broke out. It started with something trivial to me but seen by Ruud as debauchery.

At Port Said a troupe of gypsy musicians and dancers came on board to entertain the passengers with their flamenco performances. They remained on board until we reached Port Taufiq.

While waiting for Ruud to join us, I rocked Norman John in my arms as I enjoyed the performance. A foreign man greeted me in Italian, *"Come sta lei?"*

I smiled but didn't answer. Probably thinking I had not understood, he proceeded in French, *"Parlez-vous Français?"*

Again, I only smiled. He continued, *"Soy español. Habla usted español?"*

When I still didn't say anything, he said, *"Spreek u Hollands?"*

I laughed and answered in Dutch, "I'm from Friesland, but speak Spanish, French, and Italian fluently."

He was very pleased and we chatted in a mixture of the four languages. He told me he worked as a clergyman in Manila, the Philippines. I was amazed because he didn't wear a robe as I expected with a celibate priest.

The music started and we both looked to where it came from. A gypsy danced to flamenco music. The typical Andalusian music sounded compatible with Arabic music, so it felt right as our ship passed through that region. The dance performance was excellent, much better than those I saw in the square in Amsterdam.

I enjoyed myself so much I called out a request for the dancer to do *bulerias*. She obliged and carried away I shouted, *"Farruca."* Again, she happily obliged. When I called, *"Zapateado,"* the dancer, flanked by two guitarists who accompanied her, came to me. She took my hand to lead me to the dance floor to perform the *zapateado* together. At first I refused, but the priest urged me to accept the invitation. Soon the whole audience encouraged me. I thought, why not?

I asked the priest to hold my son. When he happily obliged, I joined the performers on the dance floor.

The first guitarist strummed the notes E F G F E F G A, and the other guitarist played the melody while the dancer clicked the rhythm with castanets. I began to sway with the music, then swayed and danced with fervor, enchanting the audience. They clapped and shouted for me to continue. I surprised myself as I was merely improvising, hypnotized by the music.

Ruud appeared and he didn't show his appreciation; to the contrary. "What a disgrace," he yelled while pulling me from the dance floor and dragging me downstairs.

The priest rushed after us, reminding us of our son in his arms.

I was ashamed of Ruud's behavior and how he had insulted me. A rage swelled in me that would not be easily subdued by an apology. If Ruud slapped me as he had before, I would have without doubt fought back. Fortunately, he did not.

However I had to tolerate his tirade. His red face puffed up like a pig's head while he yelled for an hour until the ship left the Canal at Port Taufiq.

Finally we reached the Red Sea, where long ago Moses had led the Jews out of Egypt toward Canaan. That was when I put an end to his shouting. I threatened to make a horrible scene if he didn't lower his voice. Aside from dealing with Ruud's ranting I was also trying to stop my baby's howling. Ruud stopped.

That evening, after we calmed down, I spoke softly to him. I initiated an apology and said I was sorry. At that moment I felt more mature than Ruud, who was much older but stunted in his mental and emotional development.

I said that the essence of a marriage was the desire and earnestness of both parties to learn their respective responsibilities and accommodate differences. Once a man became a husband and a woman became a wife, they had to find a suitable compromise through negotiation. "If I make mistakes," I said, "tell me, not through violence, but through loving words, so that I can learn not to be self-indulgent."

To my surprise, Ruud suddenly hugged me and kissed me on the cheek.

"I don't like seeing you behaving like a possessed gypsy."

I asked, "Is it a sin to be a gypsy?

"You are a civilized Dutch woman, not a barbaric gypsy."

Oh Heaven
Who will guide my steps to reach the clouds?
It seems I have been crowned
The queen of human misery.
Darkness follows me wherever I go
Attaching itself to my weakness.
I long to catch the moon in my arms
And lock it away in a safe.

Chapter Eight

We docked in Batavia on Sunday and were billeted in a military complex in Beierlaan, not far from Meester Cornelis. On Tuesday we boarded a ship to Semarang, then continued over land to Ambarawa.

Thankfully the information about Ambarawa having a cool climate was correct. Nor was it dusty like Batavia or Semarang. To the east we saw green paddy fields where finches and sparrows flew around and tweeted. We were again billeted in a military complex, this one near the Willem I Railway Station where the cool breeze from Mount Oengaran was reminiscent of a European spring.

We were assigned a maid, who was only five years older than myself but had already mastered the skills of cooking a number of Dutch dishes, from the complicated pan-fried *biefstuk* to the simple stew of potatoes, onions, carrots, and a little meat known as *hutspot*. She also spoke some Dutch, in Eurasian vernacular called pidgin Dutch. Standard words like *aanstellerig,* for flirtatious, became *anstiel; alstublieft,* for please, became *alsjeblieft; dank u wel,* for thank you, became *dankje*; and water closet was shortened to WC, and became *kak huis*, which is literally "shit-house," and was pronounced in Malay as *kakoes.*

Our maid's name was Kinanti. Since she was left-handed, she had the nickname, *Nyai Kidhal. Nyai* is a term used for native women who work as domestic helpers for Dutch families, while *Kidhal* means left-handed.

Nyai Kidhal taught me the word *matahari*. Later I spelled it as two words, *Mata Hari*, and adopted that as my new name. Western people misinterpret its meaning as "the eye of the day."

The first time I heard my maid utter the word *matahari* was when she sang a lullaby for Norman John. After she sang it in its original Dutch version, she sang it in Malay.

Terbenam matahari
Malam soedah soenyi
Boeroeng hantoe berboenyi
Di pohon yang tinggi
Koekoek koekoek koekoek koekoek koekoek
Koekoek koekoek koekoek koekoek koekoek
At sunset
When the evening quiets
The owl high in the treetop sings
Tu-whit, tu-whoo, tu-whit, tu-whoo....

I was amazed at the native people's ability to transform a Dutch tune into a Malay song by substituting lyrics. Whether it was creativity or criminality I did not know.

I had yet to learn the Malay language. I didn't know whether the lyrics were a literal translation or an adaptation. I was especially attracted to the word *matahari*, which I found particularly pleasing to the ear. "What is this *matahari*?" I asked Nyai Kidhal.

Nyai Kidhal replied, "*Mata* means eye or eyes, and *hari* means day."

Then I understood. The Malay lyrics were not a translation, but rather a trans-creation. I was very pleased to learn a very important and impressive word, which I pronounced as two.

"Madam, you mustn't say *mata* and *hari*," said Nyai Kidhal. "It's *matahari*."

"It's the eye of the day, isn't it?"

"No, *matahari* is one word, meaning in its true sense the sun. "

The word was suddenly etched into my memory. The sun represented heat or fire. People in Holland were only able to enjoy the warmth of the sun during one season, which lasted less than four months. If the fire of the sun were transferred to a woman and her demeanor, that fire would remain alight throughout twelve months of the year. And only a man would be able to test and verify the existence of this fire. I knew the fire in a woman was different from the heat in inanimate objects. For instance, if a man touched a hot saucepan, he'd promptly fling it away. But if a man touched a passionate woman, he would want to hold her longer. I was anxious to test my theory in real life.

Chapter Nine

Though Ambarawa was very pleasant, it wasn't a city where I could satisfy my social needs. The neatly planned village had a population socially identifiable by the houses they lived in. The houses either had walls of bamboo matting, wooden boards, or bricks. What I meant by "social needs" were, among other things, beautiful clothes. If I wanted beautiful clothes I had to buy the fabric in Semarang on Bodjong, the largest street in the city that was longer than any I remembered in Amsterdam.

Ever since I was a toddler my mother dressed me in pretty clothes. I grew up with these expectations. In fact, I was sure, that Wybrandus Hanstra, my first admirer, had been attracted to my clothes.

Damn. I just broke my promise not to name him.

He was a disgusting man. However he was the only person who, for the purpose of educating me, took me to the Rijksmuseum to prove the truth of the Latin proverb, *ars longa vita brevis*. We enjoyed the beauty of paintings and sculptures, and various crafts such as ceramics, furniture, and textiles. I wore one of my favorite dresses, the red frock.

On our way to see the painting by Rembrandt van Rijn, "The Nightwatch," he grabbed my hand and pulled me to Hall 217. There we looked at "The Jewish Bride," also by Rembrandt van Rijn. It was a painting of a woman in a red dress, whose modest-sized breasts were squeezed by a man in yellow attire. I was absorbed in the painting when that wretched man put his hand on my breasts, and said, "You have small breasts, like Rebecca."

I managed to pretend nothing had happened. I asked, "Who is Rebecca?"

He knew the subjects of the seventeenth century Dutch master's painting very well and replied, "The woman in the red dress is called Rebecca, and the man holding her breasts is Isaac."

"You know about them," I said.

He responded indirectly. "Her red dress is as pretty as yours."

I shouldn't have recalled that incident. Now that I lived in the East, I should drop my Western clothing habits as well. I noticed that many village women did not wear bras. In my opinion, bras represent physical constraints on women. While living there, I forgot about wearing brassieres and pretty clothes. I only worried about the parts of my body that needed protection from insect bites. I happily wore Pekalongan sarongs and Lasem *batik* clothes that covered the lower parts of the body, from the waist down to the calves. For those I didn't have to go through the trouble of taking the train to Semarang. They were sold in Ambarawa, in shops owned by the Chinese.

Chapter Ten

Whenever Ruud was on assignment away from Ambarawa for several days, I bathed at the natural springs near Kerep, accompanied by Nyai Kidhal. I took all my clothes off, enjoying the freedom and the closeness of nature to my skin. I fancied myself being the subject of Cornelis van Haarlem's painting, "Bathsheba at Her Bath."

In that open bathing place I also learned about the art of sexual pleasure from Nyai Kidhal. It began with my interest in the pineapples that grew wild under banana trees. When I asked Nyai Kidhal to get me some, she said, "Women should not eat pineapples; it makes them wet."

I was surprised. "What do you mean?"

"Madam," she said, "When a woman eats pineapples, her woman's place becomes wet and unpleasant for her man."

"You mean, her vagina?"

"Yes, madam," she replied. "According to our Javanese elders who mastered the wisdom of Soerakarta kings, a wet woman's place is not good. For that reason women are forbidden to eat pineapples, so their place remains dry and pleasurable for their men."

I was thankful for the information from Nyai Kidhal. I learned much from her about Javanese tradition. And since I liked learning different languages, I enjoyed learning the many layers of Javanese language, starting at the lowest form to the highest.

Javanese had layers, from *ngoko, krama andhap, krama madya,* to *krama hinggil,* from the everyday to the more formal, to the most refined. During the next four months I learned to string words together meaningfully and even speak a little refined *krama hinggil.*

Chapter Eleven

Ruud was often away for his work, leaving Norman John and me in Ambarawa. When he came home he always demanded sex like a hungry lion demanding his feed. I once imagined his arms and legs tied up when making love to me, and how he'd suck my nipples while unable to assault me. The fantasy came from a Peter Paul Ruben's painting in the Rijksmuseum, "Cimon and Pero." It depicted a shackled bald man sucking a woman's nipple. It was such an apt image of stupidity, the man painted as a defeated fool. Would I realize that fantasy?

I had problems with my body. I longed for a man. Only a man could physically satisfy my womanly desires. I was also aware that masculinity was closely linked to strong animal instincts, which stirred in me the need to dance and cavort without restraint.

I needed a man just as French roses need summer showers. I was not a Portuguese lily that grew wild in rocky valleys without having to rely on rain.

For this one thing I would not hesitate to beg, perhaps not with words, but with deeds. Why should I pretend not to have physical desires if physical desires were part of the beauty of humanity? When Ruud demanded sex and behaved as usual, I obliged. I had no choice. Eventually I was able to have an orgasm fairly often.

I believed that I was living a drama, a story with the eternal question of what next? Barring the issue of death, which I refused to think about in my young age, the question of what would happen next in my life became an exciting prospect.

One answer came when I became pregnant again. Instead of bringing happiness to our house, the news brought misery.

Instead of being jubilant at the news that his wife was going to have another child, Ruud told me that he wanted Nyai Kidhal to service him sexually during my pregnancy.

Fury overcame me and I dropped my coffee cup. It fell on the table, splashing its contents.

"Have you gone mad?" I asked.

"You asked me to be frank with you. Now I am."

"But that is crazy."

"I thought it was realistic."

I was speechless. This was absolutely crazy.

I knew we had to be frank with each other. But this?

I suddenly remembered what Nyai Kidhal told me about pineapples. I imagined how her knowledge about sexually pleasuring men would enable her to snare Ruud and without a doubt she'd regard me as a defeated and useless woman.

What was happening to me? Why was my mind full of such nonsensical rubbish?

What was Ruud's brain made of, to think that what he just proposed was realistic?

I decided to fight him to the very end. "What is realistic about that?" I said. "It is crazy. Insane."

"Wait," he said.

"No," I said. "If you intend to do that, I'd rather give birth to your child without its father."

I wasn't joking. I had reached the limit of my tolerance, my emotions setting my feminine pride on fire.

Ruud seemed to take my threats seriously and tried to appear reasonable. "Listen, Margaretha," he said in a gentle yet nauseating tone, "This would be for your own good, too. That way I wouldn't disturb your pregnancy."

I wanted to throttle him. "How can you say that?" My voice went up in volume. "What devilish thoughts you have in your head. You don't want to disturb me physically, but you've crushed me mentally and psychologically. I've never heard anyone utter such filthy nonsense."

He smirked and said, "Have you never heard of Abraham? This is exactly what he did with Hagar, Sarah's servant, and Sarah accepted it. It was even Sarah who suggested it to her husband. If you don't believe me, read about it in Genesis."

I was momentarily speechless. When I recovered, I said, "You are not Abraham. You are not a prophet. You are a mere human, a freethinker."

"Can't a freethinker read the Bible?" he said defensively.

"You are nothing but a sewer mouth," I said.

"Calm down," he smirked.

"I swear on my mother's name that I will never accept your insane, nonsensical, proposition."

Curiously, he said, "All right. Let's just see what happens."

I was overcome with panic and fury. "You mean you won't change your mind?"

"Please don't think I'm stupid," he said, and walked out.

I ran to the bedroom and slammed the door shut. I hurled myself on the bed, crying disconsolately while I held Norman John, who had woken with a start and began to howl.

Chapter Twelve

Where would I go for help?

Ruud hurt me badly. He drove me to take revenge, and pushed me toward divorce. I didn't know where to go. In Western countries, people went to the clergy for help and counseling. Catholics saw a priest and Protestants saw a minister. But who was there to consult in Ambarawa? If I wanted to see a priest or a minister of religion I had to go to Semarang by train.

Would they take kindly to a former Catholic who had become a freethinker? Besides, Catholic churches were not popular in Semarang. The favorite instead was the dome-roofed Protestant church in Heerenstraat. The Catholic Church often had problems with the colonial authorities, many of who professed to be Protestants and encouraged their ministers of religion to make life difficult for their Catholic counterparts. I call them "those who professed to be Protestants" because in reality they were just well dressed robbers. Many came from the northern provinces of Holland where most people are Protestants.

I saw how futile it would be going to them for help, and decided there was no use going to Semarang to see any priest or minister. It made more sense to see the governor. If Ruud really went ahead with his insane idea, I would certainly do that. In the meantime, there was something more immediate I had to address.

The following morning Ruud left for work, looking smart in his uniform. People called him Mr. GG, short for governor general, because his bald head and moustache made him look like the former governor general, Meester Cornelis Pijnacker Hordijk.

I went to my jewelry box and took out one of my gold necklaces. Then I called Nyai Kidhal. I asked her, "Are you from Ambarawa?"

"No, I am from the village uphill from here, madam. A fair distance on foot."

"How do you go there?"

"On a water buffalo cart, madam. It's called a *songkro*."

"What's the name of your village?"

"Mojosongo. It's the name of the temples there."

"What temples?"

"I'm not quite sure myself, madam, whether they are Buddhist or Hindu."

I gave her the necklace I held in my hand.

"Take this, Nyai Kidhal. This is a gift from me."

"A gift?" She was surprised and looked at me with hesitation, her mouth gaping.

"Please take it," I said.

"Are you leaving Ambarawa, madam?"

"No. Just take this now."

Nyai Kidhal took the necklace. Again she asked, "Are you leaving Ambarawa?"

"No. But I want you to go home to your village in the hills."

She regarded me with sadness. "What have I done wrong, madam?"

"You have done nothing wrong. I am worried that if you stay, I will do something unpleasant to you."

"I don't understand, madam."

"Never mind, Nyai Kidhal. I like you. You have done your work very well. But before anything happens to you, I'd rather you left us. Please go back to your village. Now."

Nyai Kidhal hung her head. She wiped her tears with the hem of her *kebaya*, restraining her sobs. "If that is what you wish, madam, I will do as you ask."

I gave her severance pay of two months salary, along with some loose change. She knelt before me, hugging my legs and sobbing openly.

"You are very kind, madam," she said. "Remember that when I came here, I had promised to serve you wherever you are and wherever you go."

I was very touched and regretted that I had to ask her to leave. I pulled her up and made her stand instead of kneel. Though a maid, she was also another human being. I didn't want to be like other colonial Dutch who emphasized the racial and social inferiority of their maids. How could I have? I never forgot that my mother was of Javanese descent. Racial prejudice of any kind repulsed me. Ruud's desire to take advantage of Nyai Kidhal sexually was a disgusting colonial attitude.

I was aware that while nationality was a fact, even a gift, it was also a curse, because it drove people to claim their rights to a country and regard it as their duty to defend it. I, on the other hand, put humanity above nationality with its inevitable borders.

That was why I was so sad when, with my son in my arms, I watched Nyai Kidhal walk away with a heavy gait. When she was out of sight, I started waiting for Ruud to come home and ask for her.

Chapter Thirteen

I was right. Ruud stepped into the house just when the sun was disappearing behind Mount Oengaran. He immediately asked for Nyai Kidhal, trying to sound casual. I was working in the kitchen carrying Norman John in a *batik* cloth tied around my neck and underarm, the way Nyai Kidhal did.

"Why don't you ask Nyai Kidhal to do this?" Looking left and right, he continued, "Where is she?"

I had rehearsed what I was going to say before he came home. Using the acting skills I learned in Sunday school presenting biblical stories, I carefully chose the words I used in the story for Ruud.

"Oh, yes," I began. "Her brother took her home to their village. Their mother had fallen very ill after being stung by bees, as did their father after being trampled by a cow. The brother took them to a *dukun*, a traditional healer, but since the *dukun* was also sick, the brother summoned all the siblings to care for their parents."

Unfortunately Ruud didn't believe me. He said mockingly, "How unlucky they are. Are you sure her brother didn't say that the *dukun* died from a snake bite?"

His remark disconcerted me. But I did not give up easily. I gave him a fierce, offended stare, and said, "You don't believe me? If you're not going to believe what I tell you, don't ask."

"When did you last play *sluip door*?" Ruud snickered.

I felt sick from anger and despair. He had referred to a Dutch child's game in which two children make an arch and the others walk through singing a song, and the one coming through at the end of the song is caught.

"What are you saying?" I asked.

"You are not the type of girl who tries to slip through anything. I never understood the fun of that game, just as I don't find listening to your lies amusing."

What a roundabout way of insulting me. My acting skills obviously hadn't done me any good. I was at a loss to decide what to do next. But before I was anywhere near recovering my wits, Ruud said gruffly, "Stop this, Margaretha. You have no acting talent. Just tell me where Nyai Kidhal is. I'm sure you sent her away."

I was completely stumped. He was right, of course. I saw no other way but to display my anger.

"Why would I have sent her away?" I yelled.

"That's what I want to know."

"I did not send her away."

To avoid making a bigger fool of myself, I took Norman John to the bedroom. But Ruud followed us.

"I don't believe you are stupid, Margaretha. You must've told that woman to go to a particular place." He stood facing me, arms akimbo.

"No," I screamed.

"Where is she, Margaretha?"

"I told you, I don't know. She went with her brother."

"Did she now? Her brother came to collect her? Extraordinary."

"Who cares?"

"You really think your story is convincing."

"If you don't believe me, it's your problem."

"No, I don't believe you and I want you to tell me where she went."

"Her brother came to collect her. I don't know where she's gone."

"You don't know?"

"Go to hell."

"We are both freethinkers, remember? We don't believe in the existence of hell, or heaven."

I screamed until I felt my lungs would burst.

Startled, Ruud turned and walked out.

I felt relieved, though I was still panting when he turned to me again. His face looked as ugly as that of a monkey. "You know, Margaretha, I'll never believe you again. You are a liar." Then he was gone.

I stood frozen. Was he expecting me to beg for forgiveness, to regain his trust? I was too hurt to turn around. I chose to declare war.

Ruud had insulted two women simultaneously: Nyai Kidhal and me, his wife. He probably figured that as a man, he had the power and money to subdue any woman.

To fight back, a woman has to use her feminine wiles to seize the power that is granted automatically to a man. After all, we were approaching the twentieth century. Women no longer retreated into the gloom. Instead, they made their presence known. We women would address men's domination over us.

If Ruud thought that he could dominate women in this modern era, he was gravely mistaken. I, for one, said, "Whatever men can do, we can match on our own," to myself and other women.

In two years we would enter the new century. While I didn't know how, where, and when, I knew for certain that the new century would see me fight back. At some point I'd twirl men around my little finger, and make them obey and serve me.

Ruud had gone too far. Once again he hurt my feelings and pushed me into a state of revenge and toward divorce. Nothing could stop me.

From the window I saw herons leaving Lake Rawapening. The past was gone forever. Thoughts of yesterday always evoked pandemonium. When I visualized the future, I saw a gray fog, with the earth holding the secret of finding a balance between the will to live and understanding the meaning of life.

I had this monologue with myself. My thoughts appealed to my mind and my mind appealed to my heart.

I pondered my own life,
I probed my own mind.
Could it be true that Java,

MY NAME IS MATA HARI

The island of my mother's birth,
Had been fated to receive female fury,
The cry of the invincible,
Oppressed but undefeatable?

At the shores of Lake Rawapening,
The small fish were unaware
That soon they'd be swallowed by herons
And flown to the mountains.

Who would care as I do
About the embryo inside me,
Soon to grow into a baby
A small human being
Who doesn't know the passage
It slipped through
While its father frequents that route
In search of the heaven adjacent to hell?

I wait for the sound
Of the echo of the past
To carry me to a place
Where the sun never sets.

Chapter Fourteen

The night came and went with no words passing our lips. Apart from Norman John's cries, outside only the sounds of cicadas, the croaks of frogs, and the occasional barking of dogs were heard.

Early in the morning Ruud rose, dressed, and walked out after playfully pinching Norman John's cheeks.

Ruud rushed down the steps and headed north, as if an evil spirit was chasing him. He even ignored the respectful greetings from Didik, who was coming toward the house.

Didik's real name was Hendrik, shortened to Endik. He was a Minahassan, one of the ethnic groups in Indonesia, which because of their light-colored skin and Christian religion, were trusted by the colonial administration to handle their provisions.

Didik, a corporal in the Atjeh wars two years previously, was brought home to Java after shrapnel blinded one of his eyes. He then married a village woman from Mendoet and they now lived in Magelang. Didik took care of the domestic needs of Dutch officers in Ambarawa. He came to Ambarawa once a month for that purpose.

He greeted me politely. "What do you need for this coming month, madam?" he asked, obviously startled by my answering the door.

"More than provisions for the kitchen and pantry, Didik. I need something to lift me from this oppressive feeling I have."

"What's the matter, madam? I don't see your maid."

"That's not what is bothering me," I hastened to answer. "My big problem stems from trust, or lack of it. I need a powerful distraction to make me forget this mental burden."

Didik regarded me without comprehension.

The birds tweeting and fluttering around the hibiscus bushes in our yard prompted me to say, "I am envious of the birds singing and dancing so cheerfully, so free from worry."

Didik interpreted what I said literally. "Do you want to sing and dance, madam?"

I laughed. "How can I when I can't rid myself of hatred?"

"I don't understand the arts of singing and dancing, madam, but I believe that sadness can be channeled into art."

"Did you say sadness?"

"Yes, madam. Pardon my asking, are you by any chance feeling sad?"

"You don't understand. What I am feeling is not sadness, but hatred."

"In that case I'd better not ask further. However, if you want to transform happiness and sadness into songs and dances, I might be able to help."

"How?"

"I know a place where people study the songs and dances that depict happiness and sadness."

"Where?"

"In Magelang my wife has a relative who performs Javanese dances at the royal palace in Jogjakarta. His name is Mbah Koeng."

"This relative, does he entertain the Sultan, the King of Java?"

"Yes, madam. Sri Sultan Hamengkoeboewono."

"How very interesting. I want to meet this man."

"No problem, madam. I can take you there any time you want."

I was suddenly seized by an irrepressible urge. I said, "Let's go now. Take me to your Mbah Koeng."

Chapter Fifteen

I decided to leave. If I stopped to think I might have changed my mind. Somehow I knew I should not leave the house, but I was not in my right mind to judge what I should do. It was however gratifying to imagine how Ruud would be worried to find me missing without even a brief note. I hoped he'd realize it was all his doing.

We took the nine o'clock train to Magelang, where Didik lived. From there we continued on to his wife's home village in Mendoet to visit Mbak Koeng's art community on the bank of the Elo River.

I wore a sarong, as I had since coming to Java. My hair was styled as that of native women, two plaits hanging across my chest. This made me less conspicuous. People who saw me walking toward the rehearsal area wouldn't stare as if I were a crazy white woman wearing a Javanese sarong, walking around braless and barefoot.

Going to see Mbak Koeng took more effort than I had imagined. From the village of Mendoet we travelled by *songkro* past a vast expanse of rice fields toward Boroboedoer. The cow cart bounced across the bumpy road. After a while we entered a cool and shady forest of big trees. Occasionally we saw food crops.

The sun had set when we reached our destination. Some fifteen meters away from where I stood, the Elo River traveled through the valley. There were *gamelan* musicians, and apparently they had been playing since five o'clock in the evening. They played compositions punctuated by the *kenong* and the gong. Around eight o'clock, four men appeared carrying a woman sitting in an open litter to the middle of the field.

I watched the rehearsal with fascination. The movements of the woman particularly interested me. She stepped down from the litter and danced among the men. After a short while she seductively shed her top, exposed her moderate-sized breasts similar in size to mine, and presented them to the caresses of the gentle night breeze.

Captivated and eager to copy the dancer's movement, I remembered the statue of Shiva in the Rijksmuseum dancing with his four arms.

Without much ceremony I asked the community leader if I could join the dance. He happily agreed. After doing a few rounds I was in such ecstasy I didn't feel my feet touching the ground. My body was the medium for Shiva, king of the dancers.

At the end of the dance, I chatted with people around me about my experience, Didik and his wife acting as my interpreters. The word "ecstasy," which Didik interpreted as *kesoeroepan*, was not enough to describe it. Finally I opted for the English expression, "in a trance." After all, my body had been a medium of Shiva. Those sitting cross-legged around me nodded.

I later learned that when the Javanese nodded their heads and said *inggih*, or yes, they did not necessarily agree with what was said, but merely acknowledged they had received the information, albeit at variance with their own opinion.

At the next session I got up again to dance, this time with more freedom and self-confidence. Those who watched me were full of praise.

I found out that when the Javanese said, "it is good," they spoke with reservation and allowed for the possibility of it meaning the opposite. Maintaining harmony was very important for these people and they did not contradict each other openly.

I was really happy being among those villagers. They were not fanatical in any religion, but had successfully synthesized Buddhism and Hinduism with their local beliefs. This had been going on since the rule of King Kertanegara, one of the first Javanese monarchs. The villagers' openness to various thoughts was compatible with my freethinking stance. I was still preoccupied with my conceptions about religion, in terms of the history of the Church in Europe. I also had not found the answer to the question why, while teaching love and goodness, religion always caused wars among their respective adherents.

However, while I was there, I wanted to take advantage of the opportunity to dance, an activity that gave me so much peace and enjoyment. I danced until the last drop of energy had left my body. Norman John had slept for three hours and I, too, fell asleep on a low bench in front of the house that accommodated the community, the cool breeze from the north bringing colorful dreams.

Early in the morning I woke to the continuous tweeting and cheery singing of birds. I looked up to the trees, where orioles, starlings, and many other species of birds busily started their day.

I got up from the sleeping bench and walked to the well behind the house to bathe. Drawing water using the leaky bucket tied to a length of rope was quite a feat. The rope was made of roughly woven grass, which was abrasive to the skin.

> *Sleep, my body, sleep.*
> *Wake, my passion, wake.*
> *Welcome the dewdrops*
> *On the thorny rose stalk*
> *Bringing the gifts of meaning and hope.*
> *I have been to the mouth*
> *Of the heavenly tale*
> *Which leapt to my heart.*
> *Today love and hatred*
> *Disappeared from my dreaming*
> *But tomorrow I shall turn into ash.*

Chapter Sixteen

In the arts community on the banks of the Elo River, I was welcome and appreciated. The leader showed how pleased he was that I also called him Mbah Koeng, the same as the other villagers addressed him.

I was given a small hut for Norman John and myself. The east-facing cottage had wooden walls and one bedroom. A turtledove sang in a cage hanging on the front veranda. It occasionally sang when the *gamelan* was playing, creating a magical ambience that I was unable to describe. I thought of staying two more days, and after that I had nothing definite planned. I still hadn't forgiven Ruud.

In two days Mbah Koeng's troupe was to perform at the foot of the Boroboedoer Temple as part of the ceremony welcoming Sri Sultan Hamengkoeboewono, the Javanese king who would be visiting from his royal palace in Jogja. He and his entourage were bringing a guest of honor from Batavia, Jacob Theodoor Cremer. The name struck me, as it was the same as that of the Dutch Minister for Colonial Affairs.

Mbah Koeng agreed to let me perform a dance with his daughter, Astri. All the other members of the community supported his decision. This gave me the confidence I needed. I hoped I would not disappoint him. I felt appreciated in this community under his leadership. At the same time I was reinforced in my stance that humanity was above nationality or ethnicity.

In terms of myself, who was I? My father was born in Friesland, a Dutch province, yet never felt part of the Netherlands. And my son, issue of my marriage with a Scot, would I refer to him as a Scot, as if he were from Scotland? I thought about the Scots, English speakers, but not necessarily a part of England.

How did I refer to myself? My mother originated from the Boroboedoer region, the cradle of Javanese civilization. No doubt I was human, and lived among other humans.

The next day I had to perform for government officials. It would be a first for me. First experiences always excited me and drove me to keep going. I didn't want to disgrace myself. I wanted to impress those important persons with my dance.

Mbah Koeng told me, "Derive the spirit of the twin dance from the relief images on the walls of the Boroboedoer Temple." I was intrigued by his enigmatic instruction and wondered which images he referred to.

That morning I rose before dawn. As soon as light came into our little house, I bathed Norman John, and prepared to go to the Boroboedoer Temple. Astri came to keep me company and help me find the images. Without her I wouldn't have known where to search in such a big temple.

Astri took me to the main wall in the second gallery, the *Gandavyuha*, which had 128 panels. There I saw the image of two dancers with nothing covering their breasts on the right hand side, facing the lead dancer in the middle. I saw nothing irregular about the image.

Astri tried to explain it to me. She spoke in village refined Javanese and at first I had difficulty understanding her. Luckily she pointed to the clothing of the characters in the image and said, "Buddha." She indicated the lead dancer, and said, "Hindu."

"Oh, I understand," I said. "This image is a bit strange because in this Buddhist temple there's a character wearing a *brahmana* attire. Is that it?"

"Yes, yes," she said.

At last we found the image referred to by Mbah Koeng. We studied it to draw inspiration for our dance. The image depicted the two dancers tilting their heads slightly upward and to the right. Their right arms lifted with elbows the same height as their chins and the forearms slanted lower, while their left arms extended forward and touched the knees elevated to the height parallel with their breasts.

This was a still stance. Now we had to define the movement prior and following this stance. Combining our imagination we developed the whole, continuous dance, merging body and soul to create beautiful art.

I should have been thinking about the king from Jogjakarta, but instead I concentrated on the official from Batavia. I wanted to know what he looked like. In the end, I was determined to impress the entire audience. Yet I was also aware that what was important was not the quality of the performance, but whether the performers were good-looking, and whether they would be willing to be seduced and used. This was conventional practice, Mbah Koeng said.

Being away from home the officers and officials took advantage of the situation and requested that their subordinates supply them with live bolster pillows to make their beds more comfortable.

Mbah Koeng's information intrigued me greatly and I wanted to meet such a person. He also said, "All high-ranking officials have two *ta-s* on their minds: *wani-ta,* women, and *har-ta*, wealth."

"What do you mean?" I asked.

Mbah Koeng explained, "Women are easily tempted by wealth. Understandably, officials are aware of this and take advantage of it."

How interesting. I knew that an official's wealth was usually obtained through corrupt practice. The Dutch East India Company was falling because of rampant corruption and the wealth gained from the corruption was used for high living with women. So much for adults and their world. A child's world is far better.

The following morning I saw the children of the community play a singing game.

I watched and listened. The words sounded simple, but contained advice to take life as it was presented because even in the luckiest situation, one still has to overcome obstacles before reaching a goal. And occasionally, despite of one's efforts, one would still fail.

Chapter Seventeen

I mused about the important gentlemen coming to Boroboedoer. What would they look like? Would they have moustaches? Would the tallest gentleman be bald? The thought of a bald man made me yawn with boredom.

Luckily, Jacob Theodoor Cremer had a full head of hair. He was neither young nor old. His overall appearance and demeanor reminded me of the Jewish people in Amsterdam who often assessed a situation by its prospects of bringing a profit or a loss.

Three other European gentlemen positioned themselves around Cremer as they toured the different levels of the Boroboedoer Temple while Sri Sultan Hamengkoeboewono waited at the ground level.

Cremer's visit was part of the endeavor to promote the temple as an extraordinary monument that every enlightened European should see.

Having completed the tour, Cremer joined the Jogjakarta king to watch the performance. The sun had set and light came from the strategically positioned torches around the field.

Someone walked to the front and delivered a speech welcoming the guests of honor. It was very flattering, and he obviously thought he was following the correct protocol. Finally the time came for Astri and I to dance.

As I expected, Cremer sent one of his guards to see me after we finished. In Limburg-accented Dutch the guard invited me to see Cremer.

I remembered Mbah Koeng talking about the two ta-s when Cremer spoke to me. As we talked, Cremer kept sneaking a look at my breasts.

"You are very good at Javanese dancing," he said.

I smiled modestly, aware he was an official of the colonial administration.

"Where are you from?"

I answered, "I live in Ambarawa," knowing that was not what he expected to hear.

"I mean, where in Holland?"

"I was born in Leeuwarden."

"Hm, Friesland?"

"Yes."

"I once bought a hat in Leeuwarden."

"The manufacturer has long gone bankrupt."

"How do you know?"

"Because the business belonged to my father."

"Heavens. Small world."

I laughed awkwardly, hoping I didn't come across like a fool.

Cremer quickly continued. "What is your name?"

I answered, "Mrs. MacLeod."

He looked serious. "Oh? Your husband is English?"

"Scottish."

"So where is Mr. MacLeod?"

"At this moment it does not concern me."

Cremer's face relaxed. "You have problems with your husband?"

I didn't answer, knowing he would keep asking and I was right.

"What happened?"

I decided to challenge him. I said, "Even if I told you, there is nothing you can do to help."

Cremer held my hands. For a moment I thought he was being fatherly, albeit with doubtful sincerity, because he also moved closer to my breasts. A certain tension in his hands made me nervous.

"Why not? I am ready to help. What happened?"

"Common domestic problem. He's old. I'm young."

"I see, I see," Cremer said in the manner of a marriage counselor. "This is a serious problem. You are still excited about life, while your husband is already aging."

I expected him to have dirty thoughts. "That's not the problem, Mr. Cremer."

"What is it then? Tell me, and I will help."

"I would like my husband transferred away from Ambarawa."

"Who is your husband?"

After I told him, he said as if it was an easy matter, "Where do you want him moved? To Batavia?"

"I leave that to you, Mr. Cremer."

"I will make the arrangements. In the meantime, I would like to contact you directly. Please write down your address and your maiden name. What is your maiden name?"

"Margaretha Geertruida Zelle."

"Hm. Yes, of course. Zelle was the brand of the hat. If you move to Batavia, you must work for me."

"Thank you, Mr. Cremer." I started to leave.

"Wait," said Cremer.

I stopped and turned around. "Yes, Mr. Cremer?"

Cremer pulled my hand toward him, placed an arm around the small of my back, and kissed my cheeks, the Dutch way, left, right, then left again. With his arm around my waist, he looked at my breasts and asked, "Are you pregnant?"

A little embarrassed, I replied, 'Yes, going on three months."

He moved his hand to my shoulder and said, "Take it easy with your dancing."

"Yes, Mr. Cremer." Very Dutch-like, I didn't show any emotion.

I heard Norman John cry in the distance. Mbah Koeng's wife had carried him the entire evening.

Chapter Eighteen

I made a point of not going home to Ambarawa until I felt ready. After what had happened with Ruud, I was emotionally distant from him. I did not miss him in the least.

I intentionally stayed with the community near the Elo River. While enjoying the fertile land and the peace with nature, I quietly hoped I would also be able to commune with my mother's ancestral spirit. I was convinced that by now Ruud would be panicking in Ambarawa.

When I returned after a week, Officer van Donck's wife reported that Ruud had been looking for me everywhere. He had even consulted a hermit who lived on the slope of Mount Oengaran, known as René du Bois. Mrs. van Donck told me that René had tried to find my whereabouts in a pack of cards.

René was a Frenchman who had come to Java twenty years ago as a Dutch officer, posted in Salatiga. The story went that René had come with another French man, Arthur Rimbaud, who was known in his country as a poet. I tended to believe the story because on the table in our house I had found several sheets of paper with Arthur Rimbaud's poetry. One poem in particular interested me. It was handwritten, titled "Départ," and talked about the poet's satisfaction with the life he lived and his readiness to continue.

I had just picked up the next sheet of paper when Ruud appeared. He startled me with his braying voice.

"Margaretha, darling," he exclaimed, rushing to hug Norman John and me. "Where on earth have you been?"

I didn't answer. It was a long story I was not ready to tell.

Ruud showered me with kisses starting on the cheeks to the tips of my fingers. "Oh, darling," he said, "I was so worried about you and Norman."

Chapter Nineteen

A Malay proverb says, "Light always comes after dark." Maybe I could rebuild our relationship from the ruins created when Ruud told me about his idea to bed Nyai Kidhal. However this was not easy. I wasn't sure if he had retracted the proposition and was prepared to mend our relationship. I still fretted about him never having said, "sorry," despite his understanding of the word.

However he never said anything. Maybe he wouldn't. Maybe he couldn't.

In any case, his apology meant nothing if he went on with his crazy idea, nothing but a futile exercise. Oh, why was I so complicated?

Little by little, I learned more about my husband. He was a difficult person to live with. His brain worked like a tangled spool of rough black rope, the kind used to bring up pails of water from the well and blistered my hands. I was left with the unresolved hurt.

I had to admit that during the next five days Ruud treated me with the devotion of a slave toward his sovereign. His behavior after my weeklong absence was more absurd than that of a crazed lover who tried to pluck a star from the heavens for his beloved's earring.

This bothered me. It was so unusual I expected to see a change any time. Deep down I still waited to hear him say "sorry" for causing me so much hurt. When this never happened, I was very disappointed. Could it be our relationship was the same as it had been in Amsterdam? I felt victorious, but not peaceful.

I assessed a man's masculinity by his ability to admit to his wife that he was wrong, and apologize.

That night, after putting Norman John to bed, I went to sit on the front verandah. Ruud joined me and put his arm around my shoulders. Elated, I gazed at the blue sky, but I couldn't find real peace of mind. Was I too hard to please?

Ruud whispered sweet endearments to me. I was flattered he made the effort. Unfortunately, flattering words only last as long as the scent of a flower. They did not represent the essence of a person's soul. Had he really abandoned the idea of bedding Nyai Kidhal?

Stroking my belly, Ruud said, "I hope this baby is going to be a girl as pretty as her mother. I'll be very proud to be her father." He continued pensively, "Perhaps I've not taken fatherhood seriously, but now love has revealed to me the magnitude of being a father to two children."

I did not respond. I suspected that this idyllic scene was not going to last. Ruud picked up my hand and kissed my fingers.

"What name will we give our child this time?" he asked, still caressing my belly.

"You don't find many people called Hercules," I joked, trying to hold on to the constructive atmosphere.

He laughed. "What if it's a girl?"

"I like Pertiwi."

"What kind of a name is that?"

"In the West people think of their country as masculine; they call it fatherland. Here in the East, people attribute motherhood to their country, *pertiwi.*"

"You like that name?"

"Yes, I do."

"I don't."

"Then why did you ask me?"

Ruud may not have been able to see my face in the dark, but if he had any sensibility at all, he should have known I was irritated.

He hastened to kiss my cheek and patted me on the back as if to calm me. And then a miracle happened. He said, "Sorry, darling."

I turned to him, my mouth gaping. I was speechless.

Ruud didn't understand my reaction. He waved his hand before my face. "What happened to you?"

I was so happy I grabbed him and kissed him. Crushing him in my embrace, I forgot all my hurt and suspicions.

If the sky can produce a full moon, I can find happiness in the future. I'm convinced that love derives from passion.

I said, "I'm tired, Ruud."

He took my hand and we went to bed.

I thought, he loves me.

Chapter Twenty

Didik came to our house at the end of the month, bringing provisions such as coffee, milk, sugar, tea, beer, and cigarettes.

It was interesting to see how a Dutch officer fared in this colony. All his necessities were taken care of by native soldiers. Take Ruud. He was never rationed like the foot soldiers, and his salary was higher than that of his indigenous counterparts. He never told me the amount of his salary. It could be five or ten thousand guilder.

Officers received an allowance over and above their salary, and the amount of the allowance depended on the person's regional ethnicity. There were three classifications: Europeans received thirty-one cents, Ambonese and Manadonese received twenty-seven cents, and the Javanese only twenty cents. Ruud's allowance was not enough to cover the cost of his cigarettes. He was a heavy smoker.

Here he always smoked Victor Hugos, a well-known Dutch brand imported by Geo. Wehry & Co. Once I tried one. It was awful, despite the motto on its packet, "Good to the last inch."

Being pregnant I didn't smoke tobacco. Neither did I drink beer. Besides, the beer that Didik brought every month was peculiar. It was called Beck's Koentji Bier. The label pictured a key on a shield with *Een Sleutel,* "A Key," written beneath.

Didik voiced his concern that I was doing everything myself, and asked if I needed a servant to help me. When I declined, he changed the subject, and invited me to Boroboedoer again, to dance with Mbah Koeng's group.

I told him that I was certainly interested. "I feel like my soul resides there," I said. "The wall of the temple with the image of the two dancers is part of my body. I want my soul to remain with my body."

"You mean, madam, you will pray to the Buddha?"

"Oh, I don't know. If I can touch his statue through the hole of his *stupa*, perhaps I should pray that my body be filled with a beautiful spirit when I dance."

"Will you dance again?"

"I'm even thinking of becoming a dancer."

I was absolutely naïve, but something inside made me say those things. Unconsciously I had expressed my desire to release myself from the physical constraints and let my soul run free. For the time being, I had no other ambition, though Cremer's face did surface for a second or two. He had asked me to write down my name and address. I didn't know if anything significant would come of it.

Didik jolted me out of my rêverie. "Do you want to be a dancer, madam?" He looked amazed.

"Yes," I said, full of self-confidence, or rather, bravado. "Dancing is an expression of the body to convey the beauty of the soul, to bring to the surface compelling desires in life."

"My goodness, madam, that is too abstract for me," said Didik.

I laughed seeing him bewildered. "You don't need to understand. An audience doesn't need to understand a dance. They simply need to feel and enjoy the beauty. This must occur naturally."

"If you say so, madam."

Again I laughed. "You know, Didik," I said, "I'm very grateful to you. Thank you for having taken me to the right place. In Boroboedoer I found my true self, my true humanity. If my mother were still alive, I'd tell her that life is short but art is eternal."

Didik remained quiet. From his facial expression I knew he had reached his limits. It is true that his job only required willing hands and not a witty brain.

Those who are smart,
Use their brains.
Those who are fools,
Use their brawn.

Chapter Twenty-one

As I entered the fifth month of my pregnancy, I thought about how horrid the last couple of months had been. There were the differences of opinion between Ruud and myself, manifested in screaming arguments, followed by name-calling. There was never any peace for Norman John and my blood pressure was consistently high.

I often stopped and pondered, and realized I had been wrong many times. Fans of astrologers would say it was in my character. I was born on the eighth of August, so I was meant to be headstrong.

When my pregnancy was in its seventh month, I began to worry that things were a lot worse than I had thought. I had gained more intuition, considering that according to Javanese customs and traditions, the seventh month in pregnancy was sacred, and marked by *mitoni*, a ritual ceremony.

During that month, Ruud went to Semarang every weekend without fail. He left on Saturday to return on Sunday bearing a gift of *dodol*, Javanese taffy. I had the strong feeling that he had another woman.

Each time I asked him about his assignment, he'd scowl and mumble something inaudible. My suspicions stemmed from the proposition he had made several months earlier regarding substituting me with Nyai Kidhal during my pregnancy. Who was to say he was not doing just that surreptitiously?

While serving him breakfast on Saturday morning, I told him that I wanted to come with him to Semarang. He was startled and said "no" too quickly.

"What do you want to come with me for? I have to work."

"Yes, I know," I said. "While you work, I'll go shopping and amuse myself."

He floundered momentarily, but quickly recovered.

"Let's do that next week," he said. "We'll make a point of having a good time. I'll come with you to the shops."

"We'll go together today." I pretended not to see his mounting panic.

"I need to make arrangements for that." His panic was increasingly visible. I tried to control my mounting suspicions.

"Why not today, or are you meeting someone else?"

His face darkened. "Who?"

"Well, I don't know."

"What nonsense is this?"

"You tell me why this is nonsense."

"No," he said, losing control over his temper.

"For heaven's sake, Ruud," I said calmly. "You are shouting. What's the matter? I only asked if you were meeting someone. There's no need to shout. The way you behave makes me think you are lying."

For a moment, he seemed stumped. "Why are you so irritating?"

"It's you who is irritating."

Ruud banged his fist on the table. "You are."

"You are," I yelled back.

Ruud jumped from his seat. Jabbing his finger at me, he said, "You are," and kicked his chair.

It fell against the table. The table shook and everything on it fell topsy-turvy. The house had turned into a battlefield.

Ruud was disoriented because I managed to remain calm.

I said, "You're hiding something from me. You're lying."

"Why should I lie?"

"Good question. You're the one who tells me there's no use in lying. Now you're lying. Why?"

The veins in his red throat turned blue and his eyes nearly popped as he barked, "Go to hell."

"Go there yourself. I still want to live in this world."

Struck speechless, he stomped out.

Chapter Twenty-two

I changed my mind about going to Semarang with Ruud. I may have been suspicious, but I wasn't going to be the caricature of a dumb wife who dutifully followed her mighty husband. I had to bide my time.

After he left, I paid a visit to Officer van Donck's wife, Saar. She knew where I could find René, the clairvoyant Ruud had consulted. I wanted information about my husband's escapades.

In the last years of the nineteenth century, Dutch people in Indonesia increasingly turned to clairvoyants when they believed their own clergy were unable to solve their problems. I was one of them.

I said to Saar, "I want to see that French clairvoyant in the mountains, René du Bois. He can show me what I can't see."

"He uses Tarot cards," she replied. "Many people have consulted him. I can take you, if you like."

Saar, Norman John, and I used a *dokar*, the simplest and smallest horse cart, to go into the hills.

René's native assistant ushered us to the front waiting room.

"The master is still with a visitor," he said.

René was not lonely in this remote location. He lived with his assistant, and during the day there were always visitors who consulted him about one thing or another. The people who came to him were like myself, those who had lost faith in the direct line to God and turned to another avenue, spiritualism.

René's house was entirely made of bamboo, very neat and tidy, oozing exoticism, right in the middle of nature in the beautifully green valley. On the front door a sign read "Maison Bambou."

As we waited, another Dutch client tried to find a loved one. Though we were in another room, we couldn't help hearing the conversation because the walls were very thin.

When it was our turn, we entered the room where René sat facing the door. Above the door hung a framed board containing a line from Rimbaud's poem, "Devotions":

A tout prix et avec tous les airs, même dans des voyages métaphysiques—Mais plus alors. (No matter how, no matter where, even in metaphysical journeys. —But *then* no more.)

René sat in his chair looking at my face, probing. He had brown eyes and must have been very handsome in his younger days. He looked like one of those saints painted by Western artists of an earlier century. It was, however, easy to imagine him as a homosexual who worshipped Arthur Rimbaud. He was so gentle, his movement so nimble and fluid. Why was I being distracted? I had come to ask René about my husband's comings and goings for the last four weekends. I showed him Ruud's photo and told him my reason.

René took the photo, placed it on the table before him, and spread the Tarot cards in front of a crystal ball the size of a baby's head. His head bowed low but his eyes fixed on me. He said, "This man is hungry for sounds and movement. The crow does not return to its branch when it is denuded by the season. His pastime is met by a never-ending war."

I didn't understand any of it. It was all so strange. "What does this mean?" I asked.

"I cannot see where he plays out his role. I feel there is a theater out there."

"You mean, he has someone else with him?"

"I'm afraid I can only give you the answer as I see it."

"And how is that?"

"Maybe the answer is yes. I'm sorry."

"Please tell me what the cards are telling you."

"In the Eastern way of thinking, what happens in some places, here, for instance, is not unfaithfulness. I perceive it as a game of seeking some kind of freedom."

"What do you mean with such obscure and enigmatic jumble of words? I want to know whether my husband is having an affair or not."

"He is merely having a physical adventure, not a psychological one."

"What are you saying?"

"That's what I see."

"So that means, it is true. Is it detrimental to our marriage?"

"I would say it is dangerous."

"Dangerous but not detrimental?"

"Nothing is detrimental in a game as long as the players are conscious that it is a game. It would be different if the players involved their soul in the game."

"How do I stop him from involving his soul as well?"

"I am not qualified to give such counsel."

"But what conclusions can I draw?"

"I can only say this, everyone can change in the face of emergency. What your husband is facing now is merely an emergency situation. It can happen to anyone, including you."

My brain hurt trying to understand him. His last sentence hit me like I'd stepped on a rusty nail. Maybe one day I would be able to work it out. Still I tried to elicit something immediate.

"What's the best thing for me to do?"

René replied, "Go home and stop worrying. When the head is hot, the heart will catch fire, and the body will burn out. When you go home, take cool drinks and sweet food, in order for the head to cool and the heart not to be bitter."

"I don't like sweet stuff. It's Ruud who likes sweets. He likes *dodol*."

"Does he?"

Chapter Twenty-three

Ruud came home on Sunday afternoon.

He tried to look as innocent as possible. It was so transparent I made a show of not noticing him.

He greeted me but I ignored him. When he went to kiss Norman John I carried in my arms, I still ignored him. I could have given him an earful about what I had learned from René the clairvoyant. However, I had to find the right time.

I decided to wait until the following week when we would go to Semarang together. I hoped to find out what Ruud was hiding then.

We took the train from Ambarawa's Willem I Railway Station to Semarang at Djoernatan. The Hotel Swatow on Pekodjanweg was only a brief walk from the station.

A pair of lion statues stood in front of the hotel. The receptionist inside stared at me, and openly looked me up and down. He was probably surprised to see a European woman wear a *batik* sarong.

Ruud and I hired a horse cart called a *cikar* and went sightseeing along Heerenstraat. This area across the suspension bridge through an area called Bodjong was part of the most important and classiest Dutch business district. In Dutch this area was called *benedenstad*, but the Chinese name for it, *pan-lay*, was more popular. If it were not a Sunday, we would have seen a more vibrant commercial area. I was disappointed because all the shops along Heerenstraat were closed. The only open establishment was the *Koepelkerk,* as the Dutch called the dome-roofed Protestant Church.

When our *cikar* passed the Koepelkerk, we heard the singing of Martin Luther's hymn, "A Mighty Fortress is Our God" from inside. The congregation was Dutch.

I felt cross and frustrated because I had looked forward to spending an enjoyable time shopping. Though seething, I restrained myself from lashing out at Ruud.

Our hotel was in Chinatown, owned by a Chinese family named Lie. However, when we returned to the hotel, I still felt it was not the right time to say anything. Maybe I'd wait until later in the evening.

We had dined in one of the Chinese restaurants that lined the street near the Tay Kak Sie temple, only five minutes' walk from the hotel. I loved Chinese food. We had noodles, wontons, fish dumplings, bean curd, and prawns cooked with Chinese vegetables and spring onions. I enjoyed the meal so much I forgot my earlier irritations. My mother had often told me not to be angry when eating.

After dinner we walked back to the hotel. Ruud went to the shop next door to buy *dodol.* Apparently that was where he purchased the *dodol* he brought back from his weekend trips.

I took a newspaper from the reception desk and went to sit in the sitting area. Meanwhile Ruud collected our key and went to the room to put the *dodol* away.

I was surprised to see the name of the newspaper: *Matahari.* It was a Malay language publication, published by Oei Tiong Ham, the sugar king from Semarang. At the end of the nineteenth century Oei had been granted permission by the Dutch authorities to cut his obligatory plait. I was further taken aback when I saw an advertisement of a cigarette by using the word *matahari.* The ad read, "Where a beam of sunlight is noticed, it is certain there are distributors of C B & K and cigarettes."

I was excited. The word matahari jolted my imagination. I visualized a life regarded as belonging to the realm of fantasy.

Chapter Twenty-four

I returned the newspaper to the reception desk. The receptionist, a Chinese man wearing a plait, a legacy of the Manchurian custom, again looked at me with amazement. "Is this the first time you stay in this hotel, madam?"

"Yes," I answered briefly. I wasn't in the mood for socializing.

"Mr. MacLeod is a regular in this hotel. He always stays in room eleven," the receptionist continued.

This took me by surprise. I was suddenly interested in chatting with him. I felt tingled with excitement as if I had discovered something important.

I knew I had to be careful and creative from that moment on. I had to appear as if I knew that Mr. MacLeod frequented this hotel with another woman.

"Who is prettier, me, or the other woman who's been staying with Mr. MacLeod?"

The receptionist made a face. "No comparison, madam. You are far prettier."

I probed on while controlling my rising bile. "Thank you for your kind compliment. Not all Dutch women are pretty."

"But she is not Dutch, madam. She is a native woman."

I was furious. I had predicted this, yet I was furious.

Just then Ruud appeared.

"Aren't you tired?" he asked.
"No," I replied loudly, and ran to the room.

Chapter Twenty-five

Three days after we had returned to Ambarawa, I still couldn't release my anger.

On Wednesday, four hours before Ruud came home, a letter came for me. My heart missed a beat when I read the sender's name: J. T. Cremer. I was even more excited when I read the name on the front of the envelope, Lady MacLeod.

Why not Mrs. MacLeod? When Cremer asked me in Boroboedoer to write down my name, I had written Margareta Geertruida Zelle. Now he addressed me as Lady MacLeod. Did I look like a lady? I wondered. Then I laughed at myself. I liked this attribute. My heart beating fast, I tore open the envelope and read the brief letter.

Cremer told me that in the following month an order would be issued for Ruud's transfer to Batavia. I began calculating the time until we'd leave for Batavia, and I realized that I would give birth to my second child in Batavia. I had no idea how my family life would fare there. Worse? No doubt. But that would be beyond my control.

When I reached the end of the letter, I was tossed further off-balance: *I believe we can work together.* He was testing me and also sending the message that he trusted me. Uncertainty and pride filled my soul.

"I won't let you down, Mr. Cremer," I said quietly. When the time came, I would prove myself to him.

I held the envelope aloft and read "Lady MacLeod," again and again and smiled, pleased with myself.

I thought of all the ladies I knew from my love of literature: Lady Bountiful in George Farquhar's play *The Beaux Stratagem*, Oscar Wilde's *Lady Windermere's Fan,* Alexandre Dumas' *Lady of the Camellias,* and Sir Walter Scott's poem, *The Lady of the Lake.*

> *Dreaming makes me feel lonely,*
> *But I am not alone.*

Chapter Twenty-six

The time came to have a talk with Ruud, a talk between a man and a woman. I knew this was going to be difficult, but it was crucial if I wanted to re-establish my dignity.

I prepared myself as if I were going to war. I positioned myself mentally in order not to lose my strength during the battle. Of course, I wanted to win, though I also knew that winning the war would not mean securing peace. Ruud had to take responsibility for his actions and admit to his mistakes and misdeeds.

After showering that evening, I asked Ruud to come to the sitting room and we sat face-to-face. "Ruud," I said. "I have delayed this moment long enough. If we don't talk now, I'll explode."

"Wait," Ruud said, disconcerted. "What is this about?"

I did not hesitate. "We are talking about what you and I can work on together."

"Like what?" Ruud asked, trying very hard to appear calm.

I crossed my legs and was ready for the offensive.

"I know that you went to Maison Bambou to ask René du Bois where I had gone. He didn't give you the answer because he knew I wasn't doing anything wrong. So he only gave you Rimbaud's poem, and asked you to be patient. However, René gave me an answer because he saw that what you are doing is wrong. You are having an affair with someone around here. So I don't have to ask around, please answer me, where have you gone the last five weekends?"

Ruud's face went white. He moved his lips but no sounds came from his mouth. He was at a loss for words. Finally, he said, "That is not true."

I was still aggressive. "That's not manly of you."

"What is not manly?" he asked defensively.

"You dare do something, but are too much of a coward to face the consequences and assume responsibility."

"What did I do?"

"I ask the questions. Not you. Answer me."

"I told you. I've been working."

"What kind of work?"

"You know; I'm an officer."

"Oh, but your going to Semarang has nothing to do with your being an officer."

"You are crazy."

"No, Ruud. It's you who are crazy, for carrying on with another woman in Semarang."

"That's not true. That's René's slander."

"What is the truth?"

"Everything René told you is a lie. All slander."

"Let's go back to my question. In fact, I have two. The first question is, where did you go these last five weekends? Then the second question is, with whom? Answer both questions like a man."

"I already told you. Work. End of story."

"That's what you're saying."

"Then why do you have to keep asking? You're being tedious."

"There's a Malay proverb, 'Even a squirrel that leaps from one branch to another all day long will slip from time to time.'"

"What do you want?"

"I want you to show your manliness by answering my questions truthfully."

"You've been duped by that French fool. That's for sure."

"You're wrong. The Frenchman is not the fool. The Scot is."

"What did you say?"

"No need for you to be angry. I am the one who can be rightfully angry, and believe me, this is my last anger. After this, the story ends. And just so you know, I didn't get the story from the French fool in the mountains, but from an honest Chinese man in town. As I said, the Scot is the fool."

"Don't say that again."

"Fine, I won't. Now speak as if you were a real officer. Be straightforward. Admit what you've done."

"Admit to what?"

I rose from the chair. Pointing my finger at him, I screamed, "You are the devil incarnate."

Ruud looked startled.

I repositioned myself for another attack. "Who is the native woman who's been sleeping with you in the Hotel Swatow?"

His face turned white, ugly, and disgusting.

Repulsed, I kicked the chair toward him. When he didn't move I screamed every swear word I could think of. At the end of my outrage, I said, "Listen carefully, Ruud. As soon as we return to Batavia, I will ask for a divorce from you in front of Mr. Cremer. You are rubbish. You are not human."

Chapter Twenty-seven

After that, Ruud tried to apologize many times. He was too late. Nothing that passed his lips could soften my heart. As we waited for the official document confirming our move to Batavia, I slept with Norman John in the front bedroom while Ruud slept in the main bedroom. All efforts on his part to win me back went unheeded. Everything he said or did only made me nauseous.

A week before I received the confirmation letter, I was startled by a piece of paper stuck to my bedroom door. When I came to examine it I saw two lines of Rimbaud's poem "Song of the Highest Tower":

Qu'il vienne, qu'il vienne,
Les temps dont on s'éprenne.
(O may it come, the time of love,
The time we'd be enamored of.)

I was going to tear the paper to shreds, but at the last moment I changed my mind and rushed to look for the sheets of paper containing Rimbaud's poetry Ruud brought home from Maison Bambou. I pulled one out with a poem titled "Morning of Drunkenness" and copied the last line, *Voici le temps des Assassins* (Now is the time of the Assassins), on another piece of paper that I attached to the one Ruud had stuck on my door.

Chapter Twenty-eight

I hoped Didik would come earlier in the month so that we could go to Boroboedoer again and visit Mbah Koeng before my departure for Batavia. I wanted to do this because it would be a long time before I'd have the opportunity again. My next visit might be the last. I never forgot the happiness and peace I experienced in the natural beauty of that region.

My wish came true, and we went to see Mbah Koeng, who was pleasantly surprised to see me in an advanced state of pregnancy. His wife came and stroked my belly affectionately. Their daughter, Astri, kept kissing my hand. They were all pleased to see me.

It occurred to me how adept Javanese people were at making visitors comfortable with their warm welcome. I was proud to be part of the culture through my mother. I wondered if the culture would outlast the passing of time. How would the Javanese be in five or a hundred years from now?

Mbah Koeng's wife recalled that around seventy years ago the region was a refuge for rebels who fought against the Dutch colonial powers. The son of one of Sri Sultan Hamengkoeboewono III's concubines led the uprising. He was such a charismatic character that even his uncles fought under his leadership.

The Javanese were willing to accept the Dutch as long as they were treated fairly. When the Dutch treated them cruelly, they quickly turned around. Yet they were happy to forget and forgive as soon as the Dutch showed they wanted peace.

The story was passed down the generations in the form of a ballad. Mbah Koeng often talked about different aspects of Javanese philosophy. There was a saying, "Don't put Javanese characters in your lap, or they will die," which meant that the Javanese people would fight back if treated badly, and would bow gracefully if treated well.

During this second visit, I sat beside Mbah Koeng's wife one night as she sang a poem called "*Ilir-ilir*." The verses offered advice on how to maintain a righteous soul by taking responsibility for one's deeds in life and remaining faithful to oneself through all of life.

Sensing that the song was a prayer and blessing for the baby, I grabbed her hand and sincerely thanked her. Then I said, "I want this child to have a native name."

Mbah Koeng responded, "If it's a baby boy, let him be called Njo, and if it's a baby girl, let her be called Non."

Pleased, I repeated the two names several times.

Mbah Koeng's wife stroked my belly and said, "That's good. I hope it's a girl. So you'll have both, Njo and Non."

"Yes," I said. "I will call this one Non."

"But," said Mbah Koeng, "would your husband agree?"

"Why would this be any of his business?" I asked crossly. "I plan my own life. And that includes choosing a name for this baby."

"But your husband is a soldier."

"What does that have to do with it?"

"Pardon me, madam. My grandfather, who fought the Dutch, was arrested in Magelang. We have been afraid of the Dutch since the time of Prince Diponegoro. We know that Dutch soldiers can be very harsh and cruel."

"But I'm not a soldier. It's my husband, soon to be a former husband, who is a soldier. I am a civilian."

"But you are Dutch."

"Ah, Mbah Koeng, Dutch people are also human. They are also of flesh and blood."

"We used to believe that the Dutch are not made of earth."

92

I laughed. "Why did you say that?"

"Well, we thought the Dutch, especially the soldiers, are made of brass, stones, asphalt, rocks, cement, and coins. They have no notion of night or day. They don't care about the people they oppress. It never occurs to them that one day these people might rise and fight back."

Again I laughed. "My husband, my almost former husband, is not Dutch. He's a Scot."

"Scot? Which country is that?"

"Scotland is in the north of England."

"My grandfather told us that the English were good to Sri Sultan Hamengkoeboewono. The English governor, I forget his name, was the one who suggested repairing Boroboedoer Temple."

I nodded.

Chapter Twenty-nine

In the small hut Mbah Koeng gave us to use, I was awakened by the swooshing sounds of flooding from the Elo River below. Apparently the heavy rains uphill had caused the river to overflow. I expected the rain would reach here too.

Two minutes later the roar of thunder shook me inside out. It felt as if my lungs dislodged. And as I'd expected, the heavens opened up. Gallons of rain fell on to the earth. The roof tore, and within no time the rain poured on us. Norman John woke up drenched. He rolled over, fell off the sleeping bench on to the floor, and started crying. He tried to stand up but his legs were unable to support his body and he fell again. My two-year-old son was still unable to crawl, let alone stand up. I didn't know then what had stopped his development.

Chapter Thirty

In Batavia our family lived in a neighborhood called the Citadel to the west of a beautiful tropical garden called Wilhelmina Park, facing the canal. From the upstairs windows of the two-story house we were able to see the tram owned by *Electrische Tram Maatschappij*, which at certain hours rode through the park toward the bank of Tjiliwoeng River.

Two days later I took a horse cart, and holding Norman John close to me on the bench seat, I directed the driver to Cremer's office. The trip turned out to be futile, because Cremer was not there.

His secretary, a plump woman who spoke Dutch with a Limburg accent, moved languidly as if she were a duck on its way home in the evening. She told me that if I wanted to see Cremer I needed to make an appointment. She found an appropriate time for me to come back three days later.

When I returned, I took another horse cart, called a *sado*. People stared. During the last days of the nineteenth century, a European woman in an advanced state of pregnancy getting on a *sado* must have been entertaining to those who walked past, not to mention unusual.

Dutch people were expected to travel on a landaulet, a two-horse covered carriage with moveable screens on its windows, or even a *palankijn*, a bigger and plusher two-horse version of the previous.

My discomfort at being stared at while carrying a small child with my big belly was compensated for by the entertainment inadvertently provided by the *sado* driver.

His eyes darted right and left as he asked me where I wanted to go. At first I was mildly insulted by this, thinking he was trying to avoid me. But when I looked closer, I realized that he was cross-eyed.

Cremer had yet to appear at his office. His plump secretary said that he had instructed her to direct me to another building, De Ster van het Oosten, a location known for clandestine meetings. Lucky for me it was just around the corner.

Cremer seemed disturbed at seeing my huge belly. I wondered what he was thinking behind that knitted brow. However, he immediately invited me into the building.

Once inside, even before we walked into the main room, I saw several gentlemen with serious, even mysterious faces, clearly putting on airs to puff up their importance. One of them came up and playfully pinched Norman John, who I carried in my arms.

Cremer later told me that those who were gathered in this building were libertines, individuals who were intellectually liberated from the Christian dogma and religious values that had dominated Western civilization for centuries. These people even refused to adhere to the Church's teaching of love and charity, because the Church criticized the power elite in the colonial administration in Batavia on these principles.

Having closed the door, Cremer showed me to a seat and then faced me from an ornately carved chair made of varnished black wood. He said, "I asked you to meet me here, so you can hear from a person who knows best about the situation in this colony. At the moment, two important matters are making our work difficult." Cremer was calm and kept his gaze on me. "Are you interested in learning more?"

"Yes, I am very interested," I said, without hesitation.

"Good." Cremer was pleased but controlled. "That means that I am speaking with the woman who, since our first meeting at Boroboedoer, convinced me that she'd work with us."

"I am glad you have given me your trust, Mr. Cremer," I said.

"Oh," he said. "Call me Jan."

"Yes, Mr. Cremer," I said, awkwardly.

"Jan," Cremer said with emphasis.

"Yes, yes," I said.

"Very well. Now let us talk business, Lady MacLeod," Cremer paused then asked, "By the way, do you like being addressed as Lady MacLeod?"

"I have no problem with that. I like the stories about the ladies, barring one lady whom I have long forsaken, the Lady Chapel."

Cremer looked pleased. I had met his approval, his personal stance being anti-religious.

"We are certainly politically compatible," Cremer said. "Now, returning to the two matters I referred to before. Firstly, the territorial defense as it is now, is undermined by the wars in Atjeh, which are costing the administration much more than expected. Snouck Hurgronje's attempt at causing a division between the warriors and scholars has not been successful in putting down the rebellion. Secondly, the war campaign has been undermined by the intervention of the Church, who accused the colonial administration of human rights violations of the native population in this colony. The Church's criticism has encouraged the natives to take up arms against the colonial authorities. The Church was inspired by the attacks launched by Protestant Pastor Hoëvell in the House of Representatives against the colonial administration."

I nodded, digesting what Cremer told me.

"Do you understand what I am saying?" he asked.

"Yes, I do." I knew where this talk was leading. "I gather that you are disturbed by the Church's criticism toward the administration in Batavia."

"You are right." Obviously impressed, Cremer nodded his head. "I like you. I have wanted a great deal yet needed little. You can help fulfill that little need of mine. You are a quick learner."

"What can I do for you?"

"My immediate need is for you to dance as you did at the foot of the Boroboedoer Temple. We will arrange for the program to take place at the Sociëteit de Harmonie in front of many important and prestigious guests, including the Protestant and Catholic clergy."

"In this condition?" I pointed to my belly.

"Of course not, Lady MacLeod. The performance will be on the thirtieth of May, the celebration party of Batavia's 280th anniversary. You must electrify the clergy. I want to know their reactions to Javanese eroticism."

I remained quiet. I tried to imagine something new, a fresh challenge.

Without hesitation Cremer touched my belly and said, "Well, Lady MacLeod, when are you due to give birth?"

"I think within two or three days."

"In that case, this afternoon you'd better ask your husband to take you to a gynecologist. Jasper Hoedt has a practice in Molenvliet. He is a good gynecologist and obstetrician."

"Mr. Cremer, Jan, MacLeod and I live under one roof, but I no longer speak to him."

"What do you mean?"

"Women often marry the wrong man. They mindlessly enter into the marriage contract for the wrong reason, as is the case with me."

"I don't understand."

"I am seeking your help."

"My help?"

"Yes, Mr. Cremer. I have made up my mind. I want a divorce from MacLeod. No arguments. No one can change my decision. I have heaven as well as hell in my heart."

"That's terrible."

"What can I say? MacLeod is not only the wrong man, the only fitting description of him is that of a pig."

"If you wish MacLeod to be given an assignment in Atjeh, I will make the necessary arrangements now."

"I don't only wish that, Mr. Cremer. I am eager for you to execute the order. Thank you."

At that moment Norman John wet himself on me.

Chapter Thirty-one

Taking Norman John with me, I headed for Dr. Hoedt's clinic in Molenvliet, about 150 kilometers to the north of the most beautiful tropical hotel in Batavia, Hotel des Indes.

Dr. Hoedt was such a comedian. When he spoke in his loud Flemish accent, one could not keep from laughing. As we progressed in the consultation, I realized why he was so loud: he was partially deaf.

Before the examination, he asked me to leave Norman John on the nearby bed and took me to another bed to lie down. He pushed my knees toward my ears to properly examine me internally while he entertained me with his jokes.

"Do you know the difference between a Chinese and an Arab?" he asked.

"No," I said, and tried not to react to his probing my body.

"A Chinese is conditioned to say yes, and an Arab is conditioned to say no."

"How's that?"

"Look at the way they read their holy books in their respective languages. Chinese is written and read from top to bottom, so when Chinese read their holy book, they nod their heads. Arabic is written and read from right to left, so when Arabs read their holy book, they keep shaking their heads."

He told and mimed his story, reminding me of the Italian clowns in Amsterdam's *nachtmarkt.*

When he finished the examination, he pulled my legs straight and rearranged my skirt.

"All is in good order," he said and took a seat at his desk. "I suggest you stay the night because I expect you to give birth tomorrow morning at the latest. There's even a possibility that the baby will come this evening."

"Really?" Pleased, I got off the bed and picked up Norman John.

"Yes, I'm serious," Dr. Hoedt said. "You may want to go home first and leave your son with his father."

"No. I'd like him to stay here with me. Besides, if I'm not mistaken, tomorrow, his father is leaving for Atjeh."

"I can imagine how busy you're going to be, living in Batavia."

"I'm used to doing everything myself even before I came to Batavia. I'd rather be busy than doing nothing and feeling lonely."

"But with two young children, you'll have more trouble than just being busy."

"I believe that trouble only visits our life, it never stays."

"You are remarkable. How old are you?"

"Twenty-one."

"You sound like twenty-one going on sixty-one."

"What's wrong with that?"

"Nothing at all. But do you want to hear my suggestion?"

"Of course."

"This is Batavia. You must have a servant."

"How do I get one? I've been here only less than a week."

"In that case, after you've given birth, go to Mr. Tan Tiong Djien in Kramat Boender."

"Who is he?"

"He provides servants to people in Batavia. You can go to his place and choose one you like. I suggest an older one. The young ones are dangerous. With their innocence, they invariably are attractive to Western men. I suspect scholars in Leiden could organize a seminar on the reasons why Western men are sexually drawn to Javanese servants."

I was suddenly irritable and angry, though I didn't know with whom.

Dr. Hoedt laughed at his own humor. Obviously unaware of my feelings, he continued, "You know, the term *Indo* refers to the offspring of a Dutch man and native servant."

I wanted to lash out at someone, but was unable to find the right person to direct my frustration and anger.

Damn.

Chapter Thirty-two

My daughter was born safely.

Dr. Hoedt said, "I want to stress the word 'safe' here, because your second child doesn't suffer from the same health problems as your first."

I asked him to explain what he meant. What was the matter with my first child?

He replied, "Don't you see that your first child has disabilities?"

I was shaken. "What disabilities?"

"Dear God. This child, apart from being lame, also has very limited vision. He's almost blind."

I remembered the night at Mbah Koeng's hut when Norman John, startled by the thunder, had fallen over and was unable to right himself. I was devastated.

"I'm so sorry," said Dr. Hoedt. "Please don't be offended."

"No. Tell me more."

"Very well. Do you want the truth?"

I looked at him, flustered. Finally I said, "Yes, please tell me."

Dr. Hoedt walked to the bed where Norman John was sleeping. Stroking his head, he said, "Your child is innocent."

"So?"

"He is innocent yet he inherited his parent's sins."

"What do you mean?"

Dr. Hoedt fixed me a serious and probing gaze. In his loud voice, he said, "Seeing that you are healthy, you are not the cause. It must be your husband. I'm sorry."

"What's the matter with him?"

"It seems that he likes to play around. Your child suffers from syphilis."

"What?"

"Your first child must have contracted the disease from his father, who no doubt frequented red light districts."

I felt weak from despair. I couldn't think of a word to say. My memory turned to Amsterdam and the conversation with Ruud's sister about Zeedijk and Walletje, and the times in Ambarawa.

I lost control. Inconsolable, I screamed, shrieked, and howled.

Chapter Thirty-three

As I prepared to go home, I enquired how much I owed the clinic. To my astonishment I was told that Cremer had paid the bills.

The immediate problem was how to carry both children to my house in the Citadel. I was still trying to figure this out when Dr. Hoedt told me that Cremer had arranged for him to call a *palankijn* to take us home.

This made me uncomfortable; Cremer was doing everything to make me indebted to him. He knew that I'd have no other way to reimburse him except by performing the service he wanted me to provide on Batavia's anniversary.

With the discomfort heavy in my heart, I was surprised to see a dark-skinned woman sitting on the stoop of my front door, looking uncertain.

When I asked who she was looking for, she replied that she had orders to find "Mevrow Miklut." This meant me. I asked who sent her, but she didn't know. All she knew was that someone from the government had told Mr. Tan Tiong Djien that she had to work for me.

The woman's name was Sarimah, Mamah for short. She was thirty-seven years old and came from a village in Buitenzorg. She had been married at the age of fourteen and widowed at thirty-six. She had three sons. The eldest worked at the Buitenzorg palace caring for the deer. The two younger ones were still dependent on her.

It was impossible to assess her character properly so quickly, but I was prepared to think positive. She no doubt had aspects I liked and some I wouldn't like, as she was only human.

Her first shortcoming was that she didn't speak Dutch. She claimed to speak some Chinese, for which I had no use.

I found consolation in that I could learn Chinese cooking from Mamah, since I liked Chinese food. But more importantly, I needed help. I couldn't be too choosy. And the gentleman from the government had paid Mamah three months in advance.

Though Sir Thomas Stamford Raffles, had banned slavery some eighty-five years ago when he was the lieutenant governor, in reality a servant had to get up at five in the morning to work non-stop until eleven at night.

I told Mamah to use the back room on the second floor.

Chapter Thirty-four

I was full of anger and hatred toward Ruud for the pain he had caused, but my love for my children was as strong as ever. This love could also be interpreted as pity. In the Malay language the two words are linked: *kasih* means love, and develops into *kasihan,* which means pity.

It seemed to me that the word "love" connoted conditions, obligations, while the Malay word *kasih* as it transformed into *kasihan* encompassed the fullest meaning of conscious unconditional love, which is compassionate and attests to sublime human greatness.

While breastfeeding my new baby, for whom I hadn't even found a Western name, I'd look lovingly and full of pity at Norman John sleeping nearby. Mamah's fanning him with a kitchen fan made of woven straw kept him cool.

I had no idea what I'd do if Ruud came back from Atjeh. I felt nothing but hatred toward him and prayed that he'd never return. If he died in Atjeh, I would put two piles of chicken manure on his headstone, along with two lines from the Song of Solomon:

The evil deeds of the wicked ensnare them; the cords of their sins hold them fast.

Nothing could stop me from getting a divorce from that pig.

"Legally you can only get divorced where you were registered as husband and wife," Cremer said when he and two of his guards came unannounced to visit me on the fifth day I was home from the clinic.

"Does that mean that I have to go back to Holland?"

Cremer confirmed such was the case. He asked, "If you want a divorce, why did you get married in the first place?"

I surprised myself with my answer. "How do you get a divorce if you haven't married?"

The expression on Cremer's face reminded me of someone watching a ridiculous performance. He said, "Your behavior defeats all norms which statistically have been accepted as facts. People make wedding vows in front of an altar while holding the Bible in order not to divorce."

"That's the ideal situation, Mr. Cremer."

"Please, Jan."

"Yes, Jan. I've tried to follow the ideal, but I failed."

"So you've taken your decision?"

"Everything has its time. The onset of the twentieth century will see me as a divorcee."

"Aren't you scared of your future with two children?"

"No. I take life as it comes."

"Sorry, but I have to ask. What's the matter with you and MacLeod?"

"He hurt me too many times to list. And he has been unfaithful so many times I don't care to count. I've never been unfaithful, not once. Now my time has come. That way, we'll reach some sort of balance."

Cremer seemed taken unaware at first, and then smiled. "You are no doubt a woman of the twentieth century, Lady MacLeod," he said, "probably even of the twenty-first century."

I laughed and so did he.

So far, I found it difficult to learn what he was thinking. My attempts at probing yielded nothing. This made me reassess my suspicions about him at the time we met in Boroboedoer. At that time I was influenced by what Mbah Koeng had told me about officials who were prone to corrupt behavior. Perhaps I was mistaken about Cremer.

I had cast the bait, but he hadn't taken it. He was as solid as the lion statue at Waterlooplein.

If Cremer was not one of those officials associated with the two tas, what did he expect in return for all he had done for me? I recalled the letter I received in Ambarawa, followed by the power he put behind

Ruud's transfer to Batavia, and most recent, the payment for my medical costs at Dr. Hoedt's clinic and the advance payment for the servant.

Was he merely expecting me to perform an exotic dance for the celebration of Batavia's anniversary at the Sociëteit de Harmonie on the thirtieth of May? I didn't know.

I waited for time to roll on through mornings, afternoons, and nights. Inside those days I danced in silence. I danced and danced, and the physical exercise helped rid me of the excess fat from childbirth.

Within three months my body returned to its original size and shape.

Chapter Thirty-five

Eventually, I settled on the prettiest Western name for my daughter, Jeanne.

I had been aware of the name since I was a little girl. But then, what European child would not have come across the character Jeanne d'Arc, the fifteenth century French heroine who had been burned alive by the Church through political maneuvering by British authorities?

I hoped my Jeanne would grow up to be just as brave and courageous as Jeanne d'Arc when defending her mother, who had carried her for nine months through buckets of tears and untold heartache.

A month after Jeanne was born, Ruud was given leave to return to Batavia and see his newborn daughter. Apparently pleased with the birth of Jeanne, he embraced me. Holding Jeanne in his arms, Ruud said, "I thought about a name for our daughter. I like the name Louisa."

"No, no," I said hastily. "Her name is Jeanne."

"In that case, let's name her Jeanne Louisa."

When I didn't say anything, he tried to sway me. "Jeanne Louisa sounds pretty, don't you think?"

"Fine. But as far as I'm concerned, she is Jeanne, named after Saint Jeanne d'Arc."

"Louisa was also a saint. Remember Louisa de Marillac, the saint who left her sumptuous home and lifestyle to serve the poor?"

So the name Jeanne Louisa was registered on our daughter's birth certificate.

Interestingly, each time Mamah rocked the baby to sleep with a Sundanese lullaby, she'd call her Non: *Non, anoe geulis tea. Non, anoe tjakep tea.* (Non, the pretty one. Non, the good-looking one.)

I recalled Mbah Koeng saying that native people called European girls Non, and boys were called Njo. Gradually I began to call my children Njo and Non as well. I continued this practice even after we left Java for Holland, where people addressed Jeanne Louisa as Non, thinking that was her real name.

Meanwhile I continued to live in Batavia with firm intentions to divorce Ruud as soon as we returned to Holland.

To move ahead in life with two children in tow was a big challenge, but I believed that women possessed the courage to confront major changes in life. As for me, I decided that whatever I did in my life, I wouldn't let people forget me easily.

> *From my mother's ability,*
> *From my mother's spirit,*
> *I was born a woman.*
> *When I die tomorrow because of destiny,*
> *Do not erase the dignity of my soul.*
> *For roses dry in time,*
> *But their scent is always remembered.*

Chapter Thirty-six

Ten days before the celebration of Batavia's anniversary, Cremer visited me in the evening. He wanted to know whether the preparations for my dance performance at the Sociëteit de Harmonie were going well. When I told him that my rehearsals had progressed, he told me about his preparations, which, of course, were taken care of by his entire office staff.

"I'm pleased to tell you that so far all of our plans show promise," said Cremer, full of optimism. "Now you have to play your part. You have to be brilliant. You must shake Batavia with your erotic Javanese dance. If you succeed, you will be the symbol of oriental eroticism to Western people." His voice went up a notch as he added, "Rooseboom is going to be there. You know Rooseboom, of course. He is replacing van der Wijck, the current governor general. Oh, how we want to see his reaction."

Catholic clergy from the south of Holland and Protestant clergy from the north were invited to watch my performance. "Are many priests and ministers coming?" I asked.

"Every congregation of the Western churches currently in Batavia is invited. The Dutch pastors of Santa Maria Cathedral, the German ministers of Willemskerk, the Anglican priests of All Saints Church, as well as the Armenian priests of St. Hovhanneskerk. All of them."

"But will they attend?"

"We hope so. However if they don't wish to, we can't force them. It is their prerogative to refuse," Cremer said soberly. "They each have a voice which is heard by the people's assembly in Holland, though they don't necessarily have the power to change the course of history. The liberal views in this century represent a modern and progressive force that will continue to move forward. Therefore, we have to be prepared to accept different views and perceptions."

"No doubt you're right."

"We want your erotic dance performance to show those who are still living in the Middle Ages that if religion is included in this colony's politics, people will rebel. They will refuse to be true to their faith, simply because they want to enjoy themselves."

"You don't like the clergy and their supporters."

"They are themselves flesh and blood, Lady MacLeod. They cannot deny that according to their religious teachings, sin lives in the flesh. In the meantime this obsession with the flesh is like a relentless shadow following us wherever we go. I want to make them see that what they regard as a problem is nothing but beautiful, natural, human desire."

"Goodness, Mr. Cremer…."

Cremer interrupted. "Jan," he said.

"Yes, Jan, pardon me. You've taught me to look ahead, to see a future I never dared dreaming of. You've encouraged me to do things I never thought possible."

"Is that true?"

"Yes, Mr. Cremer, sorry, Jan."

"I believe there is no such a word as 'no' when it comes to the will to do something."

I laughed. He was right.

Cremer looked at the clock. "I must go," he said.

Before he left, he kissed me in the Dutch tradition—on the cheek, left, right, and left—"I'll see you soon," he said, waving.

I called out as he walked away, "Jan, there is something important I have to ask you."

"Yes, what is that?"

"To accompany my dance performance, I need some *nayaga*. Where can I get them?"

"What are *nayaga*?"

"*Gamelan* musicians. At the very least, we need musicians to play the *kenong, kempoel, kendang, gendjoer, bonang, gambang, rebab, bende,* and gong."

"Maybe we could ask at the Schouwburg if they can help."

"And I need a *slendro* set. It is a scale similar to Western music. The notes are roughly equivalent to C D E G A."

Cremer shook his head, looking amazed. "You know Javanese music?"

"I have to, Jan," I said. "*Slendro* is a type of pentatonic scale which was created in Boroboedoer based on Chinese pentatonic scale, *huang mei tiau*."

"You know Chinese music, too?"

"I have to understand what I do in my dance," I said.

"Very well," said Cremer. "I will look for your *slendro*."

"Thank you. Remember, *slendro*, not *pelog*."

Cremer looked bewildered. "What on God's earth is *pelog*?"

"*Pelog* is also pentatonic, but native to Java. Its notes are roughly equivalent to C E F G B."

"Yes, you will have it. You are unbelievable."

He laughed. And I laughed.

Again, he said, "I'll see you soon."

He started to rush out, but came back. He took me in his arms and kissed me again three times on the cheek. But this time he kissed me passionately, long and tight.

I didn't want to assume a deeper meaning in his kisses although it was entirely possible things were moving into that direction.

If that were to happen, I would justify it to myself. While I was still legally Ruud's wife, I had morally and mentally divorced him.

Chapter Thirty-seven

I entered the Sociëteit de Harmonie building, known by the Dutch as the Soos and by the native people as Harmonie, and was immediately awed. The sumptuousness made me dizzy. I stared in admiration at the interior of this building. Built more than eighty years ago, it was designed by an architect named Schulze and officially opened by Sir Thomas Stamford Raffles.

It was unique. In other buildings of classical style, pillars were normally found outside. Here they were inside. They were Corinthian style, with the tops sculpted in shapes of acanthus, a plant endemic in the Mediterranean. Eighteenth century Chippendale and Hepplewhite chairs were arranged around the base of each pillar. Where I stood, the entire floor was made of marble. Beautiful Venetian chandeliers, each containing three magnificent bright glass bulbs, hung from the ceiling. Large mirrors in Baroque copper frames magnified the grandness, and cast the light in every direction.

A number of sculptures and paintings were also on display. Four paintings particularly caught my attention. They were landscapes by the Dutch masters Aelbert Cuyp, Meindert Hobbema, Jacob van Strij, and Pieter Rudolph Kleyn. One painting I first thought to be the work of the French master Delacroix, turned out to be that of Raden Saleh.

The entire ambiance impressed on those present that this was an extraordinary social meeting place in Batavia. It would be absolutely criminal if in the future an ignorant leader would cause the building to be demolished and replaced by another, as had often happened throughout the last two hundred years.

Hundreds of invited guests had come to celebrate the anniversary of Batavia. I did not ask Cremer if the European clergyman who had irritated him was also present. It was not my place to do so.

As I walked further into the room, closer to the area where plush chairs were neatly arranged for the guests, the air was impregnated with various fragrances. The scent of jasmines, roses, and tuberoses in the vases, mingled with the perfumes sprayed on the elegant evening dresses of the upper class ladies.

Approaching seven o'clock, the cavalry marched and saluted with their arsenal, accompanied by "Wilhelmus van Nassouwe," the Dutch national anthem, played by the military orchestra. Governor General Rooseboom and his wife stepped down from his official carriage and walked into the building arm in arm.

The women whispered about the appropriateness or inappropriateness of the attire and overall appearance of Rooseboom's wife. This was a common occurrence.

Gossip ridiculing the wives of high officials was fuelled by their ostentatious appearance. This embarrassing social phenomenon was triggered by the women's perception of how a high official's wife should look. Very often, instead of elegant, they looked gaudy and unnatural.

The official ceremonies began, and they seemed never-ending. I was increasingly nervous.

Finally my moment came. Cremer went to the front and as master of ceremonies, introduced me. "Distinguished guests, honorable ladies and gentlemen. We are now going to see a Javanese erotic dance performed by Madame MacLeod from Friesland."

The audience applauded, but looked uncertain. I was startled because Cremer did not refer to me as Lady MacLeod as he usually did, but as Madame MacLeod. However, I did not have time to worry because the *gamelan* music started.

I stepped onto the stage made of wooden boards measuring ten by seven meters. For several seconds I stood motionless, arms extended, waiting for the electric lights to be turned off and replaced by the glow of candles that had been placed on the stage. When the lights dimmed, I slowly raised my right hand and lowered my left. Then I began to dance. A few movements into the dance I undid and took off my Chinese-style white *kebaya*. Turning my body while lifting my left leg to hold on to the blouse, I slowly unfastened my bra. Placing the *kebaya* on the floor, I used the bra in the dance, moving it this way and that in front of my breasts. Then I placed the bra on the floor and continued dancing bra-less, free of the cloth of civilization. Next I loosened and slipped the *batik* sarong from my waist, and began the last part of my dance in only my knickers. In a few seconds these, too, were placed on the floor and I danced in front of high society completely nude in half darkness, the only light on my body coming from the candles. I couldn't tell whether or not the audience liked my dancing. What I did know was that I had danced with my body and soul fully merged, creating art. A performer must have confidence in her ability to create something beautiful, and the audience can decide to like or dislike it.

Cremer was the first to congratulate me. He hugged me tight. To my own surprise, I responded with enthusiasm, holding his body close to mine. I'm not clear how it started, but we were no longer kissing on the cheeks. Instead we were passionately tongue kissing.

Coming to my senses, I pulled myself away. "I must go home now," I said.

"Won't you wait till the end of the program?" Cremer, gently, yet firmly pulled my hands towards him. "There's going to be a *bal masque*."

"No, sorry," I said. "I must feed my baby."

Cremer nodded. "I'll see you tomorrow."

He walked with me to the door. Outside, he looked for a carriage to take me home. Before I boarded the vehicle, I stopped and thanked those who approached and greeted me, expressing their appreciation.

I recognized the man who playfully pinched Norman John when I first came to De Ster van het Oosten looking for Cremer. Clockener Brousson said, "Your dance was true poetry."

"Thank you," I said humbly.

Just when I was leaving the sumptuous building, the orchestra inside—a military group of whose members came mostly from Ambon and Menado, and the conductor from Solo—played Johann Strauss' "The Blue Danube."

Chapter Thirty-eight

I was troubled and restless as I waited for Cremer to visit me. Twice my heart missed a beat when there was a knock on the door. The first knock at seven o'clock in the morning was the baker, and the second knock at nine was the postman.

At eight, Mamah went to the market. Unlike the times in Ambarawa, where Didik delivered our provisions once a month, we bought our necessities everyday at the market.

Mamah went to the market with Njo. She carried him in a length of *batik* cloth tied around her neck and underarm. We had two options, the Gambir market to the southwest, and the Pasar Baroe market to the northeast. Both were about the same distance. And Mamah went by *sado*.

Mamah seemed to take her time and I was lonely. My mind began to wander to Cremer, hoping he would come soon, as he had promised.

Why did my longing for him intensify by the minute? I was bewildered by what was happening to me and afraid that even my freethinker self was unable to be truthful. What blocked my mind was too complex for me to see, too difficult to articulate.

I tried by asking myself if my feelings in any way related to my dance performance of the previous night. If so, it meant I wanted to hear the reaction from the audience, something which Cremer would tell me. If this was the case, then thank God the problem was simple.

But was this the crux of the problem, or was there another reason? Maybe I hoped to receive an honorarium. But was I not an amateur? What does it actually mean to be an amateur?

If I waited for Cremer to bring me reactions about my performance, it meant that I thought like a professional. In the performance world, a professional is always eager to hear reviews, be it from an ordinary audience or professional critics.

In other words, if I wanted to hear evaluations to my performance, I was no longer an amateur. Instead, I was becoming a professional dancer.

So what was the actual reason that I was restlessly waiting for Cremer? Was it because I hoped he would bring me an honorarium? If that was the reason, it was because of what he said in the letter he sent to me in Ambarawa, asking for my cooperation. Surely that meant that I was to do something to benefit him, and he was to do something to benefit me. I give him a service, and he gives me payment. This is the essence of cooperation.

Was that the reason for my eagerness to see him?

I could not answer the questions I asked myself in that torrent of thoughts. Instead of answering those complicated questions, I stopped thinking about them. My head hurt from the assault.

The hours moved on. I waited all day. The morning turned into evening, and yet Cremer hadn't come.

At nine in the evening, I lay on my bed breastfeeding Jeanne Louisa, or Non, trying to lull myself to sleep. I was not one who fell asleep easily.

This time I was unable to sleep despite being tired because I had so many unanswered questions. What was happening to me?

After Non fell asleep, I walked to the dining table for a drink of water from the jug. It was only ten o'clock and too early for a maid to go to sleep. Mamah asked if I wanted a cup of hot tea, a drink the Dutch had learned from the Chinese.

Two hundred years earlier Batavia had been hit by an epidemic of dysentery that killed many Dutch people but barely made inroads into the Chinese community. The Dutch concluded that it must have been the tea the Chinese drank daily that saved them.

Outside the night was cool from the strong wind. It was the last day in May and looked like rain. Tomorrow the dry season would officially start.

"Yes, a cup of hot tea," I said to Mamah. "Put sugar in it, but not too much."

She laughed. "Madam, if it is too sweet, it's *gioeng*."

I turned at hearing the word. "What is *gioeng*?"

"*Gioeng* means not nice because it is too sweet," Mamah explained.

With that I learned a Sundanese expression that did not have any equivalent in Javanese or Malay.

There was a knock on the front door. I jumped up and ran like a deer to open it. The object of my anxious wait stood in front of me. Overcome with joy, I lost my self-control and flew into Cremer's arms.

He responded warmly and enthusiastically.

In no time we were enveloped in a tight embrace, our mouths engaged in passionate kisses. The questions that swam in my head while waiting disappeared and were replaced by an honest admission that in each of those questions there was the immutable truth that I wanted to see Cremer because I missed him. Not as a working partner, but longing to be in his arms enjoying his kisses.

After that, I did not care where fate would take me.

Outside the wind howled.

However I knew nothing bad would happen that night.

Tomorrow was another day, along with the day after tomorrow, and the following day.

Each day inevitably brought its different problems.

Chapter Thirty-nine

Cremer sat down.

"I am in your debt, Lady MacLeod," he said.

"Wait," I interrupted. "Why did you refer to me as Madame MacLeod last night?"

Cremer smirked. "I don't know. I suddenly thought of Madame Bovary. Do you know who she is?"

"Of course. I read Flaubert's novel four years ago, in its original language. I liked it."

"Formidable."

"Not really."

Cremer and I gazed at each other. Were we thinking of the same thing?

He took several bills out from his jacket pocket, and handed them to me. "This is what I meant when I said I was in your debt. Please take it," he said.

Startled, I stared at the ten bills with "De Javasche Bank" printed on them. They were banknotes of five guilders, greenish blue, with the picture of Jan Pieterszoon Coen in the right hand corner.

"For the moment, this is all," said Cremer. "But things will be different when you become professional."

"What?"

"The director of the Sociëteit de Harmonie wants to discuss the possibility of you appearing regularly. Yes, Lady MacLeod. You are becoming professional. You will dance regularly at the Soos."

Proud and gratified,
I kissed him.
Though misery is my travelling mate,
I only see fragrant flowers
In the new light of dawn,
In the fading light of dusk,
Tomorrow, the day after,
And the day after.

Chapter Forty

Cremer was right. The director of the Soos came to my house the next evening.

"I hope you will appear on the first Saturday of each month," he said.

"I'd be very happy to oblige," I answered.

"We do have a minor problem. We don't have a *gamelan* orchestra to accompany your dance each Saturday. We can only take advantage of a *gamelan* orchestra when there is a group from Soerakarta or Jogjakarta coming to play in the Schouwburg. I wanted to ask you, and I know this is a silly question, can your dance be accompanied by other than *gamelan* instruments?"

I laughed. "You have answered your own question."

"I'm afraid so," he said. "Perhaps you have a suggestion?"

"If it is difficult to get hold of a *gamelan* orchestra, I could dance to guitar music complemented by the sounds of castanets."

Amazed, he asked, "Can you do that in a Javanese dance?"

"Not Javanese," I said. "Flamenco, the Spanish gypsy dance."

"That is indeed a good idea," he said. "But we don't have any Spanish in Batavia. Spanish culture is regarded as foreign and only holds sway in Menado. Besides, I am an adherent to van Deventer's concept regarding our ethical policy, which instills in the Dutch people an awareness of our moral debt to this colony. That awareness has to translate into showing appreciation of its culture, in particular Javanese culture, and that means its theatre, literature, music, dances, fine arts, *batik,* and so forth."

I was surprised by what I had heard, and a deep respect for this man grew in my heart.

"Very well," I said. "How many times a year do the cultural groups from Soerakarta and Jogjakarta perform in the Schouwburg?"

"They perform there in turn every three months."

"That's that, then," I said. "Once every three months I'll perform at the Soos."

"Ouch," said the director regretfully. "I had hoped an orchestra could simulate a *gamelan* group."

"An orchestra that plays Strauss waltzes?"

"Yes, but I'll ask them to simulate a *gamelan* orchestra."

"I don't think that would work. It would be as incongruous as eating *poffertjes* with *sambal terasi*."

He laughed at my mention of combining the Dutch cake-like treat with the local hot sauce.

I told Cremer of our conversation when we saw each other the following day, and he also laughed.

"You are going professional," Cremer said.

"I'll perform once every three months at the Soos."

"Excellent," he said.

I remained silent. I still had much to learn. I needed to see Mbah Koeng in Boroboedoer, to continue my studies and acquire a deeper understanding of the significance of the dance as *natya* and the dancer as *nartaki,* who merged the beauty of body and soul in accordance with the description on the temple's wall. I experienced stirrings like these when I saw the statue of Shiva for the first time.

Chapter Forty-one

Cremer had to go to Bandoeng, and he invited me to go with him.

I was thrilled. I had always wanted to see the city known as the flower of the colony's mountain resorts. However, we did not go as lovers. There were seven of us. Cremer had two guards with him and I asked Mamah to come as well, so she'd be able to look after Njo and Non.

We went to Bandoeng on a government train popularly known as the Fast Four, short for the train company's Dutch motto, "Staat Spoor Steeds Sneller," or State Trains Move Faster. Batavia and Bandoeng had been connected by railway for eleven years, via Buitenzorg, Soekabumi, and Tjiandjoer.

A small orchestra of Russian and Turkish musicians entertained the passengers with several musical numbers minutes before the train departed from the Batavia station. The Russians and Turks had been influential in the development of performance arts in the Indonesia, such as opera *bangsawan* and *komidi stamboel*.

As the train rolled forward, a vista of green rice fields opened up before us. Moving through jungles and forests, we climbed over tall mountains after Tjiandjoer. We sped through spectacular valleys and ravines, as well as through the Lampegan tunnel. We were wonderfully absorbed in the journey, where the events and drama were provided by nature while we sat in the train compartments. There was not a dull moment for me who came from a land where an incline of three meters provided as much excitement as climbing a high mountain. The highest mountain in Holland was St. Pietersberg, a one hundred meter-tall hill to the south of Maastricht, which my teacher had described as the beginning of the Netherlands.

I kept looking at my watch to confirm the popular claims that the remarkable train took only two and three quarter hours to travel from Batavia to Bandoeng. And it did, nothing more or less. The well know advertisement for the train read, "In Daendels's era the fastest postal train took two and three quarter *days* to travel from Bandoeng to Batavia, but the Fast Four now only needs two and three quarter *hours*."

As soon as we reached Bandoeng we felt the city's famous cool weather. We were met at the station and taken to the Grand National Hotel, which was not very far away.

I shared a bedroom with Non, while Mamah and Njo occupied another. Cremer had his own suite, and his two guards shared a room. That was how things were arranged, for the purpose of appearances.

Late in the afternoon Cremer had a meeting with officials at the Sociëteit Concordia building. His carriage returned to the hotel to take me to Bragaweg, an area of the city with the most European shops to be found in Indonesia, including three sumptuous establishments owned by Jewish families.

Mamah, the children and I stopped at a café in the middle of Bragaweg. It was the only café that had the coat of arms of the Dutch monarchy on its front door. I never saw any such establishment in Ambarawa, Semarang, or Magelang.

We took a seat at a table under the umbrellas on the terrace. A Dutch-speaking native waitress asked for our order. She recommended the house's cream cakes, Koningin Emma Taart and Wilhelmina Taart, named after King Willem's queen consort and their daughter, the princess. We ordered a slice of each to enjoy with our afternoon tea.

I was looking forward to having a Chinese dinner. However I was told that in this city Dutch people were forbidden to eat in Chinese restaurants because of their perceived lack of hygiene. In addition, Chinese were banned from entering Bandoeng by a law called *passenstelsel*, instituted in April 1882.

There was much pronounced racism directed against the Chinese in Indonesia. As far back as 1289, Singasari's King Kertanegara mutilated the face of Meng Ki, Emperor Kublai Khan's emissary, by cutting off his ears. Then in 1740, the Dutch East India Company's twentieth-fifth governor general, Adriaan Valckenier, massacred some 10, 000 Chinese in Batavia. More recently, Prince Diponegoro beheaded all Chinese inhabitants in Kedoe.

I found this interesting as Islam, practiced by the majority of Javanese as well as those on other islands, was believed to have been brought to the archipelago by nine proselytizers known as *walisongo*. Many believed these nine individuals were from China. What had happened in the meantime? Why were the Chinese in disgrace? However, I hadn't come to solve social and political problems.

While waiting for the sun to set, I watched the people stroll along Bragaweg. With Non in my lap, I pondered the immediate situation. Everything was so chic, French chic. Even the menu offered mostly French cuisine.

At six o'clock the elegant street lamps were lit and I was hungry. I decided to order what was written on the board, grilled mushrooms and red wine. We left the café at seven o'clock.

When we entered the hotel, Cremer had not come back.

Chapter Forty-two

While waiting for Cremer, I lay on my bed and thought about the prospects for the night. Would it be better to present myself as a simple woman, who accepted anything offered to her? But that would not be honest, because I was a brave, straightforward woman who had no difficulty showing, or expressing, my sexual desire.

First I needed to erase Ruud from my heart. What happened tonight would help reinforce my resolve to divorce Ruud. We no longer had mutual feelings for each other and there was no reason to remain together.

By coming with Cremer to Bandoeng I had taken the necessary step to show the world and myself that I no longer belonged to Ruud. I was not being unfaithful to Ruud; I was exercising my basic right to choose my own company.

At the same time, I realized I had a whore in me. What I was doing was nothing less than to justify becoming a concubine.

At one minute past ten, Cremer knocked on my door. "Did I wake you?" he asked.

"No, I wasn't asleep."

"Are you tired?"

I shook my head. He smiled and I saw a glint of naughtiness in his eyes. I was ready to be naughty myself.

He pulled me into his arms and kissed me passionately. Responding with similar desire, I opened my mouth to receive his tongue and held him tight, signaling how my body wanted him.

Cremer took off my blouse and kissed my breasts. He was not rough like Ruud. He knew how to please a woman, and how to send me into ecstasy in no time. Pushing me gently on to the bed without interrupting his kisses, he continued to undress me until I was naked. He quickly undressed as well.

What I had thought and fantasized about was happening, and I was overcome with joy. I didn't even have to say I loved him. Neither did he say he loved me. Yet we made love.

We didn't stop making love until the following morning.

> *I was drunk*
> *On a body no longer bound.*
> *With one utterance*
> *I note my passion.*
> *I look to where the spirits*
> *Of my ancestors cried,*
> *At the lake before my ship went down.*

Chapter Forty-three

Bandoeng agreed with us. Even Njo rarely cried. We spent two nights at the Grand National Hotel, until the city authorities arranged for us to move to a newer hotel on the Grote Postweg, next to the signpost indicating the city center.

Hotel Preanger was only two years old. It was built in classical style, with Ionic pillars complete with tympanon and decorated friezes. Pretty *penang* trees shaded the front yard. We spent another three days here and each night Cremer and I made love. If my life were a book, this phase would be the chapter that described how I discovered my talent to be a courtesan. Providing I didn't become pregnant, the next chapter would prove to be interesting as it would be about how I escaped my fate.

After a day in the Hotel Preanger, Mamah and I strolled to the city square. Mamah carried Njo and I held Non. A beautiful mosque was built in the center of the square. The three-layer roof showed the influence of Hindu architecture. Around the square, a number of barbers had set out their tools under shady trees and waited for customers.

We enjoyed ourselves sitting in the morning sun. It was certainly very different from hot Batavia. The surroundings were quiet and peaceful.

To the south of the square, in front of the entrance gate to the courtyard of the regent's palace, a performance of *longser* was going on. It was an integrated Sundanese theatre, very popular because of its comic acts. We went closer to see for ourselves. I was very interested in its *gamelan* music. The instruments did not seem as complicated as the ones in Central Java. I noticed that the *kendang* consisted of four units called *koelanter*. The player's hands enthralled me; the way he beat the small drums was magical.

I was the only European in the audience. I enjoyed watching the *beboeka*, the opening dance, which led to the opening of the real drama performance. It was accompanied by a three-by-three tune, known as *ketoek tiloe*. Performed with swaying hips and shimmying breasts, the movements had a very erotic effect.

I absorbed the dance. It would remain in my subconscious as part of my understanding of the traditional arts of Java. I suspected that I'd need to bring it to my conscious mind and incorporate it into my own dance movements on more than one occasion.

Someone in the audience who had stood behind Mamah, asked her while sneaking a look at me, "Excuse me, are you the servant of this Dutch lady?"

"Yes." Mamah spoke Sundanese. However, hers was a Buitenzorg version, not as refined as the Bandoeng version.

"She seems to be enjoying *longser*."

"Yes, she is," Mamah said.

I was so absorbed in the performance that I was unaware of the man behind me until he touched my back and said in Dutch, "It's nearly twelve o'clock. Let's go eat."

When I turned around, Cremer smiled at me.

Chapter Forty-four

Cremer told me that we had to return to Batavia. We celebrated our last night in Bandoeng at the hotel's coffee house. Instead of coffee we ordered Bordeaux wine, sipping it while enjoying the piano solo music. The blind Russian pianist played magnificently several numbers of Chopin's mazurka. We took our seats in the plush upholstered chairs while he played Opus 6 No. 3 in E Major.

Though we had reached a deep level of intimacy I knew very little about Cremer. So I asked, "Would you be offended if I asked you a few personal questions?"

Cremer frowned. "What about?"

"About things I don't know."

"Is there anything about each other that we don't know now?"

"Yes, there is."

"Really? We know each other very well already."

"We know each other physically. But that doesn't mean that we know much about each other."

"What do you want to know?"

"Are you married?"

"Yes."

"Where is your wife?"

"In Amstelveen. Why did you ask?"

"Just curious."

Cremer took a sip of his wine and turned around to check on his guards.

"Now I've answered your question," he said.

"There's another," I said.

"You can ask two or three," he said half jokingly.

"Why do you like to call me Lady MacLeod?"

"It's personal. You are a Dutch woman with a Scottish name. It might bring you good luck."

"Are you superstitious?"

"I don't think so."

"There's something else I've wondered about. When we met, I mentioned that you had the same name as the minister for colonial affairs, but you said you were not him."

"Indeed I am not. Jacob Theodoor Cremer the Minister is in the Netherlands. Not here."

"So you and he are not the same person?"

"In Spain many people are called Jesus, the same name as our Lord. However, some of those people are also criminals."

"It is curious that you work for the Dutch government, even the Governor General showed you respect, and you have an office in De Ster van het Oosten."

Cremer laughed aloud, but without mirth.

"You have a sharp mind," he said, and continued, "But you're making the wrong conclusion."

As we left for our room, the Russian pianist played Opus 7 No. 5 in C Major.

Chapter Forty-five

Without a warning, the good times I had in Bandoeng came to a stop as soon as I returned to Batavia.

Three days after our return, Cremer came to my house bearing a gift of cash worth 5,000 gulden. He stayed very briefly. Before leaving he kissed my cheeks and said, "No flowers, even those in Keukenhoff, can compare with the beauty of your body."

I was in awe. I didn't realize that those were his parting words.

After waiting for three weeks, I went looking for him at his office. It was July twenty-seventh.

To my surprise, his plump secretary told me that Cremer had gone back to the Netherlands.

"You're joking," I said. "Are you sure he is not at De Ster van het Oosten building?"

"Feel free to look for him there," she said dismissively.

I didn't believe her, so I did.

Clockener Brousson, the man who had praised my dance performance at the Soos, received me. "How can I help you?" he asked genially.

"I am looking for Mr. Cremer," I answered.

He was surprised. "Didn't he tell you he was going back to the Netherlands? He left on the eleventh."

Now it was my turn to be surprised. Apparently the secretary had told the truth. If Cremer left on the eleventh, he did so on the day after

134

he gave me the gift of 5,000 gulden. To save face, I said, "Oh yes, but I thought it was going to be tomorrow."

"You were mistaken."

"Well, in that case, I had better go."

I started to walk out when Brousson called after me, "Wait, Madame MacLeod."

Madame MacLeod, just like Cremer had introduced me at the Soos.

When I turned to look at him, I was struck by his good looks. He had a formidable moustache that reminded me how as a teenager I'd visualized the perfect man.

I was driven to say my name, not the name he had used, but a name I associated with a passionate nature. I said with confidence and clarity, "My name is Mata Hari." I articulated each word.

Brousson seemed startled. Recovering quickly, he sparred flirtatiously, "When were you baptized with a new name?"

"You like it?"

"It certainly sounds exciting."

I laughed.

"Are you in a hurry?" he asked.

"I have to go home," I said. "My baby needs me."

"If you need assistance, don't hesitate to look for me."

"Are you sure?"

"Of course. I will help in any way I can."

"Thank you very much. I won't forget."

Then I hurried home.

Chapter Forty-six

As soon as I was home, I felt bad spirits. My heart began to beat fast. At the front door the neighbors were gathered with varying degrees of worry on their faces. One of them rushed up and expressed his condolences in a Brabant accent.

It felt as if someone had punched me in the stomach. I rushed into the house and saw Mamah sitting limply on the floor facing the sofa where Norman John lay stiff, his glassy eyes unseeing.

I stood speechless, unable to make sense of what I saw. My son, my poor son, had been released from the shackles of illness. And he had left without saying goodbye.

When I recovered, I shook Mamah's shoulders. "What happened?"

"Njo died," Mamah shrieked, and then recounted the event.

A small native man had come to the house, and asked if this was the residence of Officer Rudolph MacLeod. When she said yes, the man gave her a bag containing *dodol*. After saying that it was a gift from a friend, he left without further explanation.

Njo discovered the sweet and made a noise indicating he wanted some. Mamah told him to wait for his mother to give it to him and went to the kitchen. When she came back Njo had opened the package and was eating the *dodol*. Before she could say anything, Njo convulsed and then went limp.

The date, July 27, 1899, has never left my mind. I learned then that the only certainty in life is death.

Chapter Forty-seven

We made arrangements for Norman John to be buried in Tanah Abang cemetery. A priest, probably notified by a neighbor, came to visit. His name was Monsignor Edmundus Sybrandus Luypen SJ, pastor since 1898. In his Limburg accent he asked if I was Catholic. If this were so, he would pray for my son's soul. I looked at him sourly. I said, "I used to be Catholic but I don't care anymore. I am a freethinker."

If I had expected the priest to retreat, I was mistaken. He said, "You're still a Christian."

"How so?" I asked, forgetting that this was not the time to be contradictory. "I don't wish to be regarded as Christian."

"Calm down, my child," Monsignor Luypen said. 'People who have been baptized and become members of the Catholic Church remain Christians, even if they are apostate Christians."

"If you like," I said curtly and let him pray, invoking the Father, the Son, and the Holy Spirit with the sign of the cross.

The only other people present then were next-door neighbors from both sides, and Clockener Brousson.

I sensed that Brousson's friendliness had ulterior motives. I would not discourage him. In fact, I welcomed him. Since the first time we met, I was struck by his handsomeness. Why would I avoid becoming close to him? I had trained myself to become a courtesan with Cremer.

Brousson hadn't only come to express his condolences and join the prayers led by the Jesuit priest, he also brought me a copy of the Dutch military newspaper, *Soldatenkrant*. Handing me the paper, he said, "I am the correspondent for this publication."

I remembered Ruud reading that paper.

Chapter Forty-eight

Njo was buried, but his memory was too fresh to recede into the back of my mind. For days on end I was consumed with sadness and anger. I needed to find a distraction if I didn't want to destroy myself. I turned to the favorite occupation of my childhood and went to the main library, the Bibliotheek Bataviaasch Genootschap van Kunsten en Wetenschap, which was in Koningsplein, far from my house but easily reached by *sado*.

The many books I read opened up a vast world of knowledge that kept me enthralled. I was increasingly enlightened. Modern women needed to do much more than make themselves attractive to men by adorning themselves with pretty trinkets the way I was brought up by my late mother. Women needed to develop and maintain healthy brains by motivating themselves to read quality books in the library. It was infuriating to see how men regarded us as chattel, because of our inability to think for ourselves.

In the new century, this had to change. My own life experience with that pig Ruud had triggered my realization. I was determined not to allow men domination over me. I had to think and stand up for myself. Without reading I would remain ignorant and vulnerable to exploitation by men. Now that I had reincorporated the reading habit into my life, I hoped this would differentiate me from animals, which were only concerned with primary needs such as eating, drinking, and keeping warm. All women need to adopt reading as a regular activity.

Chapter Forty-nine

Six days after Njo was buried, I was reading in the front room when there was a knock on the door. Mamah started toward the door, but I said, "I will do it."

I didn't know exactly why I wanted to do that. I knew it wasn't Ruud, because the news about Njo's passing would take four days to reach him, and then he still had to find a ship bound for Batavia. Perhaps I secretly hoped for a handsome fellow sporting a big moustache to come and entertain me.

When I opened the door, I was surprised to see Nyai Kidhal. Her appearance hadn't changed much, except that she had put on a little weight. If the native belief that gaining weight indicated prosperity was true, I had to conclude that after leaving my employment, whoever employed her was more generous than Ruud and I.

When she saw my consternation, Nyai Kidhal knelt and burst into sobs while kissing my feet. "Have mercy, madam," she said. "I tried to stop my brother, but he was resolute. Please have mercy, madam."

Nothing Nyai Kidhal said made the slightest sense. "What are you talking about?"

Instead of answering, she lurched forward. Hanging on to my feet, she kissed them again, and crying even louder, she said something that made me jump. "Please kill me, madam. I can't bear to live."

"Wait a minute. Please calm down. What are you trying to tell me?"

Nyai Kidhal would not stop crying. After several minutes she tried to speak again without much success.

I asked Mamah to bring a cup of water. According to native belief whenever someone was unable to speak from tension, fear, or stress, a drink of water was known to rectify the situation.

Mamah brought Nyai Kidhal the water.

"Here, drink," I said.

Nyai Kidhal hesitated, but after a while she took the cup and drank without looking up at me.

I coaxed her gently. "Now tell me, what's the matter?"

"My brother insisted, despite my opposition," she said.

"I honestly don't know what you're talking about."

"Madam, my brother brought the *dodol*, Mr. Ruud's favorite snack."

"We've discarded it."

"Madam, forgive me. My brother put poison in the *dodol*. It was intended for Mr. Ruud. But I swear by Ida Sang Hyang Widhi Wasa, I have sinned against you because it was Njo who ate it."

My breathing seemed to stop until I realized I was perspiring, though my hands and feet felt like they were dipped in ice. Questions filled my mind but never found their way to my mouth, the most pressing one being, "Why?"

Nyai Kidhal clung to my feet and sobbed. "I am ready to receive any punishment, madam. I am guilty."

"Why did your brother want to murder Mr. Ruud?" I asked.

"He was angry," Nyai Khidal answered. "I am four months pregnant."

I struggled to understand the situation. Nyai Kidhal had gained weight because she was pregnant, not from a new prosperity.

"Are you married?" I asked.

"No, madam," she replied.

"So what happened?"

"My brother was angry, and wanted to murder Mr. Ruud after he refused to take responsibility."

The room went dark.

When I regained consciousness, the room still moved like a boat at sea. My head hurt and I was unable to say anything. The pieces began to fit. The story told by the receptionist of Hotel Swatow in Semarang, about Ruud taking a native woman to room eleven. Now that woman turned out to be Nyai Kidhal.

"So it was you who went with Ruud to the Hotel Swatow," I said.

Nyai Kidhal bawled in despair. "I beg forgiveness, madam." She reached inside her bra. "Please take this back," she handed me the necklace I gave her. "I don't deserve it."

"No," I said.

For a few moments I was filled with hate, but recovered quickly. Nyai Kidhal and I had a common adversary. Ruud had treated both of us with utter contempt. I felt sorry for Nyai Kidhal, while my anger toward Ruud solidified. Though I still found men necessary, I was determined that if this were how they treated women, they now had to contend with how I treated them.

When I made myself available to Cremer, I wanted to prove to myself that women had the ability to do something reckless. I now decided to have another affair, this time with Clockener Brousson.

I looked at Nyai Kidhal without animosity. "It was not your fault, Nyai Kidhal," I said to her. "I wish it had been Mr. Ruud who'd eaten the *dodol*."

She was astonished at my words. "Madam?"

"Yes. If your brother's heart had not turned against Mr. Ruud, I would use the infernal fire in my own heart to burn him. Believe me, he is the devil incarnate."

Chapter Fifty

When Ruud returned to Batavia and learned that Norman John died after eating *dodol*, he went into a rage. Blaming me for everything, he accused me of being a useless mother. "Norman John wouldn't have died if you'd been a good mother," he shouted until he was hoarse.

I kept quiet. I was not prepared to match his performance. To be effective I had to wait for my turn to speak, otherwise we would just shout and neither of us would listen to the other.

Ruud didn't want to stop. "What have you been doing? Didn't you know Norman was in danger? What kind of mother are you? You only think about prettying yourself."

Finally I walked away. In my bedroom, I locked the door. Lying on my stomach on the bed, I cursed Ruud. "You don't know what I know. You don't know Nyai Kidhal came here and revealed your disgusting behavior," I said to the pillows.

I didn't want to use it as a weapon. I wanted Ruud to stop his ranting. Since he gave no indication that he would, I hoped that when I woke up tomorrow, his squealing-pig voice would be silent.

However, the recriminations resumed with renewed vigor the following morning. Mamah made coffee for Ruud, so I proceeded to make a cup for myself and sat down at the table ready for breakfast. I had hardly settled in my chair when Ruud started ranting again. "You should have known that children of Norman's age need to be watched closely.

Servants are only good for bathing and hand-feeding them, changing their clothes, and waiting while they poop. You have to do the rest. But you, useless woman, you're good at nothing. All you do is make yourself pretty. You are cheap. Only a cheap woman would let her teacher take advantage of her."

As if it weren't enough to admit that I'd made a proper mess of my life by marrying Ruud, I had to be reminded that I'd lost my virginity in the most stupid manner.

It shook my resolve to keep calm. "Shut up," I screamed, my hand holding a cup of hot coffee. "One more word from you, and I'll throw this in your face."

Ruud's eyes nearly popped from the threat.

I realized immediately I had made a mistake. I should have just tossed the coffee. Now I had advertised my move.

He banged his fist on the table. "You think you can threaten me? You little trollop."

I had to move fast. I threw the cup at him, but missed.

He jumped and slapped me hard across the face.

I fell to the floor. However, having gathered enough energy from anger and hatred over the years, I quickly got back on my feet. Employing the most powerful weapon of a woman I started to scream.

Ruud tried to stop me, but only rendered me more hysterical.

"Quiet," he yelled, emptying his lungs.

When I kept screaming, he grabbed me and threw me against the door.

I managed to open the door and ran out of the house.

Several neighbors burst out of their houses. They were fellow Dutch people. Usually keeping very much to themselves, they were now unable to curb their curiosity, a characteristic they must have adopted from the natives.

I saw an opportunity to publicly embarrass Ruud and continued to scream while heading for the street.

I am winning.
Oh, tell the rational world,
How the heart has torn the veil
Protecting the face of the tyrant.

Chapter Fifty-one

Ruud did not give up. He rushed after me and caught me.

I struggled free and ran.

He caught me again. His grip on my upper arms hurt me, and he shook me hard. "Get in, quick," he snarled.

I screamed from pain and anger as more neighbors came out of their houses. "No. Let go of me." I ran.

Again he chased me. Seizing my arm he made me stagger, nearly falling on the pavement. "Quick, get inside."

Fighting back, I tried to pull my arm free. The number of spectators had grown. Ruud was obviously disturbed by the situation. "Aren't you ashamed of your behavior? Neighbors and strangers are watching," he scoffed, looking like a predator about to devour his prey.

"Do you think I care? You are the one who should be concerned. I'm going to embarrass you in front of everyone."

He grabbed my hair and pulled with brute force. I lost my balance and Ruud gained physical control. Dragging me by my hair, he twisted my arm, rendering me powerless.

I screamed in pain.

Ruud continued dragging me. Close to the front door, he loosened his grip and I tried to struggle free again.

"Don't try anything silly if you want to stay alive," he threatened.

I had reached a hysterical point and nothing could stop me. "Let go. You no longer have any rights over me. You're not my husband any more. I've started divorce proceedings. Do you hear? I'm no longer your wife."

We had made ourselves a public spectacle. Ruud looked uncertain and his grip loosened.

That was when three of our neighbors approached. Two of them pulled Ruud away from me, and the other pulled me to one side. When Ruud tried to break free, another man held him back. Temporarily disabled by the physical restraint, Ruud lashed out at me. "Norman John died because of your negligence. You refuse to admit your fault."

I moved toward him, but the neighbor held me back. So I shouted, "Norman John died because of you."

"Don't try to wriggle out of your responsibility," Ruud said with a sick arrogance, and moved toward me.

The three men stopped him. One of them put his palm on Ruud's chest, and said, "Calm down."

Ruud ignored him. He continued to hurl abuse at me, and blamed me for Norman John's death. "You've killed my son."

"Norman John was disabled, or he would have understood not to eat the *dodol* intended for you. But he couldn't hear, couldn't speak, and couldn't walk properly. He was the victim of your reckless behavior. You contaminated his blood with the syphilis you contracted from frequenting Zeedijk."

Ruud went pale and began to howl at no one in particular.

"No," he roared. "That is not true."

Bitterness made me cruel. "Ask Dr. Hoedt, the Belgian doctor. You are the killer of my son."

Ruud continued to holler, "It is not true."

"The *dodol* was intended to kill you because you're an irresponsible bastard. Nyai Kidhal's brother brought the *dodol*. He put poison in it because you made his sister pregnant. Now what do you have to say?"

Ruud stood as if he was glued to the spot. His mouth moved several times but no sounds came out.

I struggled free from the neighbor's grip on my shoulders and rushed to Ruud. Punching his face as hard as I could, I said, "You are evil. Your father is Lucifer and your mother is Beelzebub. And you are cursed."

The Brabant man came forward to hold me back again, while trying to cajole me into going back inside my house. In the meantime, the three men who held Ruud had to retighten their grips because Ruud had gone into another rage.

Consumed with a passion for revenge, I broke free and rushed toward the crowd. "Look hard, ladies and gentlemen. This is Rudolph John MacLeod. He was my husband, but is no longer. I'm divorcing him. You must know who he really is. He has tortured me physically and mentally. He sired a child with a servant in Ambarawa. The servant's brother tried to kill him by putting poison in a roll of *dodol,* but my son ate it instead. Look hard, ladies and gentlemen, this is the man. Call the military police to arrest him."

The Brabant man tried to calm me. In a typical Brabant accent, he said, "What you think is everything is actually nothing, and what you think is nothing is actually everything."

I was grateful for his caring attitude. In fact, he was the only one among my neighbors who had been friendly toward me. I really appreciated his presence. If it were not for him, I would have been in a much worse situation in the altercation with Ruud.

> *I am grateful.*
> *Yes, I understand,*
> *Thoughts of goodness*
> *Reside in a pure heart.*

Chapter Fifty-two

I don't know who notified the military police, but two officers took Ruud to their headquarters. However, the press knew of the charges before they did. The journalist who came was none other than Clockener Brousson. He only had time to exchange a few words with me, because the military police officers took me in also.

Ruud and I were seated side by side at a long table. The picture of Queen Wilhelmina and a Dutch flag of red, white, and blue bordered with orange tassels, Orange being the ruling dynasty in Holland, hung on the opposite wall.

I undid the top button of my blouse, revealing a hint of cleavage. Then I calmly recounted my story to the examining officer with as much detail and drama as I could.

He was touched by the fact that Ruud had caused our son to be infected by syphilis, and was angered that my husband had made the servant in Ambarawa pregnant only to abandon her.

Then came the question I had waited for: What did I expect to do next?

"Divorce," I said, without hesitation.

"Are you one hundred percent convinced that's what you want?"

"Yes, and I have discussed it with Mr. Cremer. He said it would have to be done in the Netherlands."

"I'm afraid he was right."

Ruud interrupted. His face resembled a dried-up orange as he pleaded, "Margaretha, please."

The sight of him and the sound of his voice repulsed me. I ignored him.

The officer asked again, "Are you sure you want a divorce?"

"I have gone through enough. And I don't want to get syphilis as well. I want a divorce."

"I understand."

I felt gratified, especially because he said it in front of Ruud, whose face flashed crimson from anger but immediately changed to dark and shrunk like a beaten animal. He remained that way until the end of the interrogation.

I was allowed to go home to take care of my baby, while Ruud was detained in a police cell. I had to restrain myself from cursing him aloud, "Rot in hell."

Chapter Fifty-three

When I stepped out of the interrogation room, Brousson was sitting on a bench facing a Eurasian soldier. The soldier regarded Brousson with great reverence. Apparently, Brousson had followed me, and waited until the military police had finished their interrogation.

Brousson rose as soon as he saw me. "How are you?" he asked.

"I'm fine," I replied.

"Very good." He gallantly gestured for me to walk ahead of him.

"Come, Mata Hari. By the way, were you serious when you said you changed your name to Mata Hari?"

"Of course," I said.

"Come," he invited me into his waiting carriage. "I will take you home."

Pleased, I boarded the carriage.

It was a type of landaulet with a collapsible roof, drawn by two horses and driven by a dark-skinned groom. We were soon on our way to my house.

Brousson told me about the Dutch East Indies administration's continuing problems, and the situation of the KNIL soldiers, KNIL being the *Koninklijk Nederlands Indisch Leger*, the Royal Netherlands Indies Army. Ruud was in the vulnerable section in Medan, a city ruled by the sultan of Deli. Medan was the logistic post of the KNIL forces on their way to Koealasimpang on the border of Atjeh.

Being full of anger with Ruud, I said, "I wish Rudolph MacLeod would die in the wars with the Atjehnese. I hear they are tough warriors."

Brousson threw me a sideways glance, but remained silent.

I asked, "Are the military police going to keep MacLeod for long there?"

"Maybe," answered Brousson. "Generally, an officer who makes a servant pregnant undergoes a lengthy interrogation."

"Is this a common problem?"

"It has happened before. After the interrogation, the officer is usually ordered to take responsibility, and marry the servant carrying his baby."

"That's a good policy," I said. "After all, servants are humans, and so are their babies."

Brousson was taken aback. He regarded me carefully before nodding.

The carriage stopped in front of my house, and I alighted. I had started to walk away when Brousson asked, "Do you have anything planned for this evening?"

"No," I said, excitement rising in my chest.

"We can go to the Soos if you wish."

"Oh yes." I was pleased by his invitation. I needed distraction, somewhere to relax after such a harrowing day.

"Good," said Brousson. "I'll be here around eight o'clock. See you soon."

"See you soon," I repeated.

The carriage moved away.

Chapter Fifty-four

Brousson knocked on the door at eight o'clock.

I'd been ready for half an hour. After I fed Non, I left instructions with Mamah regarding what to do if Non were to wake up. I looked forward to relaxing at the Soos. I opened the door to the handsome, smiling Brousson. "Are you ready?"

"Yes," I said, stepping out.

Brousson held out his hand to help me climb into the carriage. He followed and ordered his driver to take us to the Soos. We had not traveled very far when Brousson complimented my dress. "You look particularly stunning in red," he said.

I felt flattered, even though my dress was purple. However, we were in the enclosed space of the carriage and it was twilight. I also began to like the man sitting across from me.

"Thank you. So you like the color?" I asked.

"Red always attracts attention."

I smiled. "The dress is actually purple, not red."

"Yes, you're right," he said, laughing. "I am hopeless at telling colors. I often see purple as red."

I offered him consolation. "There is a significant red element in purple. A painter in Amsterdam told me that purple is a combination of red and blue."

Brousson was pleased. He took my hand and said, "I'm impressed by your knowledge of colors. You know, the natives are also hopeless at colors. They call brown beans *katjang merah,* which means red beans."

"There's no word for brown in Malay. They use the word *tjokelat,* borrowing the word chocolate for its color."

"I really like you," exclaimed Brousson. "You are beautiful, and have a good mastery of languages. How many do you speak?"

"Only seven," I replied, a little embarrassed.

"That's remarkable." Brousson brought my hand to his lips and kissed it. Just then we stopped in front of the Soos.

Brousson quickly stepped out and offered me his hand to alight. As soon as we entered the building, we heard the Spanish song, "La Paloma," composed by Sebastian Yradier, whose name had been known to music lovers since 1877. Several couples were dancing.

We headed for the left corner of the room where three men sat around a table. Brousson introduced me. "These gentlemen are on the editorial team of a publication we are setting up in Batavia. It will be operating shortly. This is Johan Tehupeiory, a most brilliant student of STOVIA, the medical school here. He is originally from Ambon. This is Prince Harjo Sosroningrat, captain of the Pakoe Alam Legion of Jogjakarta. And this is Nawawi Gafar Soetan Ma'amur, a teacher at the Kweekschool, the center for teacher training at Fort de Kock."

They all shook my hand and uttered the appropriate greetings.

Brousson pulled me a chair and asked, "Where is Wiggers?"

Almost at the same time, Tehupeiory and Nawawi replied, "We're waiting for him."

Soon after, the man they called Wiggers entered with two women dressed in frippery. One was tallish and looked Eurasian. Her father was probably Dutch and her mother a servant. The other was shorter and looked like a native from eastern Java. She had dark brown skin and was well built. I thought she was pretty.

Brousson introduced me to Wiggers. He shook my hand. Looking straight at me, he said, "I saw your erotic dance at Batavia's anniversary celebration the other evening."

I nodded, without saying anything.

He continued, "It's a unique Javanese dance."

Prince Harjo Sosroningrat frowned. Perhaps he thought I was just another arrogant white woman like the ones he often met. Shifting his eyes between Wiggers and me, the captain of the Pakoe Alam Legion cynically asked in Dutch, "Are you adept at performing erotic dances?"

I answered in refined Malay. "Yes, your highness, I learned and trained at Mbah Koeng's arts community at Boroboedoer."

My response seemed to put the prince ill at ease. Again he spoke in Dutch, "Do you speak Malay?"

"Yes, your highness, my mother was a Javanese woman."

Sosroningat laughed. Relaxed, he said, "You have shamed me. You speak our language very well."

The waiter set down the glasses of beer that Brousson had ordered while I was talking with Sosroningrat. I didn't like beer; it looked like horse's urine. Out of respect for Brousson and his friends, I said nothing.

I realized that the men were meeting to discuss work when Brousson said, "Let's drink to our baby, the magazine, *Bandera Wolanda.*"

They raised their glasses and toasted, "Salud," before finishing their drinks in one gulp. Brousson turned out to be the editor-in-chief of the magazine.

On a low platform at the dance floor, a band of ten musicians finished one number and started playing Strauss' "Tales from the Vienna Woods."

As the band reached the fourth bar Brousson held out his hand inviting me to dance with him in front of the band.

I felt a little awkward because I was used to the French version of waltz, while Brousson danced in a German style called *schottische,* which was more of a two-step.

Each time he swung me I hugged him tight in a seductive manner and eventually aroused myself. I wanted to kiss him. And since I was not going to play a teasing game, I kissed him there and then. Had I not liberated myself from the constraints of tradition and convention in terms of sexual behavior, through my initiation with Cremer?

> *I know I exist*
> *Because other people exist.*

MY NAME IS MATA HARI

I want to find shelter
In a worldly home.
My heart wants to find shelter in mortality
By landing sexually in a dream,
As lust manifests in dreams.

Chapter Fifty-five

Inside the carriage after leaving the Soos, Brousson and I transformed into a pair of birds. Whether parakeets or doves, we took turns nipping at each other's lips and our tongues explored each other's mouths, exchanging saliva.

The first flushes of our amorous exploits were interrupted when the carriage stopped in front of my house. When I started to step out, Brousson held me back and ordered the driver to go around Koningsplein, the park.

The driver obeyed and we duly returned to the realm of Eros. Other people may have called what happened as lovemaking. Not I. Other people probably saw sincerity in our exploits. But I no longer did.

Some would think that we had progeny in mind, or regarded what we were doing as our contributions to guaranteeing the continuation of society. Not I. To me, we were engaged in pure physical enjoyment, well-deserved fun.

I derived three kinds of pleasure from Brousson. First, sex with him was balanced. He was gentle and appreciative, and he looked so handsome that I was lost in the ecstasy of being with him. Secondly, he was always exciting in the intellectual realm. I learned a great deal from him about the social aspects of humanity, drawing on his store of knowledge as a journalist. His profession not only provided him with various disciplines of knowledge, but in order to do his job properly he always had to explore and discover. Last but not least, something still important for me as a woman: he always gave me cash at the end of each month. Admittedly the amount was never greater than what Cremer had given me as his parting gift, but it exceeded the allowance I received as an officer's spouse.

Brousson provided the cash I needed to buy beautiful clothes in Passar Baroe.

Our relationship lasted nine months, full of fun and sexual pleasure. It was I who decided to terminate it.

At the close of the New Year's Eve party at the Soos, I thanked him for his very enjoyable companionship, and told him that now was the time to say good-bye.

Brousson looked crestfallen, though he did accept my decision.

"I mustn't force you," he said. "We are partners, not enemies."

I was pleased and proud of him. He was a man who was able to take an upset without losing equanimity. I admired that quality in him.

Brousson was my initiation into a way of life in which I could end a relationship at will, and without lamenting the loss of enjoyment and pleasure it had given me. Again, I was increasingly aware that I was becoming a courtesan.

I whisper in earnestness
The amorous words
Wrapped in the fear of loneliness.
Rolling from one bed into another,
I seize the illusion of satisfaction.
Rocked by the music of hunger
All for the purpose of revenge
I will never run out of self-love.
I am free of boredom
A torture and curse
To the voice of serenity.

Chapter Fifty-six

I was increasingly adept, and more skillful, in sexual relationships with men who were not my husband. I no longer regarded this as adultery. I had undergone a fundamental change. I was now Mata Hari.

The saint's names given to me by my parents were now buried. It was only natural that I changed. My attitude to life stood apart from most people around me. My values of enjoyment and contentment were vastly different from those held by people in my community. In particular, I regarded sex as a means of attaining pleasure and physical ecstasy. I subscribed to Chinese and Indian thinking relating to this issue. They were two ancient civilizations that openly discussed sex as a refined art of living pleasurably.

When the Western races were yet to be civilized, the Chinese had already written books about the beauty of physical pleasure.

I refused to regard this fixation on sexual pleasure as a kind of disorder, as if it were deviant from the normal mindset. Sex had to be performed by a healthy body. In order for those engaging in the act to have maximum enjoyment and reach the plateaus of fulfillment, it had to be explainable as a science.

I was fully conscious of what I wanted in this respect.

What I wanted, and indeed was getting, was to find in the beauty of the act a real freedom of the spirit. I had never been as free as I was then.

I knew that the lack of freedom was a cultivated crime. For that reason, it had to be opposed. And I opposed it.

I had been stupid to believe in the Western style of marriage that was tied to the rule of the Church, and made one swear that only death would release one from the binds and allow the pursuit of another partner. I had also been made to believe that the sacramental rite uniting a couple was a formidable fort to be defended until death.

All that sounded good. However, I'd learned through my own marriage that in practice it did not work. Ruud would do anything he pleased, and my place was to accept the situation.

Extreme disappointment and anger had strengthened my resolve to fight back. Now I was free from the mental agony that had tormented me and tied me to the Church. I had broken out of those constraints with my sexual affairs, first with Cremer, then Brousson. I was ready for another affair with another man whom I deemed would give me what I wanted.

I was intent on making this game a profession. If I had to go back to the Netherlands for my divorce, that was what I intended to do. I would use my body in dance performances as well as in providing physical pleasure to men who were eager for the service.

Having closed the chapter with Brousson, I turned to Wiggers.

Wiggers was not as handsome as Brousson, but I overlooked a man's physical appearances and concentrated on his wealth. In his case, I made sure there was no love in our sexual encounters. Furthermore, no orgasm was necessary on my part. Women are able to fake it. And I was good at faking it. I groaned and moaned as if lost in ecstasy, bringing my sexual partner to reach the climax and ejaculate in no time. I was well trained.

When I was tired of Wiggers, De Bruyn was waiting for me. Then came Zuuderhoff, Vinck, Bijleveld, and Hoos, in uninterrupted succession.

The latest was Van den Bers.

In those days I could choose any man at the Soos, and nominate any sumptuous hotel for our sexual encounters. There were a number of hotels in Batavia suitable for my purpose. Hotel des Indes and Hotel der Nederlander were in the immediate vicinity of the Soos.

I went to the hotels with Dutch officials and in their company forgot the past images of happiness for the purpose of indulging in today's enjoyment. I enhanced my femininity by allowing men who were not my husband to derive pleasure from me. As time passed I became more convinced of a woman's sexual power, which served me well.

Betrayal had to be matched by betrayal for justice to be done. I didn't dwell on words and I proved my theory with deeds. I had overcome the weight of Western civilization and traditions heavily dominated by the Church. I had succeeded in snubbing God and His mysterious ways. I had begun a new history where I was free from the domination of the Church, which I believed belittled individual personality and will. I was now free to be different. I was able to choose my sexual partners. I no longer disguised or suppressed my sexual drive.

Chapter Fifty-seven

The last day of December 1902 was also the last day of my dalliance with Van den Bers. When the sun rose in the eastern sky on the first day of January 1903, I made further changes to my life. Some things had to change again.

When we entered the New Year, which was celebrated with fireworks at Koningsplein and paper trumpets along the roads in Weltevreden, Non was nearly three years old. Time had hurtled on while I pursued my adventures in Batavia after Ruud had been sent back to Medan.

Non was different from Njo.

Mamah had taught her to sing *"Jali-jali,"* a Malay-Betawi song, played on a pentatonic scale after the Chinese *huang mei tiau.*

The way she sang the song was so cute I wanted to hold her tight and never let her go. I was very proud of her.

Mamah had worked longer for me than Non was old, and she was a very good servant. While she couldn't speak Dutch like Nyai Kidhal, she was influential in my learning to speak bazaar Malay.

I never heard again from Nyai Kidhal. The child she was carrying must have been born and about two years old by this time. I wondered how they supported themselves. As for the child's father, not only did I not know, I didn't want to know. I hated him as if he were a knot of vipers that I wanted to expel from my soul.

Why would I want to know about him when I didn't even know what happened to the men who were my seasonal sexual partners during the dark years of Governor General Rooseboom's administration?

When I thought of the men, remembering them by name, Brousson, Wiggers, De Bruyn, Zuuderhoff, Vinck, Bijleveld, Hoos, and the last one Van den Bers, I had to confess that over those years, each had given me different kinds of joy and sadness. Only three out of the eight individuals had celebrated New Year's Eve parties with me at the Soos.

This year it was Van den Bers. We passed through the doors of the Soos at ten o'clock, and proceeded to drink and dance. Van den Bers had bought paper trumpets outside from the street sellers who were supplied by small Chinese factories in Sawah Besar. The tradition of blowing paper trumpets on New Year's Eve in Batavia went as far back as the time of French occupation, when Napoleon Bonaparte defeated the Netherlands.

When the clock struck twelve midnight, we blew our trumpets, and sang the Scottish tune, "Auld Lang Syne." We then walked out of the building, got into our various carriages, and continued blowing our trumpets along the streets in Weltevreden.

Van den Bers didn't know that our sexual joys together were coming to an end. He had a surprise coming when he took me home.

In front of my house he tried to kiss me.

I refused. "We end our relationship here."

He was downcast. "Why?"

"Because I said so," I said. "We've come to the end."

"What have I done?" he asked pathetically.

"The end of a satisfying physical relationship, like what we had, isn't necessarily preceded by a fault or a mistake. We can end the relationship amicably."

He looked at me, uncomprehending. Just then the first lightning bolt heralding rain flashed across the western sky.

"Please," he said, holding my hand. "Please don't say that."

I pulled my hand away. "It's going to rain soon."

I opened the carriage door, stepped down to the ground, and walked to the front door.

Van den Bers jumped out, ran after me, caught me at the door, and held me.

The second lightning bolt flashed across the western sky.

"Tell me you're not serious," he said.

I freed myself from his embrace. "We have to stop here."

"I don't understand." He tried to grab me again.

"I'll never understand, either," I said, moving away. "Time has dictated its term to my heart."

"Can't your heart contradict him?"

"It's not a *him*, and it is too powerful. Human hearts are bound to do its bidding. We humans are nothing but slaves to time. We voluntarily shackle ourselves to it and can never be liberated. We can only adjust ourselves when it changes. *Tempora mutantur nos et mutamur in illis.*"

"You're wrong. We are blessed with intellect. We can fight time."

"That is futile, a waste of time. We can't even compete with it. We have never understood the secret of time. The distance, the length, or the depth of it."

"You and I still have a long way to travel together. It's only the first of January and April is still ahead. That's when the leaves will be growing, flowers blooming, bees swarming, and fireflies will be lighting the nights."

"But we can't avoid the dry season in September: flies on piles of rubbish, mosquitoes in monsoon drains, cockroaches everywhere. So before stepping into a world forever changing, let's stop in January to prevent falling in love out of boredom."

At that moment the dark sky brightened. The third lightning bolt preceded the rain.

"I'm not bored," he pleaded. "I really love you."

"Thank you," I said, without emotion. "But I'll never love you. I had fun with you. And take note, fun is seasonal. Now the season is over."

A roar of thunder opened up the heavens and all the water they held fell to earth. I opened my front door and rushed in, leaving Van den Bers looking dazed outside.

Alas, men are prone to make fools of themselves because of women.

Don't ask me why
Men insist on going to sea
With dilapidated sails
Unheeding the lessons
Of the power of the tempest.

Chapter Fifty-eight

Barely three steps into the house I was paralyzed by fear. My knees nearly buckled.

The Christmas tree decorated with strips of colored crepe paper, gleaming glass balls, angel dolls, silver stars, and lighted tiny candles, was on fire.

As soon as I recovered my wits, I shouted for Mamah.

No answer came from her room in the attic and I panicked.

I remembered the heavy rain. Grabbing the trunk of the tree, I rushed outside and threw it as far as I could into the street, where the rain promptly put out the fire.

Van den Bers was gone and I stood alone in the rain, drenched. I turned around and reentered my house to check if Non was safe in her bed. But when I opened the bedroom door and looked in, she was not there.

I ran upstairs and tried to open Mamah's bedroom door. It was locked. Terrified, I rapped on the door.

"The door is locked from outside, madam," Mamah said from behind the locked door.

I heard Non cry and breathed a sigh of relief, though I was still confused. Without thinking I kicked the door repeatedly with all my might. When it finally flung open, I rushed in and grabbed Non from Mamah's arms.

"Who locked your door?" I asked.

"Mr. MacLeod, madam," Mamah replied.

I was furious and immediately suspicious. "Where is he?"

"I don't know, madam. He came here with two women."

With Non in my arms, I went to the front bedroom on the second floor. The door had no keyhole and was locked.

I kicked the door open and was confronted with a nauseating scene. On the bed Ruud was having sex with one woman while the other watched, giggling.

"Hey," I roared. "Do you think this is Zeedijk?"

They froze.

I was sick, tired, and my head spun.

Holding Non tightly, I turned around and went downstairs, only half-conscious of my feet on the stairs. I walked straight out of the door. We were soaked in no time, but I kept walking.

Where should we go?

I didn't care.

Chapter Fifty-nine

I reached the bridge across the Tjiliwoeng River on the edge of Rijswijk, while Non cried and shivered in her wet clothes. We found shelter under the eaves of the house belonging to the family of the Brabant man who always helped me. Would I inconvenience them if I knocked on their door? It was nearly dawn. Anyone who had not celebrated New Year's Eve would be fast asleep.

I was cold and miserable, and Non still cried. Finally I knocked on the door. I felt silly and guilty because despite having been neighbors for so long I only knew the man by his first name, Jan. I never asked him for his surname, but as someone much younger I shouldn't call him just Jan. And calling him "Mr. Jan" was not culturally appropriate. I decided to call him "Mr. Breda" because that was the name of the Dutch suburb where he came from. I hoped he wouldn't mind.

Mr. Breda opened the door after I knocked several times while calling his name. He looked surprised. We must have been a sight. He seemed to know immediately that we needed help.

From inside the house I heard his wife ask who was at the door this late.

"Come in." Mr. Breda's family sat at the table playing cards. His wife rose from her chair after putting her cards down.

I thought she felt sorry for us, seeing the state we were in, but I was very mistaken.

Mrs. Breda faced me with her hands akimbo, a very Dutch stance. "We have barely entered 1903 and you're already making trouble. What do you want from my husband?"

Dazed and disoriented, I was ashamed and offended as well. Yet I didn't know how to react to the situation. I wanted to walk out, but my feet refused to obey. It was as if I were under a powerful spell.

I heard Mr. Breda admonish his wife, "That was uncalled for. Don't you have a heart?"

His wife turned to him angrily. As usual with a wife who henpecked her husband, she began to rant. Her voice resembled the noise of a series of firecrackers.

"Why do you let her manipulate you?" She pointed her finger at my face. "You want to be another of those foolish victims of her exploits?"

"For goodness sake, use your head," Mr. Breda said.

"It's you who've lost your head. Why do you let this woman in my house? Lucifer and Maria Magdalene possess this woman. Get her out of here immediately or I'll drench her with hot water."

I trembled. What a dreadful woman. How different she was from her husband.

I saw my mistake. Why had I knocked on their door and gone inside? I quickly retreated out the door and rushed to find shelter under the eaves of the house next door. I needed a few moments to think, regroup, and gather my wits. How to address the situation, how to confront those pigs in my home?

Despite being cold and wet, and trying to soothe a whimpering baby, I calmed down.

I should have stayed in my home and defended my territory, and kicked those pigs out. Mr. Breda's wife had given me a cruel idea. Hot water!

I headed back to my house with firm, definite steps. At the door I shouted for Mamah.

A muffled voice came from the kitchen.

Mamah was tied to a chair with a cloth stuffed into her mouth.

"Where have they gone?" I pulled out the cloth from Mamah's mouth.

"Mr. MacLeod and the two women left, madam," Mamah replied, breathless.

"Where did they go?"

"I don't know, madam."

"Damn," I cursed.

Chapter Sixty

Early in the evening on New Year's Day, before I knew what had happened, Ruud was back in the house. I had fallen asleep from exhaustion.

Ruud's voice singing "Silent Night, Holy Night" woke me up and for a moment I thought I was having a nightmare. I had a terrible headache, and couldn't believe he was so shameless to return.

I jumped out of bed and walked to the kitchen, bent on practicing Mrs. Breda's threat. I looked in the kettle to see if there was hot water. Most Dutch families in Indonesia had kettles that were wrapped in a quilted cover specially made for them to retain heat.

Satisfied that the water was still hot, I took the kettle to the side veranda where I heard Ruud singing. I was ready to throw the kettle at him, aiming for his head. But I was stopped short. He had Non in his arms, turning around and around as if they were dancing.

I leaned against the wall. I couldn't throw the kettle, but I could approach him quietly and hit his head from behind.

What if he dropped Non?

I put down the kettle, went up to him, and grabbed Non.

He resisted until I kneed his groin as hard as I could. While he bent over grimacing in pain, I seized Non.

I was pleased. A completely unplanned act finally yielded the desired result. I shouted, "Get out of this house, or I will scream in the streets until someone calls the military police to take you away."

Leaning against the back of a chair and nursing his groin, Ruud said, "No need to threaten me."

"You are disgusting. You have no shame. Get out," I yelled.

Ruud sat down instead. "Don't be so arrogant. You have no shame yourself. Everyone in the neighborhood knows who you really are. Every night you go to the Soos to snare a man and move in and out of Hotel Des Indes or Der Nederlander. Puh!"

He spat.

I froze. I was unprepared for this.

I quickly repositioned myself for another offensive. What I had done was a result of his deeds. I had withstood multiple assaults from him, starting when we were in Amsterdam.

"I'm damaged because of you. You gave my children and me syphilis. I hope you rot in the military prison at Ngawi."

"Don't be too cocksure, you whore. If I rot in Ngawi, you'll be in Bubakan," said Ruud, referring to the prison for European civilians.

He came toward me.

I moved away quickly.

"Get out of this house. I am sick of you. I hate you!" I shouted.

"This house is in my name," said Ruud. "You are my wife, and as my wife you'll do as I say. I determine your fate."

"Definitely not," I said. "If you don't get out, I will."

Crossing his legs arrogantly, he said, "Go ahead."

The house was no place for me. Ruud had brought bad luck to it.

Despite my exploits with men I met at the Soos, I never once brought them into this house, where my daughter lived.

Chapter Sixty-one

I told Mamah to start packing. All of my and Non's clothes were put into a big trunk. We packed bits and pieces of women's items in a smaller suitcase. If there was anything I needed and forgot to pack, I planned to come back after I had found another house.

We walked out without any hindrance. Ruud showed no interest. With Non in one arm and a small suitcase in another, I left the house with Mamah, who carried the big trunk.

Outside it was very windy. The sun was retreating into the darkening sky. Birds flew toward Wilhelmina Park. It would soon rain.

Mamah and I trudged to the bridge over the river, hoping to find a horse-drawn carriage. We were weighed down with a toddler, a trunk, and small suitcase.

A number of carriages usually parked in front of the Soos waiting for passengers. But it was too far to walk with the baggage. We looked for passing carriages on their way to a stop near the Stadsschouwburg, the arts house, but found none. So we walked eastward across Wilhelmina Park. I was too tired to keep carrying Non, and slipped her to the ground asking her to walk. She was over three years old and when she wanted to, she could even run.

It was getting dark when I saw the light from the lantern of a *sado* in front of the cathedral. I called out to the carriage, clapping my hands.

Mamah joined me. "Here, brother, come here," her strident voice called to the carriage driver.

But the carriage didn't move. Maybe the driver was deaf. While we walked to the carriage, I made up my mind to ask the driver to take us to a cheap hotel, either in Tanah Abang fairly close, or Chinatown in the suburb of Kota Tai further away.

Mamah complained in vernacular Batavian or Betawi, "Hey, brother, we called you many times. Why didn't you come?"

The man jolted out of his rêverie, and nearly dropped the hand-rolled cigarette from his mouth. "Why do you startle me like that?" he exclaimed.

I laughed despite being irritated. I thought, here is a deaf joker with weak concentration.

The driver said, "Sorry young woman, I'm waiting for my *babah* passenger who is inside the church."

I was very disappointed. The *sado* was already booked for the evening by a *babah*, a Chinese-Malay man. This *babah* had apparently left the traditional religion of the Chinese, *Sam Kauw It Kauw*, and turned to Christianity.

"Can't you take us in the meantime?" asked Mamah.

"Where do you want to go?"

"My employer wants to find a modest hotel."

"Goodness, my passenger works at Hotel Krekot. You go this way to Pintoe Air, through Pintoe Besi, and turn left."

"What are you saying?"

"You and your employer had better stay at that hotel. Of course it won't be the same as Des Indes or Der Nederlander."

"Will you take us to Krekot?"

"I have to wait for my passenger. He's booked me for the evening. I can't."

"Ah, you're full of sweet talk."

The man laughed.

I was exasperated. Then something strange happened. I felt encouraged to go into the cathedral to look for the priest who had prayed for Norman John at his funeral. I turned to gaze at the building.

It must have been the devil whispering in my ear, because under normal circumstances I wouldn't dream of going into a church. I was a freethinker. I was past going to church, where I believed the devil wielded his power. Had I changed or was I moving closer to the devil?

"Let's go in," I said without hesitation and pulled Non toward the door of the cathedral. There was no front gate. The message was that anyone was welcome to enter.

In a Dutch colony where anti-Catholic Protestants dominated the colonial administration, the Catholic clergy made use of their church to lure people to their side. They were welcome to seek counsel and emotional solace when in trouble, as indicated by the exhortation, "Come to me, you who are tired and troubled, for I will give you peace."

Tired and troubled, I approached, albeit with heavy steps. In front of the double door entrance, I stopped. Staring at me was the statue of Mary.

This was the first time after many years in Java that I had stood in front of a church, not to seek God, but to look for the priest who had prayed at my son's funeral.

It was dark inside. Even the entrance was unlit. I tried reading the plaque in Latin on the right wall which was full of praise for Dutch East Indies Governor General, Leonard Pierre Joseph Burggraaf du Bus de Gisignies, who was originally from Belgium. After a while a priest came from the side carrying a candle. He walked toward a statue of the Piéta. When the candle lit his face, I knew he was the man I had come to see. "Father," I called.

Monsignor Luypen stopped and raised his candle to have a better look at me. He seemed to recognize me. "Oh, it's you." he said.

"Yes, Father, it's been a long time," I replied.

"Yes, it has," he said. "You look troubled, and in trouble."

"I am indeed, Father," I said. "But I haven't come because of financial destitution."

"That's good to hear," he said. "So what brought you to church? The statues must be astonished, not to mention the angels in heaven. They'd send for an orchestra to welcome an apostate."

I laughed. He had lightened my heart.

I said, "Apostate sounds more feminine than hypocrite, Father."
The monsignor laughed. "I like that reasoning."
Outside the rain started falling.

Chapter Sixty-two

I told Monsignor Luypen what had brought me to the church of the beloved Mother assumed to Heaven.

Concerned for my welfare after hearing my story, Monsignor Luypen promptly wrote a letter to Mother Superior at the Groote Klooster in Noordwijk requesting her to provide me with a room for the night. He even lent me the horse carriage belonging to the presbytery, complete with a native driver, to take us to the convent.

At first I demurred. I hadn't entered the church to obtain free accommodations.

"That is not my intention, Father. I have money to stay in a hotel," I said, startled at my arrogance.

But Monsignor Luypen didn't seem affected, nor did he heed my protest. "Whether you have money or not is not the issue," he said. "This is a case of a shepherd taking care of a lost lamb. Your money cannot buy peace and rest. It may be able to buy many things, but not everything. If you care to, stay a day or two in the convent. Let's hope you'll find dignity and the essence of the soul by learning to meditate in silence. That's something money cannot buy, my child. When peace comes, it comes free of charge. But you have to seek it by praying. Prayers are a dialogue between you and God, not a monologue between you and your ego. If you believe in the power of prayer, you can shift mountains."

I kept quiet and remained non-committal. He didn't pursue his argument and I liked that.

While we walked toward the carriage house, he said in a fatherly manner, "Stay and relax as much as you can in the convent. As I said, you are a lost lamb, and it's my task to guide you back to the path of God."

I still didn't say a word.

The rain fell on us, and we were wet by the time Non, Mamah, and I boarded the carriage. So was the monsignor.

Before the driver got the carriage moving, Monsignor Luypen said, "About your husband. Someone will take care of him."

I didn't understand what he meant, but didn't feel the need to ask for an explanation. I only responded with a smile filled with gratitude.

Then the carriage moved westward into the night through the heavy rain.

Chapter Sixty-three

I woke feeling awful. I had caught a terrible cold and every joint in my body was stiff and tender, and combined with a pounding headache. This was the result of running about in the rain, flustered and troubled, and a very restless night's sleep.

As my vision alternatively blurred and shimmied, I tried to find my bearings. I was not in any room of my house in Batavia. In the bedroom at home, a framed sampler in Old English script hung on the wall and said "Home Sweet Home," but I only found a cross with the inscription "INRI" beneath. I did not belong here.

I sat up slowly and breathed with difficulty. My throat was very dry. As soon as I stood, I nearly doubled over coughing. A sharp pain in my chest made me sit again.

Mamah came in. "You're awake?" she said, and sat down on the floor before me.

"Yes," I said.

The day had begun hours ago. After lying awake all night, I'd fallen asleep near daybreak. "I'm sore all over, Mamah," I said.

"Would you like me to give you a coin massage?"

"No, thank you," I looked for my daughter. "Where's Non?"

"She's playing with the nuns outside, madam," replied Mamah.

It dawned on me then that I was in a room in the Ursuline convent, which explained the cross on the wall.

"Has Non had a bath?" I asked.

"Yes, and she's had breakfast. It's well past ten o'clock, madam."

There was a knock on the door. The director of the convent who had received us the previous night stood at the threshold.

"You have guests," she said.

"I do? Who is it, Sister?"

"It's a couple. They said they're your neighbors. Otherwise I wouldn't have allowed them in."

I was confused. Who in my neighborhood would want to see me? As far as I knew, only the monsignor knew where I was.

Consumed by curiosity, I dressed and went to the anteroom where Mr. Breda and his awful wife were waiting. I nearly retreated from the room when Mrs. Breda rushed to hug me. "I apologize for having been so rude," she said, tearfully.

I felt awkward and didn't know what to say. Her apology was completely unexpected.

Mr. Breda started to explain. "We went to church this morning and Monsignor Luypen told us your real situation."

His wife added, "I am really sorry. I know now what a beast your husband is."

"Before we left we saw the military police taking him away," said Mr. Breda.

"All the wives in the neighborhood are very angry and disgusted," his wife added crossly. "We hate men like him. We hope he'll be sent to Ngawi."

I was speechless, but pleased. I felt better already.

"You looked so miserable and lost yesterday," said Mrs. Breda.

I still didn't respond.

"When the officers came to take your husband, he had three native women with him," said Mr. Breda.

"So disgusting." Mrs. Breda reached for my hand. "I apologize."

I was touched by the sincerity in her display of friendship. Could I call it friendship? I didn't even know her name. I said to her, "Please, madam, there is no reason to apologize."

"Call me Elsa."

I returned her hug and the hard feelings from the night before melted away. "I'm so glad," I said.

Elsa held my hand and said, "Let's take you home. That house is yours by right. Don't abandon it. When a wife leaves her home, she is defeated and admits that her husband is more powerful. Don't consider defeat. We're in the twentieth century."

Jan Breda remained quiet through our spirited conversation.

Despite my bad cold and cough, I was happy because there was hope for the future.

> *I have no desire to ask who I am*
> *When I see myself breaking in half.*
> *It is best to play the mute*
> *While pretending to understand*
> *The verses that dismiss the moonlight.*
> *Without a mirror to erase my doubt*
> *I see my broken self giving birth to*
> *A woman conceived with tears.*

Chapter Sixty-four

Back home, I enjoyed the solitude of my bedroom where "Home Sweet Home" hung on the wall. During these moments I found a deeper meaning of life. I realized that despite living among other people and maintaining my individuality, I needed to fall harmoniously into place, to swim with the flow, yet be strong enough to follow my beliefs, my concept of truth.

At the onset of the last week of January, Mamah reminded me that the thirtieth was Non's birthday. So I began to plan a party. I invited the neighbors who lived in the houses across Wilhelmina Park.

I thought of Brousson. I had tried to forget him. After all I had only used him for my debut into the world of the courtesan. He was, if there was such a thing, merely my temporary lover. However, I couldn't deny that I thought of him, even missed him. This was proof that Brousson was extraordinary. He had left a deep impression on me. I had to go and look for him.

At the office of *Bandera Wolanda,* Brousson was missing. His Ambonese associate, Tehupeiory, told me Brousson had gone to Semarang to see Brooshooft, a supporter of van Deventer's ethical policy and the editor-in chief of *De Locomotief,* the largest newspaper in Indonesia, which now, in mid 1903, was in trouble and heading for collapse.

During my visit to Brousson's office, I met an Englishman who was placing a business advertisement in *Bandera Wolanda.* He greeted me

183

politely and, attempting to compliment me in Dutch, said, "What you look at is beautiful," instead of, "You look beautiful."

I laughed. When he seemed embarrassed, I switched to English. "Are you an Englishman?"

"Oh, yes." He looked pleased and offered me his hand. "My name is William Perkins."

I took his hand. "Mata Hari. Nice to meet you."

He kept my hand in his for longer than was necessary, looking into my eyes. Having gone through several lovers, I recognized that look. He was interested in me, and I liked the attention.

Perkins asked for my address and I gave it to him. I even obliged when he asked for directions. But when he said he wished to visit me, I told him I preferred meeting at the Soos.

Becoming involved with him would be another adventure. As a businessman who imported musical instruments and sports equipment, he was worldly and interesting. He was not bad looking. Though he was older than me, his brown hair was still mostly dark. I saw several advantages in our age difference. He was courteous and would no doubt spoil me.

To ask him the whereabouts of his wife and children would only have spoiled the fun. I was better off not to know.

Two days after Non's birthday party with the neighborhood children who were older than her, I had a rendezvous with Perkins at the Soos, and we waltzed the night away.

Our first dance was fairly uneventful, though the orchestra played Johann Strauss II's "Perpetuum Mobile" exquisitely. Only during the second dance did I begin to feel aroused. I longed to kiss and be kissed. However, nothing happened.

At the end of the evening Perkins took me home in his carriage. In front of my house before I stepped out, I asked, "Aren't you going to kiss me?"

Even in the dark I saw his face brighten. He looked at me intently, then moved to kiss me. "Of course," he said. "I like kissing you."

I pulled his head toward me and met his lips with mine.

"Good night," he said. "Sweet dreams."

"Dream of me."

"Oh, yes. I dreamt about you last night. Rose up in the morning and slipped between your thighs."

"You're in luck."

"Why do you say that?"

"Because I love you." I held him tight and kissed him again. We never stopped.

It rained hard all night.

Chapter Sixty-five

Perkins and I did not last long.

It became clear we were incompatible after I discovered that he wanted to marry me. His wife had passed away three years earlier in India and he'd been looking for a woman to replace her. That would not be me. Apart from the fact that I was not looking for a permanent relationship, I was made uncomfortable by Perkins' churchiness. He went regularly to the All Saints Anglican Church in the suburb of Pangarangan near the Tjiliwoeng River. When he tried to cajole me into coming with him, I said, "Don't try. I don't belong to any church."

This only made him try to discuss his faith with me. "You object to the Church's communion with the Archbishop of Canterbury?" he asked.

"No."

"Then why?"

"I'm a freethinker. More than that, I'm a materialist, a positivist, an agnostic, and an atheist."

"That's crazy, nonsense."

"Nonetheless I have a strong intuition in my beliefs."

"What intuition?"

"Intuition that one gets in natural reality."

"What reality?"

"That God is dead."

His mouth gaped as if he'd seen a ghoul.

Despite our differences, just to show my appreciation of his humanity, not his religion or nationality, I agreed to go with him once, the first and the last time.

Stepping on to the church's front yard gave me goose pimples. The large spreading trees effectively prevented any sunlight from coming in and caused a gloomy and eerie atmosphere. It felt like being in an old graveyard. In fact, headstones surrounded the church, some belonging to the graves of English officers who had fallen during the wars in Indonesia.

Just before entering the building, I felt uncomfortable, thinking that hundreds of people in the congregation would stare me at as if I were a curiosity. But once inside, I was surprised.

No priest led the service. For the last twenty-five years no permanent clergy had been on regular stipends to lead the church service. The pews were empty. There were only seven people, each with one leg very close to the grave. Spread throughout the room, the seven worshippers all looked earnest. When Perkins and I walked in, they were singing "Rock of Ages." Then a man with a beard down to his chest read from Isaiah 1:18 in a Scottish accent. He read:

"Come now, let us settle the matter, says the Lord. Though your sins are like scarlet, they shall be as white as snow; though they are red as crimson, they shall be like wool." I liked what he read. As for the hymn they sang, it reminded me of that awful teacher who had taken my virginity. He often sang that hymn too.

I came away from the church pondering the words of the scripture reading. I found in the words justification for what I was doing, adopting fornication as a hobby with the intent to turn it into a profession.

What was so terrible about committing a sin?

After church, I was resolute to end my relationship with Perkins. I planned to find another man who cooperated with me in committing sins as crimson as sins could be.

"Good-bye, Perkins."

So long.

Chapter Sixty-six

I returned my attention to Brousson.

It was noon when I entered his office, but only the editorial secretary was at her desk. I asked for a piece of paper and wrote Brousson a brief note that said, "Do you have time to see me tomorrow evening at the Soos? Mata Hari. PS: I'll be waiting for you at eight o'clock."

I left for the Soos at seven and Brousson was waiting for me. We gave each other Dutch kisses and walked to the right corner for seats, a fair distance from the orchestra so the music was not so loud.

"I knew we'd see each other again," Brousson said.

"So did I," I answered.

"I hear you're marrying that Englishman, Perkins."

"That's not true. I plan to return to the Netherlands. This August I'll turn twenty-seven and I have to make changes in my life. Not here, but there."

"What about Rudolph?"

"I don't know."

"He's going to be released from active duty in November."

"Where did you hear that?"

"Don't forget that I am a journalist."

"I'll start the divorce proceedings with him there as well. Then I'll be well and truly free."

"Haven't you been free to do whatever you want?"

"No. How can I say I'm free when there's an uncertainty in my mind that weighs me down? When I'm officially divorced, I'll be free without any doubts or fear. Doubts and fear kill any creative energy."

"Hmm."

"Why are you laughing?"

"I'm not laughing. I'm amazed."

"I meant what I said. With the divorce I'll be completely free to be creative. I want to go to France and dance in Paris. I'm better than the dancers at Moulin Rouge."

"You can dance in Batavia. You're having a sensational success here."

"But I can't grow and develop. There are limitations to income and fame."

"You are known here."

"Being known is not the same as being famous."

"What kind of fame are you after? That of a head of government, like a governor general?"

"They are only talked about and respected while in power. On retirement, they suffer from anxiety because nobody cares about them any more."

"Then what do you want?"

"I want to be famous as an artist, admired and respected during my lifetime, always in the limelight. And when I'm dead, I want my name to be remembered, recorded in a cultural encyclopedia, and remain respected. Only in the arts does the Latin proverb, *ars longa vita brevis,* apply."

"You can achieve that here."

"Batavians have no appreciation for artistic creation. You, for example, have you ever written about my achievement as an artist in your paper?"

"My paper is read by military people."

"I am a military officer's wife."

"True. But an officer's wife is not the same as an officer himself, in terms of understanding military signals."

"What signals?"

"War signals."

"How's that?"

"When an officer is ordered to lie down, he'll immediately stretch out on his stomach, while an officer's wife will spread on her back."

"You cheeky sot," I laughed.

Brousson looked pleased with his own joke.

I continued, "There is a difference between men and women regarding their understanding of war. For women, war is a discovery, while for men, war is a search."

"No," he said. "A war is not an idea, but action. For men, action is recreational, while for women, it is reproductive."

"That's very patronizing to modern women. It sounds as if we are equal to donkeys. A modern woman is more feminine than a Spanish horse. This is the twentieth century. A feminine woman no longer regards a battle as a consequence, but she can actively cause it to happen."

"Yes, yes. I know you're no donkey. You're a Spanish horse. So when can I ride the horse again?"

I pinched him hard on the arm. He was so infuriating.

"Wait," I said. "You still need to know what this twentieth century woman thinks. You need to hear my opinion about those war signals you mentioned. In a war, a signal for advancing for men is countered by a signal for attack by women. Since men are not prepared for that, they become overwhelmed, lose direction, and the capacity to continue. They are quick to raise the white flag of surrender."

Brousson laughed, and I felt gratified.

"That's not always the case," he said. "The best outcome is both win and both are defeated."

"I agree. That's the essence of the Chinese book *Su Nu Ching* and the Indian book *Kama Sutra*."

"Have you read them?"

"I'd like to, but I can't. Indian and Chinese characters are extremely difficult. I was only able to read the reviews in English in the main public library."

"Do you go to that library often?"

"Yes. Did you think an exotic dancer has no need to read books? Typical. Modern women have to read books in order not to be gullible or vulnerable to men's deception, and powerless when treated as objects. We are just as much entities as men."

"Remarkable. I have underestimated you. The way you talk, you're ahead of our era."

"I want to build my fame in Paris. In Batavia the sky is limited and unable to accommodate too bright a star."

"You want to be brighter than the sun."

"I am Mata Hari."

"What more do you need?"

"There's no space to grow here. Everything is gauged by morality. This is the influence of the local mores that are collective in nature. Even a mistake is collectively committed. As a consequence, I can't be myself. And in the dance circle here, there isn't enough competition to push me in developing my creativity. In this field competitiveness is very important."

"You are remarkable. You're so impassioned. You're no longer a star. You are the sun."

"Don't forget, my name is Mata Hari."

"So you are the sun. What can I do to match you?"

"Be the galaxy which allows different lights to shine. As the sun, I move around the center of the galaxy."

"Do you have to be so enigmatic? Give me something simple."

"What would you like to be?"

"As a man, I'm a bee, and as a woman, you're a flower."

"If we become a bee and flower, we'll never be human again."

"In that case, let's just remain a man and woman."

"I guess that's realistic."

"Realistic in a naturalistic way."

"Now, as a man, would you accompany me, a woman? Before leaving for the Netherlands, I want to visit the Boroboedoer Temple once more."

"Why?"

"I promised Mbah Koeng, my Javanese dance teacher, that I'd return, and I want to go there with you. Like you said, we were fated to meet again."

He smiled and I smiled.

The orchestra still played its music.
We walked across the room to dance.

> *The rhythm of the waltz*
> *Made me refuse*
> *To enter the beginning of the world*
> *East of Eden.*
> *With an ephemeral lover*
> *Love is woven into uncertainty.*

Chapter Sixty-seven

Brousson, Non, Mamah and I went to Semarang, before continuing to the village of Boroboedoer. In Semarang we stayed overnight at Du Pavillon, the best hotel in Central Java. Our stay was free because Brooshooft, editor-in-chief of the Locomotief, the largest Dutch language newspaper, arranged it and knew every official and businessman in the city.

In the hotel Brousson and I revisited the joys we knew years ago, this time with more passion, in the spirit of what he described as both winning and losing, with three encores.

The following morning, we left the hotel that faced a large square that the locals called Ya'ik, and went to Djoernatan Railway Station. We traveled to Magelang via Kedoengdjati and Ambarawa, and rode a horse-cart to Mbah Koeng's home on the banks of Elo River at Boroboedoer.

However, Mbah Koeng, had gone to Jogjakarta, to stage nightly performances during *sekaten*—the word derived from *syahadatain*—a grand ritual organized by the Royal Palace to commemorate the birth of the Prophet Muhammad, peace be upon Him. Mbah Koeng had taken his entire troupe and followers. Only his wife was left behind.

What to do?

Go to Jogjakarta and while there, experience *sekaten*. But we needed transportation. It would be dark soon, and getting to the main road was a real problem.

Mbah Koeng's wife said, "Stay here tonight. Tomorrow morning you can go to Jogja. The opening of *sekaten* is in the evening."

I told Brousson what she had said. He wasn't pleased. His face showed signs of exhaustion and exasperation.

I finally persuaded him to stay in a small hut which Mbah Koeng's wife prepared in a hurry. When he didn't stop complaining, I became irritated.

"I can't believe you're this crazy, tormenting yourself to the extent of foolishness," he said.

"Am I tormenting you?" I asked furiously.

He tried to evade the ire. "You're tormenting yourself. It's beyond me how you can have so much respect for a race that, for their stupidity, we've colonized for three hundred years."

I could not speak. How could someone who wrote for a newspaper with a staff consisting of educated native intellectuals, harbor such a disgusting sentiment?

Finally I said, "You're not only a colonialist like most Dutch soldiers, you're also a racist."

"Don't blame me. It's a reality. The inhabitants of the Dutch East Indies, which you always call Indonesia, are like vegetables. Nothing more, nothing less. If you insist on calling them human, maybe they can be regarded as primitive creatures, from the era of *Homo erectus*. Even the adults behave like children because they are not smart. It is true what the Dutch say, that for them the abbreviation KNIL does not stand for the Royal Netherlands Indies Army, but for *Klein Niet Intelligent Leger*, small unintelligent soldiers."

"Enough! That is utter nonsense."

My shouting stopped Brousson. Until that moment I had never spoken harshly to him.

While he was still speechless, I repositioned myself for another offensive. "For your information, my mother was from Java, and she was an ordinary human being, not a vegetable."

He looked at me uncertainly, unable to utter a single word.

I walked out and went to the edge of ravine above the Elo River to stare at the orange sky.

Brousson approached slowly and touched my shoulder. "Forgive me," he said. "I went too far."

I gazed at the western sky where the sun had set, without responding.

"Will you forgive me?" he asked.

"I have forgotten it."

At least Brousson was manly enough to apologize to a woman. His vocabulary was richer than Ruud's.

Chapter Sixty-eight

The next morning we left by horse-cart and reached Jogja at noon. On the advice of the driver, we took rooms at the Hotel Toegoe on Toegoesche Weg.

After resting for a few hours, I enquired at the hotel front desk for the exact time of the opening ceremony. The hotel staff didn't know. They suggested that I ask the staff at the Exhibition for Arts and Crafts building across the road.

I was informed that the ceremony began at eight o'clock, in the courtyard of the mosque in front of the Royal Palace. We walked the fair distance to the palace at the town's square where there were two banyan trees named Kyai Widjojodaroe to the north and Kyai Dewodari to the south. The square was already crowded.

We were lucky to be in front of the mosque before eight. I saw Sri Sultan Hamengkoeboewono enter. This was the second time I'd seen him, the first time when he came to Boroboedoer with Cremer. Clad in his full ceremonial attire, the sultan went inside for the speech of the head cleric about the Prophet's life. Previously the sultan had gone to the spot where the set of *gamelan sekaten* was kept, and showered the grounds with *oedik-oedik*, coins mixed with yellow rice believed to have supernatural power.

When the speech was over, the sultan completed a ritual called *djedjak banon*, stomping on a pile of bricks. Later the crushed brick was spread around the mosque's courtyard to be grabbed and collected by the local people for use in amulets.

Enthralled by all I saw, I felt privileged to see this important cultural event. I thought of Brousson and asked him, "What do you think of the ceremonies?"

Suspicious he might be miserable and bored, I was afraid he would respond with something infuriating. To my surprise he said, "I'm glad I came with you. Otherwise I would be completely ignorant of all this."

Nonetheless, I found his answer a little strange since he had introduced me to Prince Harjo Sosroningrat, the captain of Pakoe Alam Legion, who was on the editorial staff of *Bandera Wolanda*.

I asked, "You mean Prince Harjo never talks about this?"

"I'm not surprised," Brousson replied. "The Pakoe Alam and Hamengkoeboewono are involved in a rather complicated and extended animosity and conflict."

I was immediately curious. "Do you know the history?"

"The current situation is a result of generations of animosity between them," Brousson answered. "Pakoe Alam separated himself from Hamengkoeboewono at the beginning of the nineteenth century during the reign of the senior sultan. Then Raffles gave his endorsement to this separation when he came to Jogjakarta."

Brousson quickly changed the subject. "Now let's find Mbah Koeng. Come on."

We walked the perimeter of the square, weaving through the crowds that had come for the night's festivities. There were children's games, folk entertainment, and food and drink stalls. People had come from every corner of the city.

Mbah Koeng's group performed on the eastern part of the square. He was extremely pleased to see me. His daughter, Astri, kissed my hand over and over again, showing her appreciation.

When I told them that we'd stayed at their home the previous night, Mbah Koeng was happy. He felt respected and appreciated.

I told him I had come to learn more about dance as it was depicted in the relief images of the Boroboedoer Temple, and I also planned to stay a little longer. I confessed that I hadn't altogether grasped the soul of the dance.

Mbah Koeng said, "You will become skilled when you've done it over and over again. Have you done that?"

"Do you mean, whether I've been practicing?"

"One doesn't only practice before a performance. The performance is a practice," he answered.

"Yes. Once every three months I dance at the Soos in Batavia."

"Excellent," said Mbah Koeng. "But you must remember, the skills you demonstrate are only the outer skin of a performance. What makes it come alive and filled with the power of beauty is the merging of the movement and your inner soul. And you must respect your audience. That's what binds them to you."

"That's why I want to learn more, and seek deeper. When can I do that again at your school?"

"We perform here for three nights," he said. "After that we'll go home."

I looked at Brousson.

"It's your decision," said Brousson. "I promised to come with you."

I said, "If you want, go back to Batavia. I'll stay for a few days in Boroboedoer."

"I've told you, I'll stay." He shrugged, using the gesture to show he was serious.

I was happy. I liked his demeanor. While dressed in military uniform he had stripped himself from all militarism and behaved like a civilian.

Chapter Sixty-nine

The four days we stayed at the village I spent every moment practicing and studying the dance movement depicted in the temple images.

Brousson, Mamah, and Non enjoyed their time living in the rustic world, listening to the tunes sung by the different birds in the trees and the crowing of roosters in the distance. At night, lamps fueled by coconut oil provided dim lights that attracted insects to rush in and die there.

We retraced our steps to Batavia. From Magelang we took the train to Semarang, and on to Batavia. I was exhausted and satisfied. I achieved what I had intended. My time with Astri taught me a great deal about dancing. I was challenged to prove that I had gained a deeper understanding of the aesthetics of dance. I was eager to do so at the Soos.

December 1903 was my last performance there. Though unintended, my relationship with Brousson lasted longer than those with any other lovers. I celebrated New Year's Eve with him at the Soos, and decided to return to the Netherlands the following year.

Mr. Breda told me that Ruud would be sent back to Holland before March 1904. I could get the divorce proceedings going in the next three or four months. I was happy.

However I was sad to leave Java. It was in this land of my mother that I had discovered my true self. Yet it couldn't give me the guarantee of becoming the *matahari* of my dreams.

Though I spelled the name in two words, I did associate it with *matahari*, the sun. And I wanted to shine. Being *matahari* in a land where there were only two seasons, the rainy and dry season, and the sun always shone in both, nobody noticed my sun. I wanted to be *matahari* in a land with four seasons, where after summer people sought the sun, and its presence was noticed and appreciated.

I had to forget all my lovers when I returned to the Netherlands. From Cremer to Brousson, each had shaped my life in Indonesia. I looked forward to beginning a new history, with new people in Paris, Berlin, Madrid, Rome, and on and on.

I left for the Netherlands in April 1904. Spring had begun. Ice no longer covered the earth, and different flowers were in bloom. Life was tinged with hope.

> *I'm going home*
> *To leave great confusion*
> *And head for the splendor*
> *Of the Blue Mountain's peak.*
> *Blue meaning high*
> *Blue meaning deep.*

Chapter Seventy

Non and I sailed through the Suez Canal and took a long train journey from a southern Italian port into Holland. We went to my hometown, Leeuwarden, and found that my father hadn't changed. He was still deeply resentful of the failure of his hat manufacturing business.

I was disappointed that he didn't show any grandfatherly affection toward Non. We went to see Ruud's sister in Amsterdam and I told her what happened to my marriage with Ruud. Her attitude toward me had changed, and the chill emanating from her was so overwhelming I decided to leave there, too.

In the newspaper were advertisements for houses to lease. My financial situation was such that I was able to afford a decent home in the Jewish quarter of Amsterdam, where geniuses like Rembrandt and Spinoza were born. From our house Non and I often walked across the bridge behind the Royal Palace, to the Dam where we strolled and window-shopped.

Two days after we moved in, I visited Ruud's sister to give her my address so she could inform Ruud where Non and I were when he returned. I expected him to contact me so we could start the divorce.

One thing I missed was the lifestyle in Java, where I had domestic servants. I scoured the newspapers in Amsterdam, reading advertisements placed by people seeking domestic work. Since the last century people had imported servants from Indonesia. In the weekly magazine, *Koloniaal Weekblad,* I found an advertisement by a Javanese servant in 's Gravenhage who wanted someone to take her home. She was prepared to work for several months in Holland, before returning to Java.

I contacted her and received a reply by post four days later. I decided to go and see her myself.

She wanted to go home as soon as possible; I wanted her to stay longer. I spoke to her in Malay and we came to an agreement. She was happy to work for me for two months, but after that time she'd go home. I saw her determination and acquiesced.

Two days later Ruud finally arrived in Holland. He immediately came to me, swollen with bravado. I wasn't interested in an idle chat. As soon as he entered my house, I stood behind a chair and gave him a stern look. I said, "We have to start divorce proceedings now, without delay."

He tried to come near me, but I told him not to move any closer. He complied, and said, "We'll do that."

I was relieved.

The divorce was easy. However, I had to pay a high price. The court granted Ruud custody of Non. It regarded me as incompetent to raise children. The wording of the ruling was hurtful and disappointing. It said that anyone who was driven by the ambition to be a famous performer was incapable of looking after a child.

The judge said, "Women who want to be famous are more preoccupied with self-love than with caring for their children. For that reason, the court grants custody over Non or Jeanne Louisa to her father, Rudolph John MacLeod."

I was furious and completely powerless. I screamed to let out the frustration, and fainted.

When I woke, I was at home and alone.

Chapter Seventy-one

I had to find an *avocat*, or lawyer, who would lodge an appeal against the ridiculous verdict. How could they think the separation of a daughter from her mother was fair? Non's place was with me. I wanted her with me.

I delayed my departure for Paris, where I intended to be an exotic dancer, because I was needed in Amsterdam for the court battle. Apart from that, to find work in Paris I needed a competent representative.

For four months I tried to persuade Ruud to allow Non to live with me. She wanted to be with me, but Ruud wouldn't give in, saying he must follow the court decision. He wasn't a good father. Driven by the desire to punish me and make me suffer, he was intent on showing me that as a man he remained the powerful one.

Ruud's display of manliness made me sick. I was consumed with anger for his terrible behavior, yet I knew that I couldn't live without men.

In the middle of the St. Nicholas festivities, a typical Dutch event, I read in the newspaper an advertisement by a Jewish clairvoyant. I was lost and frustrated, so I went to her practice at the end of Jodenbrestraat, not far from the Portuguese synagogue.

The clairvoyant was a middle-aged woman who reeked of myrrh. I had no misgivings about seeing her. The idea of consulting a clairvoyant appealed to me, as I no longer was associated with the conventional church. Clairvoyants were able to offer things the clergy were not. Through Tarot cards the clairvoyant satisfied my needs.

I posed two questions: would I win back my daughter, and would I be successful in becoming a dancer in Paris and other cities in Europe? I received a negative answer for the first question and a positive one for the second.

"You will have your success next year," she said.

"Wait," I said. "There are twelve months in next year. Which month?"

"It's very close," she said. "Snow still covers the ground. Before leaves begin to grow on the twigs and branches."

It was too enigmatic and too vague for my liking, but since I was more inclined to believe clairvoyants than the clergy, I said, "Fine, I'll hold on to your predictions."

"Believe me," she said. "No other people can predict the future as accurately as we, the Jews. We are the chosen people and the cursed race all at once."

"I don't want to be involved with the problems of your people. I just want my child back, and my career successful. That was why I came to consult you."

"You have my predictions," she said.

"What am I supposed to do while waiting for this year to end?"

"Avoid buying before you have cash in your hand."

"What does that mean?"

"Just wait. You may learn the art of waiting from fishing. You can't catch a fish when it is not hungry. A fish will only bite when it is ready."

"Meanwhile what should I do?"

"You must pay me."

I handed her the money.

She took the guilders, shook them gently, and blew at them. I didn't understand what that was all about. To be honest, I'd never understood the Jews.

Chapter Seventy-two

One afternoon in an attempt to escape from my unrelenting frustrations, I walked to the Rijksmuseum. There I gazed at the statue of the god Shiva, King of the Dancers, which had always fascinated me. Before I left for Indonesia, I had been mystified at the Hindu god's four arms and wondered how the dance was choreographed. After studying the images of the Boroboedoer Temple and training under Mbah Koeng, I knew how to turn it into a real-life dance by accessing the power of my subconscious. I had learned to move my arms and hands in such a subtle and beautifully nimble manner that I enchanted my audience into thinking they saw two pairs of arms.

I was deep in rêverie when a voice jolted me back to reality. I turned around to see a pleasant and smartly dressed man who greeted me, smiling.

"You seem lost in admiration," he said.

I told him I was.

"What is it about the statue that captivates you?"

"I once admired the sculptor who translated his imagination into this, a god dancer with four arms."

"Once?" He was quick to hear the nuance.

"Before I had the opportunity to learn the dance in Java, I thought I needed two pairs of arms to create something as beautiful in my dance," I replied, and demonstrated with arm and hand gestures.

"I see," he said appreciatively. "You are a dancer."

"Yes," I was pleased to be speaking with someone who caught on quickly. "As I said, I learned in Java."

"Where is Java?"

"In the Dutch East Indies, which I call the same as Adolf Bastian named it: Indonesia. This includes Soematera, Java, Bali, Borneo, Celebes, the Moluccas, and the other islands."

"I hear they are very exotic," he said.

"Eastern culture is exotic for those in the West. As for myself, I perform exotic dances derived from the exoticism of Central Java, Boroboedoer."

Looking pleased, he offered his hand. "My name is Gabriel Astruc."

I took his hand and said, "Mine is Mata Hari. I'm planning to perform in Paris."

"Who is your agent?"

"I haven't got one yet."

"What a coincidence." He released my hand. "Perhaps we could work together. I can be your agent."

He gestured for me to walk alongside him. "On the thirteenth of March, there's going to be an East Asian arts exhibition in Paris. If you want to, you can perform one or two of your erotic dances at the Musée Guimet."

"I'd love to." I said. "Let's arrange that."

"Let's discuss it over coffee." Astruc quickened his steps.

I had to quicken mine too, to catch up with him.

We went to a café in the right wing of the museum.

"Would you be ready to dance in March?" Astruc asked after the waiter placed our cups of coffee on the table.

"Absolutely," I said. "I was hoping for someone to manage my performances."

"Well, you've found him," Astruc said. "More accurately, you found me, and I found you. That is an excellent basis for collaboration. We need each other. Performance management must be based on mutual needs and trust. We'll begin with a contract."

"That's fine."

Chapter Seventy-three

Two days later Astruc delivered the contract. After signing the document, he said, "We forgot something."

"What's that?" I asked, concerned.

"I have no doubts that you are a dancer. But I haven't seen you dance, and I have no idea what a Javanese exotic dance is like."

"I also forgot an important issue. Where can we find a *gamelan* set and players to accompany me?"

"That is difficult," Astruc said. "Even if the instruments are available in Leiden or Bronbeek, we won't be able to take them to Paris."

"What will we do?" I asked.

"I don't know. Can the *gamelan* be substituted with a more accessible type of orchestra?"

"In Batavia, I insisted on *gamelan* or nothing. But now that I'm in Europe I have to be realistic. I could substitute the *gamelan* with other instruments, but they must use the correct scale. In *gamelan* music two types of scale are used. One is *pelog*, native Javanese. The other is *slendro*, heavily influenced by Chinese music."

Astruc sought out musicians. He found a student at the conservatorium, and arranged a meeting.

The next day we went to the student's house on the Prinsengracht. I explained the music to him by humming the notes of *pelog*—almost equivalent to C E F G B—and those of *slendro*—almost equivalent to C

D E G A—and he made copious notes in his notebook. I also explained what *patet* was in *gamelan.*

I said, "It's possible to slide from *slendro* to *pelog,* by *slendro patet manyura* to *patet barang,* or from *slendro patet nem* to *pelog patet nem.*"

"Jesus Christ, I'm lost," the student exclaimed.

I repeated my explanation, humming the notes where necessary. He made more notes in his book, and then went to his piano and tried some of the phrases.

"Not bad. Not bad at all," I said.

He composed musical parts and phrases for me to carry wherever I went, so different musicians could follow and play them. While he developed the parts and phrases I danced near him. I did the whole dance starting from the first movement while fully dressed to the last movement completely nude.

"Now you see what I mean," I said at the end of the exercise.

Astruc applauded.

"Very exotic indeed," he said. "The audience in Paris will regard this as a new addition to the cultural world."

Chapter Seventy-four

The morning was very cold. December 1904 would soon be behind us. Snow had been falling since five o'clock. I went to Ruud's house around ten and again tried to persuade him to allow me to take Non for a vacation to France. But Ruud held fast.

He refused to let me see Non. I didn't know where he was hiding her from me and despaired.

At my request, Astruc had come with me and he saw what happened.

When we left Ruud's house, I was quietly angry. The snow and the cold did not help the situation.

Astruc took me to Rembrandtplein, the major square in Amsterdam lined with shops and cafés. We went into a café for hot coffee and sausage rolls. "You need to be rational in addressing your problem," Astruc said when he saw what an emotional wreck I'd become. "At this stage it seems unlikely you can win custody of your daughter. To keep trying is futile and you'll only exhaust yourself. You have to believe that a solution will be found eventually."

"I need an *avocat* with compassion and a conscience, who can see how miserable and tormented I am by not being with my daughter," I said. "But where can I find such a man?"

"What do you mean by conscience?"

"When I was a believer, the conscience was God's eyes in a human heart. The *avocat* has replaced God with money. All he has in his heart is the desire for money. Everything can be made to happen if the money is right. I don't trust the legal profession. Not one bit," I said infuriated.

"Don't generalize," Astruc said. "When we get to Paris, I'll introduce you to a man who has more than money on his mind. His name is Maître Edouard Clunet."

"But my case is in Amsterdam, not Paris."

"It doesn't matter. You can ask Clunet to come here. As for the conscience, there's a universal understanding of it, though named differently in different cultures."

"My question is whether today's *avocat* has a conscience."

"Let's hope Clunet does," said Astruc.

I smiled though unconvinced. Slowly sipping my hot coffee I wondered whether the coffee came from Indonesia. Did it come from Lampoeng, Bali, or Toraja? Perhaps it came from Neverland.

Chapter Seventy-five

We were ready to depart for Paris. That night we stayed in Amsterdam to celebrate New Year's Eve. On the second of January 1905 we left, and the following day we saw the devout commemorating Sainte Geneviève's Day, Saint Geneviève being a French saint, the protector of Paris.

A week later, Astruc took care of two important issues. First, he took me to see the can-can dance at Moulin Rouge. Then he introduced me to his friend, Edouard Clunet, the *avocat*.

We were trying to decide what to name my dance in our publicity.

After seeing the dancers at Moulin Rouge, Astruc commented, "They were erotic. You are not. Though you also take off your clothes on stage, you are an exotic dancer. Can you see the difference?"

"Certainly," I said. "What's called erotic is sexual simulation, which is suggestive and risqué, while exotic is something not native to the country, something other than Western tradition. True, like an erotic dancer, I, too, take off my clothes, but that is natural in the Hindu-Buddhist tradition in Java. Unfortunately, there are aesthetical elements in exoticism that are usually regarded as erotic."

Astruc was satisfied with my explanation. We were in agreement. "How would you like to be described in the publicity, as erotic or exotic?"

"I don't mind either word," I said. "But I prefer the term exotic, because it represents more accurately what I do. If you look at Gauguin's paintings of nude women in Polynesia, you'd call that exotic because it is natural according to the local mores."

Astruc hoped Clunet would solve the custody problem with my daughter Non in the Netherlands.

We went to see Clunet in his office. The *avocat* was not young, but after getting to know him I realized he had a formidable spirit. With him I had a new experience, a sexual relationship with a man over sixty. He made me concede the truth of the Malay expression, *Toea-toea keladi, makin toea makin jadi,* which was roughly similar to the French expression praising aged wine.

Our relationship was brief. He was very busy with his work in Paris. Twice we arranged to go to Amsterdam for the purpose of lodging an appeal regarding the custody of my daughter, but on both occasions something more urgent needed his attention. I was very disappointed because I had always complied to his timing whenever we arranged a tryst. Exasperated by the imbalance, I ended the relationship after a month during which we had at least five sexual encounters in various hotels.

After a dinner at a restaurant on Boulevard de la Reine, I said, "We've come to the end of the road. We must say good-bye."

For a moment Clunet was silent, but then kissed me on the cheeks. As if addressing a little girl, he said, "You've been very nice."

I saw him again in March, the day of my debut at the Musée Guimet. He congratulated me, and I thanked him. Clunet left without attending the opening reception. And I met other men.

> *Life must be traveled,*
> *And people choose short distances*
> *As only the heart can travel far.*

Chapter Seventy-six

In the Musée Guimet I walked around to observe the crowd, who appeared to study and admire the statues and other sculptures of the East. I couldn't help wondering whether they actually appreciated Eastern cultures and traditions. The guests whom Astruc had invited were military officers from various European countries. I wasn't convinced that military officers had the capacity for cultural appreciation, especially the fine arts, and especially non-Western fine arts. In their day-to-day life and professional duty, these men who devoted their mental and physical energy to conquering their enemies, were often filled with contempt for the enemy countries and cultures. They destroyed cultural items and establishments without hesitation.

My doubts were more acute because the art on display belonged to countries that were conquered and colonized by the West for the last three hundred years. It was inevitable Westerners believed that anything Eastern, or non-Western, was uncivilized and uncultured.

I was greatly disturbed by this misconception. I had a deep appreciation for Eastern culture, in particular coming from Indonesia where Eastern cultures, spanning from Western Asia to Eastern Asia, germinated and grew, hence the name *nesia* and *indo*. In addition, I was convinced a part of me originated there. I felt this belonging when I was still in Java. And now, in Paris, the center of Western culture, that feeling was even more acute.

Eastern culture was more complex and more difficult to understand than its Western counterpart. One could trace Western cultures to the Renaissance, where the pagan roots of Greek civilization met the Church's concept of "God is love." In earlier centuries, this was apparent in the endeavors to make the teachings of Aristotle and Plato compatible with Christianity.

Eastern culture was more diffuse, and large segments of various regions grew in Indonesia. Western Asia, Arabic countries, and Persia were basically Muslim, which had deep roots in Indonesia. Central Asia and India were Hindu and Buddhist, and these religions also spread to Indonesia. Eastern Asian cultures such as *Sam Kauw It Kauw*, a mixture of Taoism, Confucianism, and Buddhism, spread there as well.

All those elements were part of everyday life in Indonesia, but were displayed like brides in the Musée Guimet. I tensed in anticipation of individuals coming forward to mouth savant explanations like instant experts.

I spotted two men in civilian clothes, but I knew they were military officers. I heard their voices from where I stood. They spoke English with different accents. The blond one was German and the dark-haired one French. I made the distinction based on their pronunciation of r's and l's.

They looked at a statue of Nayaka and Nayaki coupling. The image was created from the description in the *Kama Sutra*, the male half standing with his right leg raised, and the female sitting in his lap, her arms wrapped around the man's neck. The statue was a replica of the original in the Kalniga-Konaraku temple, labeled *Latanwestitakam.*

I silently stood behind them obscured by a large statue of Shiva that was the centerpiece of the room. The conversation quickly turned coarse.

"Look at this," said the French man. "This Indian sculptor had no idea of anatomical balance."

"What's wrong with it?" the German asked.

"It's such a caricature. How could it be possible that his cock is longer than that of a horse?"

"You should travel more, Ladoux," the German mocked. "Everyone knows that the men in the Arab and Indian regions have gigantic cocks."

"Even so, this is primitive. Just think, von Bayerling, where would you find a woman with hole to fit it?"

"Your knowledge about a woman's anatomy is also nil, Ladoux. You think a vagina is like a shoe with its fixed size. It has an elasticity that can accommodate any size."

I cleared my throat to attract their attention.

They stopped their conversation and walked around the statue of Shiva.

I pretended to be seriously studying the statue. But through the veil of my hat, I glanced at the two men now standing near me.

Ladoux pointed and said, "You seem very interested in this."

I turned to face them. "Yes."

"This fascinating work is from Madoera," Ladoux said with authority.

"No," I corrected him, "this is not from Madoera, but from Madurai."

Both men were surprised.

Ladoux then asked, "What's the difference? Here it says Madoera."

"That's a mistake. The card should state Madurai."

Von Bayerling stepped forward and assumed an autocratic stance. "What's the difference?"

"Madurai is in India, Madoera in Indonesia."

"Where is this Indonesia?" Von Bayerling's question infuriated me immediately.

"Are you German?" I asked in a provocative tone.

He took the bait. "Why? Do you feel uncomfortable speaking to a German?"

"No," I said, "I respect Germans."

Von Bayerling was pleased and barely disguised his arrogance. He said in a jovial tone, "*Deutschland über alles*—Germany above all others."

I gave him a faint smile.

Ladoux did not react.

Von Bayerling returned to the topic of Madoera and Madurai. "You haven't told us the location of Indonesia."

I felt driven to test this man. "Maybe you've heard of the German professor, Adolf Bastian, who in his book refers to the Dutch East Indies as Indonesia?" I was certain he had never heard of Bastian.

Von Bayerling tried to disguise his ignorance with more of his arrogance. "Which book of Professor Bastian are you talking about?"

I replied without hesitation, "*Indonesien: Oder die Inseln des Malayischen archipel.*"

He was bewildered. He probably never thought that an attractive woman would read serious books.

Looking embarrassed, he asked in German, "You read and speak German?"

I replied in his language, "Certainly."

He continued, "Very pleased to meet you."

"Thank you," I replied

Ladoux was nonplussed at the lack of attention. He looked at me, shrugged and pouted, and walked away while mumbling in French, "The way they carry on. As if I cared."

"What did you say?" I stopped him by speaking French.

Ladoux turned back. "You speak French, too?" he asked in French.

"Yes, I actually do. Don't worry. Listen to me. Walk in the path of intelligence."

Ladoux stood with his mouth gaping. When he recovered, he asked, in French, "Who are you?"

"My name is Mata Hari."

"Ma-ta Ha-ri?" Ladoux and von Bayerling repeated.

"Yes, that's it," I said.

Chapter Seventy-seven

Ladoux and von Bayerling looked like failed marathon runners. Their faces shrunk as if they'd been pickled when an elderly general appeared, and said, "Come, my dear child. I've reserved a table at Maxim's for after your performance." He took my arm and we walked toward the door.

Ladoux and von Bayerling lowered their heads and stood at attention for my escort.

Astruc had introduced me to the general earlier, and though he called me "child," we were lovers.

After a few steps, I dropped my handkerchief. When I bent to pick it up, I stole a glance behind and saw Ladoux and von Bayerling as if glued to the spot staring at me.

I was pleased. I understood men very well. They liked to watch a woman's swaying behind while fantasizing being in bed with her. As for myself, I enjoyed looking at men, not only from behind, but also from the front, sides, and any other angle. The two men behind me were equally attractive, albeit in different ways.

My taste in men had evolved. I once only liked men with moustaches, but now I found the clean-shaven Ladoux and von Bayerling very attractive. Did I fantasize about being in bed with them? I never said no to fun in those days.

Because life,
Which echoes in the mind,
Searches continuously
For short-lived rapture,
And only ends when
Arriving at the grave.

Chapter Seventy-eight

The freezing weather outside had lost its bite inside the Musée Guimet. The warmth generated by the large number of guests—important men and perfumed women—was certainly comforting. The crowd had come to see the debut of a dancer who specialized in Javanese exotic dance, a part of the exhibition of fine arts of the East.

On the invitation I was mistakenly named in English as "Eye of the Day," a literal translation of the Malay *mata hari*.

Before I stepped onto the stage, Astruc impressed upon me how important it was to perform flawlessly. This made me so nervous that my fingertips turned ice cold.

"You have to be perfect," Astruc said. "This is Paris. If you're successful here, you'll become famous throughout Europe. That means Berlin, Vienna, Rome, Madrid, and anywhere else."

"I know what I'm doing," I said.

As I stepped onto the stage, I felt so heady I couldn't feel my feet touch the ground. I stood behind the curtains and waited for the music, a rendering of *slendro*, to be played by the makeshift orchestra in front of the stage.

The music started and Astruc introduced me to the audience. "Ladies and gentlemen, we will soon see an exotic dance from Java, an island in the Far East. Performing the dance is a new star who will change the cultural landscape of the West. Ladies and gentleman, I present Mata

Hari, the dancer from the East. Ladies and gentlemen, please give Mata Hari a round of applause."

The music rose in volume.

The curtains opened slowly.

I danced in the middle of the stage.

Ladoux and von Bayerling were in the audience, and likely to be extremely surprised. They were the first men to whom I introduced myself as Mata Hari before being announced by Astruc.

My dream of mystifying an audience was coming true. Enthralled, the guests silently watched every movement of my dance. The music based on the pentatonic *slendro* scale captivated and transported them far away, while being enchanted by my presentation of Javanese eroticism that was in my blood.

In Holland my dance might not have been a surprise as Java was a part of what they called the Dutch East Indies. However, in Paris, Javanese eroticism presented in a dance by a Dutch artist, was a completely new experience, especially seen in a live performance.

While I saw my future as a respected dancer in the West coming to reality, I promised myself never to stop perfecting my art. I had to guard against being lulled into self-satisfaction, which was a dangerous enemy for any artist.

That night began my career in Paris, a city that had haunted my dreams for years. The exuberant and reverberating applause from the audience was an opening to the world I sought to enter. I saw myself as a Westerner with an Eastern soul. I had yet to find and develop new forms and stances to incorporate into dance. I had much work ahead to perfect them while maintaining the dance I performed that evening. Only time would tell of my success or failure.

Ladoux and von Bayerling came backstage. They expressed their appreciation of my performance with many words of praise.

"Thank you," I said. "I hope you'll come to my next performance."

"We most certainly will," they said.

Chapter Seventy-nine

I was pleased to see my picture postcards sold in souvenir shops in the central business district of Paris, and other places such as the Boulevard de Rochechouart, where the Basilica of Sacré Coeur was being built.

Now that my name was known in Paris, I worked for even more recognition. I wanted artists of Montmartre to fill canvases with my image. I don't mean the Fauvists, but painters in the classic tradition of Rembrandt, Goya, and Da Vinci. I also wanted my postcards sold in Berlin, Rome, and Madrid. I wanted to be recognized and respected as a talented dancer and receive abundant remuneration for my unique performances so I could afford the good living I desired.

The years passed and I became better known than I thought possible.

I never expected to maintain my popularity for ten years, dancing in many European cities. I met high-ranking officials as well as rich businessmen and developed relationships with them.

My ambition to see my postcards circulated in many cities soon materialized. Wherever I performed, photographs were taken, made into postcards, and widely sold and collected.

They were even sold in Leeuwarden. I was annoyed that my father, who had been unemployed for years, also sold the postcards. I hoped the cards were sent to Indonesia so that my friends and lovers over there could see them, too.

I never forgot Indonesia.

I longed to return to Java and commune with nature, along with the spirit that made me who I am.

> *I converse with my soul*
> *And leave no room for resting.*
> *Truth is created*
> *From flickering candlelight*
> *In the mist of years.*
> *The windows are open*
> *To the wind from all directions.*

Chapter Eighty

Throughout these years I never gave up hope to be reunited with Non. Between performances I went to Holland to see her, but to no avail. At Ruud's house I quarreled with his sister. The following day Ruud placed an announcement in the local newspaper complete with my photograph:

I request that all and sundry not supply goods or services to my former wife, Margaretha Geertruida Zelle, the so-called famous Mata Hari. This evil woman has deserted me.

I cursed Ruud loudly in private. What could I do to stop his defaming me through the press? I should have taken him to court. But I knew that any legal proceedings would take time and drain my creative energy. I had come to Amsterdam to see Non, not to engage in a legal fight with the bastard.

The last time I had a glimpse of Non was at the Central Station. Ruud was with her. She had grown into a teenager with a full face, her hair cut with a thick fringe on her forehead. She saw me, and when I waved to her, she waved back hesitantly. She was probably scared of her father. I worried that she had been brainwashed by Ruud to hate me.

Chapter Eighty-one

In those ten years, I had sex with untold numbers of officials from France, Germany, and Spain. My lovers ranged from ministers of state, generals, and colonels, to captains and lieutenants; all of them enjoyed our time together.

I met these men as I moved from one city to another to perform at prestigious venues. No man from any social class is strong enough to fight the temptation laid in his path by a woman, as women gave men the highest pleasure.

I always took care of my body. It was the main tool of my trade.

I still followed the Javanese wisdom regarding maintaining sexual desirability, which had been passed on to me by Nyai Kidhal, my former domestic servant. I often wondered how she was faring with the child Ruud had sired.

Mindful of her advice, I avoided eating fibrous, acidic fruit and drinking too much water in order not to cause excessive wetness inside. Among the dignitaries who fell for my sexual charms were very powerful individuals; some were handsome and pleasurable in themselves, others disgusting. There were those who acted very aggressive in public and turned absolutely passive in bed. Then there were the snorers, the pregnant pig snorers, and the quiet snorers with pneumatic mouths like a duck's backside. And many, many more. They slept; I did not.

The pleasant men included France's Prime Minister Aristide Briand, senior official at the Ministry of Foreign Affairs Henri "Robert" de Marguérie, and Minister of War Adolphe Messimy; General Traugott von Jagow and General Moritz Ferdinand von Bissing of Germany, and also the Crown Prince. Out of all the men I slept with, the only one to steal my heart was Flight Captain Vadim Maslov, a Russian who served for France.

Vadim was very courteous when making love. He was also very tidy and scrupulous regarding his uniform. During foreplay while we were still kissing, he made sure that his uniform stayed neat and unwrinkled. While I waited for him in bed, he undressed slowly and methodically, and draped each piece of clothing carefully on a chair. Watching him aroused me no end. I never experienced this with the first military officer whom I'd married, the Scot bastard, Ruud MacLeod.

I loved Vadim with all my heart. When I had sex with other men I pretended I was making love to him. I understood now what René du Bois on the slopes of Mount Oengaran had called adventures with the body, not the soul.

> *Come, oh amorous desires*
> *Of many names.*
> *My soul is open to only one,*
> *The one who renders me drunk*
> *With the wine of Dionysus.*
> *Words will reverberate*
> *Tomorrow in the clouds.*
> *Yesterday polluted the forests*
> *And I don't care if my garden floods.*

Chapter Eighty-two

One French officer with whom I had a loveless tryst throughout 1914 was Ladoux, whom I met earlier at the Musée Guimet.

The relationship with Ladoux was significantly beneficial for me. He liked to boast and introduced me to a number of generals, some of whom, unbeknown to him, also met me regularly in luxury hotels in Saint-Germain-des-Près and Champs-Elysées.

Knowing these officers intimately meant that I was privy to a great deal of information on the world affairs. My knowledge was not limited to the realm of politics, such as the Calmette-Caillaux affair that scandalized France, but also included developments beyond France in science and technology. For instance, I knew about J. H. Jeans' embryonic work on radiation and quantum theory, Joseph Conrad's literary work *Chance*, and Irving Berlin's new composition "Watch Your Step," as well as events related to the world economy, like when the Bank of England was authorized by the government to manage illegal currency circulation.

While I became aware of various problems, be they in politics, economics, social or cultural, I never neglected my skills at providing sexual pleasure. The combination kept me in demand despite my age. Perhaps I could break the myth that declared, "Woman's intelligence is in her good looks, and man's good looks are in his intelligence." As a woman, I maintained the balance between good looks and intelligence, and I also had the ability to create beautiful art, despite being a courtesan.

While I received payment for my sexual favors, I avoided being despised. Instead I received respect and adulation.

I had to attribute much of my achievement to Ladoux, although he was rather naive. At first he thought I only slept with him. When he finally discovered the truth, he didn't show any resentment.

One evening he came to my house and invited me to dinner at the Palais Royal gardens.

While waiting for me to get dressed, he looked at my list of performances for 1914 that I had written on a piece of paper and stuck to the back of the front door.

"You're performing in Berlin in July?" he asked when I joined him.

"Yes, I am," I said. "Shall we go now?"

As we walked out Ladoux said, "The train trip will be lonely without a companion."

"Not necessarily," I replied.

"I think you need someone to help you."

"I already have an agent, Astruc."

"What about a personal assistant for your performances and the household?"

"That is a splendid idea," I said. "I'll find one when I am in Holland."

He drove us to le Grand Véfour, a well-known restaurant that had been established in the eighteenth century.

Ladoux was particularly romantic that evening. He didn't behave like the guileless person I had ascribed him to be. I was surprised when he displayed jealousy toward a handsome, dark haired young man who sat at a table across the room from us. The man kept stealing glances at me. And I reciprocated while quietly studying his face and overall appearance.

Noticing what was happening, Ladoux asked, "Do you recognize someone you know?"

"Why do you ask?" I responded unemotionally.

Indicating the man with his eyes, Ladoux said, "He's been looking at you."

"Really? It doesn't bother me," I said, wiping my mouth with my napkin. The man was very attractive. I didn't know his name and didn't care. Is a name important when one is infatuated? I hoped we would meet again under more conducive circumstances.

Chapter Eighty-three

I left for Holland on the train. Ladoux drove me to the station. He was very solicitous. Before the train departed, he reminded me to find a personal assistant, someone on whom I could rely to care for my needs. I was bewildered by the change in his attitude. When I asked him to explain himself, he said, "We want you to work for France."

I took it as a social proposition. "I've always wanted to stay in Paris. I've had that ambition since I was in Java. France has given me what I wanted."

"Excellent," Ladoux said. "Contact me as soon as you return from Holland. We need someone with your intelligence."

"Thank you."

With that, I departed.

While I hoped to see Non, I tried not to be too optimistic. However, I did find a suitable woman to be my personal assistant. Her name was Anna Lintjens. She gained my confidence immediately. She was exactly who I needed to manage my personal needs, as well as those of a dancer. When Anna expressed her willingness to work for me, I was compelled to tell her about Mata Hari. I did not want her to be surprised by what I did, the dancing and providing sexual favors.

I asked her, "Do you know what I really do?"

"Everyone has heard of Mata Hari, love."

I loved how she talked to me as if I were a little girl. "Very well. Are you aware that I have many lovers?"

"A beautiful woman with extraordinary dancing skills automatically attracts many men, love," she said. "I adore you myself."

I had no misgivings about hiring Anna as my personal assistant. She was smart and understood enough English, French, and German to be useful. She understood what I thought without needing a lengthy explanation. I was so happy with her work that I regularly gave her ten percent of the fees from my performances, in addition to a set monthly salary. Life was much easier with Anna around.

Over the last decade, I had successfully maintained my appearance. When I looked at photographs taken ten years earlier, even further back when I lived in Batavia, and compared them with how I looked at present, I had to say I hadn't changed. I had remained youthful. However I wanted to avoid the term "youthful." It reminded me of a type of dog called a *telomian*, which in Indonesia was a common village dog. It was described as having a youthful appearance and people believed that from the moment it was born until the moment of its death, the dog looked the same. Why were women so scared of aging?

I didn't remember how many military officers and state officials had found their way into my bed during my thirty-eight years of living. They had not only given me sexual pleasure, they had also revealed state secrets that had been entrusted to them. From them I learned about the prejudices the power elites of different nations had toward one another.

I returned from Holland, with Anna in tow. Ladoux and I saw each other often. One night we went out to dinner at Le Jules Verne, on the second level of the Eiffel Tower, with a view of the city beneath us. During the meal we fell into a rather serious conversation that taught me more about the current political situation.

"Of course, you remember Karl von Bayerling," Ladoux began. "You met him at the Musée Guimet."

Instead of recounting the German's dismissive manner that irritated me, I said, "Yes, I do."

"He and I are fencing partners," Ladoux said. "We've been friends until he recently went home to Germany and came back somewhat changed. He's suspicious about France. So our different nationalities have become an issue."

"I see," I said. While a sense of nationality was important, it certainly caused conflict between people.

Ladoux said, "I'm afraid that something unpleasant is going to happen between France and Germany. But I hope that I'm wrong so that von Bayerling and I won't have to face each other as enemies."

Again I was noncommittal.

Chapter Eighty-four

It was July 1914. Anna and I left for the beautiful city of Berlin, which also had a reputation of being a cultural center. In the Dahlem district was a museum with the biggest collection of Rembrandt paintings in the world.

On the night train, Anna and I sat in the dining car with Traugott von Jagow and Herr Griebel of the Berlin police. They both loved my dancing and my body. Two tables across from where I sat, a handsome man in his mid-thirties send me flirtatious glances as he looked up from his Vienna newspaper, *Neue Freie Presse.* The murder of Archduke Franz Ferdinand of Austria and his wife by Gavrilo Princip in Sarajevo two days earlier was still on the front page.

Von Jagow and Griebel carried on an animated conversation about the incident. I was certain the handsome stranger overheard the conversation though he didn't appear interested. He continued reading and making eyes at me. Meanwhile, the two Germans speculated on the motive for the double murders and the consequences that were likely to manifest themselves during the next two weeks.

"The situation will deteriorate quickly. There may even be war throughout the continent. Austria-Hungary will no doubt accuse Serbia of being responsible for the murders," von Jagow said.

"Will we be involved?" Griebel wondered.

"That goes without saying," von Jagow responded. "Germany won't stay out of this. We are, after all, a part of the Triple Alliance with Austria-Hungary and Italy. For some time now we've been aware that the Triple Entente of France, Britain, and Russia is the main cause of the chaos in Europe."

"Russia made a point of getting involved, helping Serbia when Austria attacked Belgrade," said Griebel.

"And we were very disappointed when France and Britain extended assistance to Russia."

"So what does it all mean?"

"It will accelerate the outbreak of war."

"Can Italy be relied on to continue backing the alliance?"

"Like you, I have my doubts. I suspect Italy might jump sides."

I listened to this exchange and couldn't help smiling. I drank my wine and wiped the sides of my mouth with the white napkin.

Von Jagow picked up the bottle of wine and asked, "More?"

"No, thank you." I glanced at the handsome man at the other table. He somehow reminded me of the man I had seen at the le Grand Véfour when I dined there with Ladoux. Could he be the same man? For unknown reasons, he aroused me.

When he rose and walked out of the dining car toward the rear compartment, I hoped he'd glance at me as he walked by, but he didn't. This only incited me more.

Moments later I excused myself to von Jagow and Griebel. Anna acted as if she had not noticed anything unusual.

He stood in the corridor in front of my compartment, and when I passed by, he moved aside a step or two.

I went into my compartment and left the door open as a signal for him to enter after me. I was now certain that he was the man at the restaurant in Paris. He entered and closed the door behind him.

I looked at him in the dim light of the wall lamp. He took me in his arms and we kissed passionately. He eased me into a chair and took off my clothes. After removing my bra, he fondled and suckled my breasts. Within no time we had sex without either uttering a word.

The rhythm of the metal wheels on the rails synchronized beautifully with the movement of his body on top of me until the movement stopped.

Drowned in ecstasy, I hadn't noticed the door of the compartment open and someone throwing a poisoned dart into the handsome man's buttocks. His limp body rolled onto the floor, his mouth gaping. He died almost instantly.

I ran screaming out of the compartment with my clothes in disarray.

We were interrupted before we finished and I didn't even know his name.

Chapter Eighty-five

At the Berlin railway station, two policemen waited to arrest me, and manhandled me during the process. I had no idea who notified them.

Von Jagow and Griebel watched the procedure, and then left me alone. Why did they condone this? Were they afraid of becoming involved? Were they disappointed in me? I could not come up with a single answer to the questions that ran through my mind.

I suspected the police officers who arrested me belonged to the class of state officials that were infected by the ruthless and cruel ideology of communism. They were driven more by social resentment than mere racial prejudice, which I associated with German people.

One policeman pulled my arm to hurry me from the train while the other pushed me from behind.

"Quick, get off," he ordered.

I shook his hand off my arm and shouted angrily for him to stop pulling my arm.

He ignored me and pulled even harder, so hard I nearly fell to the ground.

An old woman looking like a sick tart pointed a dirty finger at me and cheered the police. "Take her away," she said. "I know damn well she was the killer."

Who was that woman? I grabbed the train's door and turned to look at her, but I was distracted by an angry outburst from Anna.

"Shut up, you ugly hag. Mind your own bloody business."

The old woman scowled and turned away.

The policemen let go of me when I stepped onto the station's platform. They allowed me to walk beside them to the station where I was told to sit and wait at a desk that belonged to the police commander, who was nowhere to be seen.

Later a man in his fifties strode in, dropped into the seat facing me, and placed his hands on the desk. He was the commander.

I wasn't able to tell whether he was smart or stupid. I knew that the French loved satirizing their police officers on stage. I hoped he was smart so he wouldn't fall into conventional thinking or be influenced by rumors. I waited for him to speak.

Leaning back in his chair, he began. "Did you know the man who died in your compartment?"

"No."

"He was our best secret agent."

"I didn't know him."

"You don't know the man who made love to you?"

"That is correct. He didn't introduce himself to me, and I didn't introduce myself to him."

"But you had relations with him."

"Is that against the law?"

"You don't find it strange that you had sex with a stranger?"

"Have you ever gone to a prostitute?"

"I am asking the questions, not you."

"And I was trying to answer, Commander. There's no need to know each other if you use the service of a prostitute."

"But you are not a prostitute, are you?"

"I wouldn't be insulted if I was called a prostitute. There is nothing wrong with having sex based on mutual consent and attraction."

"That's part of the communist philosophy."

"No. That's part of my philosophy."

"You came to Germany from France?"

"That's correct."

"But you're Dutch?"

"I am."

"Did you come here in connection with the Spartacus League? Maybe you're here to see Rosa Luxemburg and Karl Liebknecht?"

"No. I don't know those names. Who are they?"

"They're the founders of the League and communist agitators."

"To hell with them. I hate communists."

"Then why did you come to Berlin?"

"I have a dance performance here."

"What's your name?"

Before I could answer, Karl von Bayerling appeared in the doorway. We had met at the Musée Guimet ten years earlier. On seeing me, he called out, "Mata Hari."

The police commander looked at me closely.

"Mata Hari?" he said, as though he wasn't sure. "You are Mata Hari?"

"I am."

He rose and held out his hand to shake mine. He became very friendly and said, "Please accept my apologies. It is an honor to meet you."

I replied, "You are very kind."

Chapter Eighty-six

Von Bayerling offered to take us to the hotel where I was going to perform the following evening and I gracefully accepted.

His car was a convertible with the top down and driven by an awkward-looking chauffeur, who was nonetheless German. The July weather was just right for that kind of vehicle. The soft breeze was very pleasant. Anna enjoyed the ride as well.

Von Bayerling and I didn't engage in an easy conversation. Everything seemed controlled and contrived and I hoped that I was being too sensitive.

"If you hadn't come to the station, I'd probably still be answering ridiculous questions from the commander," I said in an effort to start a conversation as we sped along a tree-lined boulevard.

"Asking ridiculous questions is part of their job. That's the nature of the police," von Bayerling said.

He backed away toward the edge of the seat and faced me. In a forced respectful tone he asked if I was performing in Berlin.

"Yes," I replied. "At the Metropole."

"That's not a prestigious venue," he said.

"I know. I want to prove that pearls will remain pearls even if cast before swine."

Von Bayerling glared but controlled himself. "Oh?" was all he said.

Realizing my error, I said, "I'm sorry. That was presumptuous of me."

"No, no. Every artist should have the necessary self-pride."

"You think so?"

"Yes, of course," he responded with animation. "Everyone should have a particular stance. That's the basis for national pride."

That's a German for you, I thought.

After that our conversation flowed more freely. I was pleased he didn't patronize me. Yet I still felt the need to test him. "You don't think I'm being arrogant?"

"No," he said. "You may boast, but boasting is needed by artists for self-publicity. In military terms, that's equivalent to a provocation to war, like our present situation."

The car stopped at the bottom of the steps to the front entrance of the hotel. All eight steps were covered with red carpet. Von Bayerling jumped out of the car and gallantly opened the car door. "Allow me." He held out his hand to help me out.

"Thank you," I said.

Von Bayerling kissed my hand to say goodbye.

I started up the steps. When I turned, von Bayerling stood watching me, which made me uncomfortable. I continued to walk when he came after me.

He halted at the bottom step and stared at me uncertainly.

"Yes," I waited for him to speak. "What's the matter?"

"In an hour, there's a train leaving for Enschede via Hannover," he said. "I think you'd better leave Germany immediately."

I looked at him, uncomprehending. "But why?"

"You better not become involved."

"I don't understand. I came here to perform."

"The man who died in your compartment was part of a plan to get you involved."

"I am a dancer. I don't want to get involved with any side, neither Germany nor France."

"In that case, I'll say goodbye."

"But I hope you will come to my performance."

"With pleasure," von Bayerling said. "Until then."

"Until then," I said. "Don't forget.

Chapter Eighty-seven

That evening I went with von Bayerling to the theater. A full bosomed singer bounced energetically from one table to another, singing the popular German folk song, "*Güter Mond, du gehst so stille.*"

Dear moon, you drift so quiet
In the evening clouds.
You're so calm
While I'm restless.
Woefully my gaze follows
Your quiet, carefree course.
Oh, how hard is my fate
Because I cannot follow you.

Von Bayerling asked me if I liked the song and the feisty singer. I told him the performance gave me headache.

"Which part of her singing is so troublesome?"

"She reminded me of a wild Soemba horse," I said. "Soemba is one of the many Indonesian islands. The native people believe, though it has never been proven, that the milk from the mares is an aphrodisiac."

"Sounds like you're a horse lover."

"Not really. Talking of horses reminds me of the Javanese tendency to use horses in their proverbs. There's one that goes '*koeda peladjang boekit.*' It refers to someone who's only appreciated when needed, and discarded when his or her usefulness is spent."

"You make me want to see the Dutch East Indies."

"There are so many beautiful islands: Java, Borneo, Soematera, Celebes, and the Moluccas, just to name a few. I've found eternal beauty, which I've incorporated into the choreography of my exotic dance, at Boroboedoer in Central Java."

"I'm really fascinated by your stories."

"About the horse or proverb?"

"About everything. Providing there is no outbreak of war, I want to go to the Dutch East Indies, especially Java."

"Will there be war?"

"I think a world war is inevitable."

I was struck by what von Bayerling had said. He believed that the murder of Archduke Ferdinand and his wife would cause a world war. I knew that France, Britain, and Russia were suspicious of Germany.

The cabaret singer continued to sing and I was bored. Performers who were no longer young often seemed unaware that applause did not always mean that the audience liked the show. Sometimes it meant that they were glad it was finished.

When the singer left the stage, I presented an exotic dance, just one, so I wouldn't bore the audience. My real performance was not until the following night.

Around ten o'clock von Bayerling suggested we leave. He was eager to be somewhere else.

"Where are we going?" I rushed after him.

"To a place where I will show you something beautiful," von Bayerling said.

"Does it have to do with fine arts?"

"As a matter of fact, it does."

We climbed into his convertible and he drove in the direction of Potsdam, past what looked like a lake. The roads were very dark. I wasn't sure whether the body of water was a lake or a river.

Von Bayerling told jokes to keep awake as well as to entertain me. When he ran out of jokes he sang the cabaret songs we had heard earlier.

Finally he slowed to turn into a large front-yard. I had no idea where we were as von Bayerling stopped the car and turned off the engine.

There was just one light shining in the building in front of us. It was so dark that when I got out of the car, I stepped on top of a low shrub mistaking it for solid ground. I nearly lost my balance and screamed.

Von Bayerling rushed to help me. We held hands as we walked toward the building.

What I hoped was a gallery turned out to be a stable. On entering we were met by snorting horses and the strong odor of their urine.

Von Bayerling pulled me further into the stable until we entered an area where there were no horses. He lit big candles so I could see more clearly. We were in a large room with paintings all around. It was an artist's studio. I suddenly understood: von Bayerling was a military officer who painted.

His paintings displayed the styles of different masters. In the limited candlelight, I saw a replica of a Raphael leaning against one of the walls.

"Please, look around." With a hand wave, von Bayerling invited me to inspect his studio.

On a table in the left corner lay a copy of a Dürer. I stood it up, looked, and then put it back in its original position.

A canvas covered by a cotton sheet filled the right corner of the studio. Von Bayerling followed me carrying a candle.

"I want you to look at this one," he said, pointing at the canvas on an easel.

I innocently turned to him.

"Have a look." He raised the candle in his hand above his head.

I stepped forward, pulled the sheet down, and gasped. It was an image of me copied and magnified from one of my postcards.

"You painted me?" I was flabbergasted.

He gazed at me in the candlelight.

I prepared myself to be kissed. There were only the two of us. But he didn't kiss me; I had to do it. I hugged and kissed him, and walked back to the parked car.

"Wait." He ran after me and grabbed my hand.

"Take me to the hotel," I said.

We got inside the car and he drove to Berlin.

As we approached the first lit building, which turned out to be a store, he asked hesitantly, "You didn't like my painting?"

"It is not your painting," I explained. "I just don't like that pose. The postcard with that picture is sold by my father in the Netherlands and distributed throughout the country. Unfortunately that is the pose I hate most. Anyway, it's an old one."

"I'm sorry," said von Bayerling.

"Forget it," I said.

> *An apology uttered*
> *Signals a green light*
> *To deny one's ego.*
> *I fly a banner*
> *And the wind blows it eastward,*
> *Where I steal a touch of rustic life.*

Chapter Eighty-eight

Anna and I went to the theatre where I was performing, and saw to the preparations. These included the decor, set, props, the musician's corner, and especially the lighting that was very crucial to the visual aspect of my performance.

The organizers had placed a replica of "Shiva, King of the Dancers" as a backdrop on stage. I had requested four young dancers to be my entourage. They were all there and I was happy after rehearsing with them.

In our opening number the dancers filed behind me, invisible to the audience. When the curtains opened and the music started, the spotlight only fell on my face. As I raised my arms above my head, the four dancers behind me moved theirs slowly up and down like wings. This gave the audience the illusion that I danced with five pairs of arms.

At first the audience was quiet. After a moment or two, they gave a riotous round of applause.

The master of ceremony came on stage and addressed the audience, "Ladies and gentlemen, we present the goddess of Javanese dance."

I stole a glance at the auditorium. Every seat was taken. Although I couldn't see very well with the spotlight on my face I knew there were important people in the audience, military and civilian alike. Before the curtain call for the next number, the master of ceremony said, "Ladies and gentlemen, out there war is brewing, but in here the exotic Mata Hari brings you peace."

The curtains opened, and I presented a dance mixing movements from the *bedhaya* and *gambyong*. The audience was quiet as if entranced. I had performed enough to know that when a dance was delivered with the perfect combination of physical nimbleness and the inner aesthetics of the soul, it never failed to captivate audiences.

Chapter Eighty-nine

The following evening von Bayerling and I danced after dinner at my hotel. The orchestra sat at the entrance of an open arcade visible from below. We danced the tango to the "Heidelberg Stein Song" by Gustav Luders. Although this was not a tango tune, the orchestra played it with a tango beat. At the beginning of the century, most likely since the first gramophone records were manufactured in the United States in 1903, Germans had taken to this Latin American dance style.

My dancer's body responded rapturously to the dance steps, especially the syncopated rhythm of the staccato notes, and von Bayerling and I drew people's attention. Some couples stopped dancing to watch how I executed the *habanera* movement, the essence of tango. When the music stopped, everyone clapped.

The next piece the orchestra played was a waltz.

Von Bayerling and I returned to our table adorned with a candle and vase of flowers, along with two glasses of Rheinegau, a German wine.

We toasted and sipped our wine. After a short pause I said, "Can I ask you a few questions?"

"Of course," von Bayerling replied.

"First, is tonight's encounter planned?"

"What makes you think that?"

"Because on my first day here, I was detained and arrested for the murder of a stranger. You suddenly appeared in the middle of my interrogation and I was released.

"The second question is, why did you ask me to return immediately to Holland? You knew I came here from France.

"The third is, why did you paint me?"

"You seem to be suspicious." Von Bayerling raised his glass. "Let's drink," he said.

I picked up my own glass, and asked, "Will you answer my questions?"

Von Bayerling looked like a schoolboy whose teacher demanded he answer a question he didn't fully understand. He smiled. "Those were just coincidences."

"We met by chance at the police station. By chance you asked me to return to Holland. And by chance you painted me."

"You really are suspicious."

"I'm just curious."

Von Bayerling shifted his focus from me to the stairs.

Two older men flanked a middle-aged woman. I found her intriguing. Not that she was beautiful or pleasing to the eye, but because she was ugly. She reminded me of a hippopotamus.

The man on her right was taller than the average Western male. His hooked nose resembled a parrot's beak. He had the pointed ears of a bat and his droopy eyes gave the impression of perpetual sleepiness.

Who were these unusual individuals?

The man on the woman's left turned out to be the hotel manager. "Mademoiselle Mata Hari, permit me to present you to our guests. This is Fräulein Dr. Elsbeth Schragmüller."

I rose and shook the woman's proffered hand, smiling as a simple gesture of respect.

Next the hotel manager gestured to the odd-looking man. "And this is Herr Wolff."

Again I showed my respect by giving the man a smile and holding out my hand, which Herr Wolff brought to his lips. His name reminded me a predatory animal. I wondered if it was spelled with a single f or two. Either way, the pronunciation was the same, "wolf," a predator.

Inadvertently the man and woman provided the answers to the questions I had asked von Bayerling, though in a somewhat indirect manner.

Herr Wolff enlightened me when he said, "Herr von Bayerling, thank you for blazing the trail for us."

I threw enquiring looks at von Bayerling and Herr Wolff.

Dr. Elsbeth, who was the more senior of the two, clarified Wolff's enigmatic comment. "Indeed, von Bayerling, we're grateful for your cooperation," she said. "You may leave now."

He immediately obeyed the ugly woman. This disturbed me. I had bad feelings, not only about von Bayerling but also about the woman. I asked crossly, "What is going on?"

Von Bayerling left without a word.

While studying Dr. Elsbeth and Herr Wolff and trying to understand what was happening. I called out to him. However, von Bayerling did not turn around. Dr. Elsbeth laughed and dismissed the hotel manager with a wave of her hand.

I became increasingly suspicious. I understood that nothing in the series of events during the last two days were coincidences as von Bayerling had claimed.

"I'm beginning to understand," I said under my breath, but Dr. Elsbeth heard me.

"Good," she said. "Congratulations."

"Mysterious," I said.

"What is mysterious?"

"Political maneuvering."

She laughed and regarded me with friendliness, almost tenderness, which scared me.

I had no idea what would happen, and I was powerless to address the situation even if I wanted to. It was like being instructed to enter a dark cave and behave as if I were doing it on my own volition.

My throat went dry.

I can't hear the singing
In the longing echo

Of my mother's words.
Perhaps the moonlight
On my umbrella
Will erase revenge
From the horizon.
The fragrance
Of incense and oil
Still guide my steps.

Chapter Ninety

I fell under the spell of Dr. Elsbeth, a woman devoid of femininity.

She invited me to ride in her car to her home. She drove with complete disregard of other vehicles on the road. We first had to drive Wolff to his office in the district of Unter den Linden before going to her house at the end of the Tiergarten.

From our conversation during the drive I learned that Dr. Elsbeth was a psychologist working for the German military and wielded enormous power.

"You are a professional," she said. "And would not be interested in accepting assignments without significant remuneration. Tell me if I'm wrong."

"You're not wrong," I said. "I work for money. Nothing is more powerful in life than money."

Wolff turned around to face me and said, "How right you are."

"Yes," I said. "There is no difference between old money and new money. The new money may smell fresh and the old a bit musty, but both have the same value. Money replaces dignity with a price and converts principles to usefulness."

Dr. Elsbeth snorted. "Sounds like we're in agreement, and this is essential for conducting business. Don't you agree, Herr Wolff?"

He obligingly replied, "Yes, I do."

"Mata Hari," Dr. Elsbeth said, "We offer you twice as much as your current highest fee."

"I don't work for a fee," I said. "I receive an honorarium. And you know, honorarium is derived from the word 'honor' which implies respect, admiration, glorification, and so forth."

"Very well," Dr. Elsbeth said. "I apologize if you found the word 'fee' offensive. Let's call it an honorarium. We are prepared to offer twice the amount of your highest honorarium if you work for us."

"Who is us?"

"Germany."

I pretended not to understand. "But I am in Germany."

"We know you trust France very much," she said. "After all, Paris sent you into the realm of the stars. But von Bayerling told us that you also respect Germany. The Dutch national anthem states that you are of our bloodline."

I was perturbed.

"There you are, Mata Hari," said Dr. Elsbeth. "Germany will pay double."

"What do I have to do for this?"

She turned to Wolff and he nodded. "We'll discuss it at my house," she said. "I'm also anxious to see your beauty more closely."

As planned, we left Wolff in Unter den Linden. I moved to the front passenger seat beside Dr. Elsbeth, and we continued on to her house.

Dr. Elsbeth lived alone. She did not like men. Dr. Elsbeth liked women. I felt more than uncomfortable. I was very much aware of her enormous political power regarding the imminent war. She recruited men and women "to work for Germany" and negotiated their remuneration.

Dr. Elsbeth opened her gramophone, wound up the machine, and set the needle on a record. Within seconds the room filled with Irving Berlin's "Ragtime Violin," which had been popular for the last three years.

She invited me to dance and there I was, dancing with another woman. This was very unusual where I was concerned. When the music came to an end, her arm still wrapped around my waist, Dr. Elsbeth pushed me gently to the sofa.

"Let's continue our business transaction here." She caressed my cheek and played with my hair. "Name the amount of your honorarium, dearest."

"Wait a minute," I said. "What is it you expect me to do?"

"No doubt you're aware the war will begin this July," said Dr. Elsbeth. "Germany has declared its support of Austria for an attack on Serbia after the murder of the archduke. Germany, in its own right, will also declare war on Russia on the first of August, and on the third of August, on France. Along with Britain, Russia and France are members of the Triple Entente which has flagrantly disregarded and insulted Germany by denying our rights to the territories we have long desired."

"I'm not interested in politics," I said.

"But you understand the situation. We know you're intelligent. We've also been informed that you know many French officials intimately."

I frowned and snapped, "Is that a sin?"

Dr. Elsbeth laughed. "You don't believe in God. Only believers are afraid of committing sins."

"Who said I don't believe in God?" I asked querulously, surprising myself. "People who don't believe in God, such as Nietzsche, are actually stupid. When they say God doesn't exist, they admit the existence of God. I am not a non-believer; I am a freethinker. In my heart and mind, I declare God dead. That's different from not believing in God."

"I don't want to get into a lengthy debate."

"As you said, you want to discuss business. So what are you expecting of me?"

"Your closeness to France's high-ranking officials can help us."

"You're mistaken," I said. "I've never been close to any of them."

"Haven't you slept with those men?"

"I sleep with any man I deem beneficial or profitable to me without concern for their political positions or status. My sleeping partners are not only French officials, but also German officials. I am like a ship. A ship stays in a port for as long as necessary. When business is completed, it continues its voyage and finds another harbor."

"We all have to adjust to new circumstances. In war we behave differently from the way we do in peace. Soon pandemonium will break out. Your association with various officials has a particular meaning."

"Why is that?"

"France and Germany are enemies," Dr. Elsbeth said. "Ladoux and von Bayerling used to be fencing partners. Now they represent different nations and will become each other's enemy."

I remained quiet as Dr. Elsbeth's hand moved from my hair and cheeks to other parts of my body. Instead of being aroused, I was nauseated. Deep down I had mercenary qualities. If Dr. Elsbeth was prepared to offer twice my current highest honorarium, I had no problem demanding much more.

When her hand moved between my legs, I stopped her and said in a businesslike tone, "We haven't finished discussing your offer."

"You don't accept the amount?" she asked, removing her hand.

"Seven times more would be attractive," I said. "Based on the honorarium I'll receive for my performance in Berlin."

Dr. Elsbeth nodded. She appeared very calm.

It was I who was shaken when she said, "Very well, if that is what you want."

Chapter Ninety-one

On the way back to my hotel, Dr. Elsbeth answered my questions and confirmed my suspicions. She said, "Everything will be arranged by von Bayerling."

I knew then that when von Bayerling put everything down as coincidence, he had lied. Everything, including my sexual encounter on the train with the stranger, was orchestrated. The staged murder was used to take me to the police station for interrogation, only to be followed by the sudden appearance of von Bayerling, who arranged my release. I was convinced that everything that happened afterward was also part of a carefully written scenario, von Bayerling pretending to be concerned about my being in Berlin, then taking me to the studio and showing me his painting. I no longer had any doubts that I had been chosen to work for Germany in the coming war.

I was disappointed at von Bayerling's deception. I wondered how he would behave in bed after what he'd done.

Chapter Ninety-two

After breakfast the following day, I told Anna to request a car. I wanted to go shopping at Kurfürstendamm, Berlin's main shopping district. At eleven, a bellboy knocked on the door. The car I had ordered was waiting.

At the hotel entrance the car glided to a stop in front of me. A doorman rushed to help me into the car and we headed toward Kurfürstendamm. However, a few minutes later the driver reduced speed and drove slowly toward Brandenburg. I became suspicious and said, "I asked you to take me to Kurfürstendamm. Where are we going?"

The driver wore a Martin Luther-style hat and wide dark glasses. He replied innocently, "I thought you wanted to see the sights of Berlin, so I brought you here. After this I'll take you to Charlottenburg Palace and Havel Lake."

"Didn't they tell you at the hotel that I wanted to go shopping at Kurfürstendamm?"

"No, they didn't."

"How ridiculous. Turn around and take me to Kurfürstendamm, immediately."

The driver followed my order and resumed driving at high speed. I leaned back and closed my eyes. My mind wandered back to the conversation with Dr. Elsbeth the previous night.

Several minutes later I opened my eyes, thinking we had come to Kurfürstendamm. However when I looked out, we were in the country. Instead of shops, I saw trees and bushes. I was furious.

"Are you stupid? Where are we?" I exclaimed.

The driver turned around and took off his hat and dark glasses. "Here we meet again," he said.

It was von Bayerling.

I shouted and gleefully slapped his shoulders and his back. I was so happy to see him. "You crazy man," I said, pinching him hard. "Where are you taking me?"

"I told you, we are going to Havel Lake."

"You are mad."

Von Bayerling laughed, got out of the car, and opened the back door. "If you don't mind, move to the front and sit next to your crazy driver."

I obliged and we continued our drive to Havel Lake, a popular holiday resort for Berliners. Apparently this was the lake I saw the previous night.

Von Bayerling rented one of the several boats moored at the bank. He took my hand. "Come on, jump down," he said.

"Where are we sailing?" I asked.

"To Java."

I laughed. "Before we get to the North Sea, the boat will sink in the Elbe."

Von Bayerling took an oar and rowed. "Who cares if the boat sinks provided I am with Mata Hari?"

"Selfish bastard," I said.

He laughed and kept rowing until we reached the opposite shore.

Von Bayerling moored the boat to a post. At his challenge we ran toward a large house resembling a castle. A very strong wind, unusual for July, stung our faces as we headed for his stable-studio. The housekeeper welcomed us.

Von Bayerling pulled my arm. "Come in."

I knew what would happen as soon as I saw the large bedroom we entered. And I was ready. Dr. Elsbeth had told me that von Bayerling was in charge of pleasure and business.

We looked into one another's eyes and von Bayerling held me tight. I returned his embrace. We kissed, gently at first, but passion overtook us and drove us to the bed in the middle of the room.

I had very satisfying sex, and an orgasm. Only certain men made me play out my own desires in sex and reach climax. With most men I thought about other things while they were busy with my body. This attitude rendered me a professional.

Chapter Ninety-three

On my last day in Berlin, I met with von Bayerling, Dr. Elsbeth, and Herr Wolff. We discussed what I was to do in France. After all, I was retained by Germany and my fee was seven times the amount of what I received for a performance.

Dr. Elsbeth said, "You are H-21."

"That's your agent code," explained von Bayerling.

"Why not R-23, S-69, or Z-77?" I asked.

"Do those letters and numbers have a particular significance for you? Luck or some such thing?" replied Dr. Elsbeth.

"No, I was only wondering."

"We picked that combination at random," she said.

But von Bayerling disagreed. "I believe the code H-21 is lucky for us."

I stared at the doves on the pavement vying for food.

That evening, Anna and I would leave Berlin and travel west to the Netherlands. From there, I was to continue to France. I didn't tell anyone except Anna, whom I trusted, about my mission.

Von Bayerling and Dr. Elsbeth drove us to the Zoo station. We had our tickets by six o'clock and the train left at seven. I hoped to sleep on the train, provided I didn't meet another handsome man who would be murdered while I enjoyed his body.

Chapter Ninety-four

Anna and I returned to Paris with a full pocketbook. I had added another dance to my repertoire: I spied on the French for German marks. I wondered if it occurred to von Bayerling and Dr. Elsbeth that, if I, as a dancer, concubine, and prostitute, spied for Germany, I would do the same for France.

Was I doing this for the money? Apart from money, which was very nice indeed, I also wanted to make a point. I placed little importance on nationality and nationalism. The emphasis on the difference in nationality, race, or ideology too often led to swords and guns.

I hated the tendency of some people to worship a nation and disregard basic human rights. The imminent war stemmed from the rising sense of nationalism. It seemed we were going backward. I continued to place common humanity above all else. Besides, if pressed to take a stance on nationality, where would I stand as a Dutch woman with Javanese blood?

The world was an open stage where each character played his or her role while moving toward the union of flesh and soil.

When war broke out in August 1914, I was performing in Paris. The theater was full. I didn't have the opportunity to scan the audience. While I was in my changing room after the first act, there was a knock on the door. Anna started to answer but I stopped her. "Tell them I'm changing and resting, and can't be disturbed."

But then a familiar voice said, "This is Ladoux."

"Let him in," I said to Anna.

Ladoux carried a bouquet. He kissed my cheeks and handed me the flowers.

"I didn't know you were in Paris," he said.

"I didn't want to be in Berlin if a war started."

Ladoux found my explanation credible. "Wars were inevitable." He smiled. "Paris is now under military jurisdiction."

"You must be pleased," I said. "War is irresistible to a soldier."

Ladoux changed the topic. "When will you finish?"

"At ten."

"We want to discuss something important. I'll wait for you in the audience."

After the performance finished, Ladoux drove us to the Hôtel Régina at Place des Pyramides with its statue of a triumphant Jeanne D'Arc in front. General Emile Fayolle and General Paul Maistre were waiting in the lobby. The two older men introduced themselves.

I wondered if Ladoux wanted me to extend sexual favors to them in this Art Nouveau hotel. If that were the situation, I was wary. Even as a prostitute I preferred sexual encounters with younger men.

Ladoux gestured to me to sit near the generals, but I chose to remain standing until Maistre took the initiative.

He was the more eloquent of the two. Maistre paid me compliments that, typical of an urbane French gentleman, sounded flowery and old-fashioned.

"My beautiful lady," he said while rising. He took my hand and brought it to his lips. "It is summer, yet I see a rose in front of me, fragrant and beautiful, bringing back the spring."

I responded gracefully to his gallantry.

"In the meantime, please sit down," said Fayolle.

After settling into one of the plush chairs, there was a change in the atmosphere. Maistre's charming elocution turned businesslike.

"We want to hire your services, Mademoiselle Mata Hari," he said.

"Thank you," I said, matching his tone.

I looked straight at him, signaling that I understood the nature of the proposition but not the details.

"Let me explain, mademoiselle. We are aware that as a prima donna of exotic dance, you are known and admired by everyone."

I still didn't know where this conversation was going.

"When you were recently in Berlin you were admired by Fräulein Dr. Elsbeth Schragmüller and Herr Wolff."

I was immediately on guard, although I tried to remain calm.

"Indeed," I said. "Also von Bayerling."

"What do you think of them in matters which might interest us?"

"Dr. Elsbeth is a lesbian."

They looked at each other probably thinking of things they never thought of before. Ladoux caught on quickly. He must have suspected something happened that made me mention the lesbian issue. He redirected the conversation to the original topic started by Maistre.

"Allow me to explain," he said. "Germany's military strategy is largely designed by Dr. Elsbeth. She is the most powerful consultant of the German defense policy. She also knows the psychoanalytic theories of Sigmund Freud in depth. Our generals are hoping you will take advantage of her admiration of you for our benefit."

Maistre was quick to add, "We understand that you will need to be compensated."

"Costs would not present any problems," said Fayolle.

I couldn't help smiling. There it was. Why should anyone pretend not to be interested in money?

"You can discuss the details with Ladoux," said Maistre.

I turned to look at Ladoux, thinking the conversation should be conducted in bed, as it required pillow talk. The attitude undoubtedly rendered me a whore.

> *The echo of boredom never knocks*
> *On the door of professionals*
> *At the table of Beelzebub*
> *In the house number 666.*
> *It is proper I take leave of the Western altar*

For the culture growing in my heart
Is a window welcoming
Doves from the East.
Behind the fog the rainbow
Reminds me of the time
I washed the lamb's feet with fragrant oil.
Trying to believe in love during darkness
I refuse to doubt myself.
Ah, listen to this arrogance.

Chapter Ninety-five

Self-awareness led to self-congratulation. I deemed myself having self-respect. My conscience made me hate this quality. Yet when I thought deeper, I loved it. Alas, I swear on my mother's grave I didn't understand myself.

I had become a chameleon.

The quality in me needed justification. I don't think it was easy to be a chameleon. It needed other skills different from what a prostitute required.

The aptitude to be a whore came from recklessness and boldness. Both qualities enabled a woman from a normal and respectable family like myself to become a prostitute. The ability to be a chameleon was based on the need to survive mentally and physically.

I realized that talent of mine because I hated people that interpreted nationality in a very narrow-minded fashion. They ignored human rights and their stance had caused wars.

The irony was that these people were the ones who provided me with money. Apart from that, I loathed living in poverty. I wanted to be rich.

The Germans paid me marks; the French paid me francs. It was my ambition to buy a beautiful house, a miniature palace, not in Europe where too much importance was given to rational thought, but in Indonesia where people relied on feeling and intuition. I have always believed that the potential of the human soul does not lie in reason, but in feeling. It is the heart that weighs good against bad, while the mind addresses this discourse with reason.

The native people were more inclined to use their hearts than their minds. Everything was measured and marked by the heart or *hati*.

I made a list comparing English words with their Malay synonyms:

English	Malay
Unwillingly	*setengah hati*
Glad	*besar hati*
Annoyed	*sakit hati*
Haughty	*tinggi hati*
Humble	*rendah hati*
Grieve	*makan hati*
Encourage	*membesarkan hati*
Darling	*jantung hati*
Contented	*senang hati*
Attention	*per-hati-an*
Conscience	*suara hati*
Determined	*bulat hati*
Eager	*suka hati*
Satisfied	*puas hati*
Unanimous	*satu hati*
Careful	*hati-hati*
Heart	*hati*

I wanted to live peacefully, unburdened from hatred or fear in a land where people appreciated what one felt in one's heart. I longed to return to Java and build my dream palace near Boroboedoer.

There I wanted to reside until I died. How idyllic it would be to pass my days watching sunrise and sunset, listening to the birds chirping and singing as my hair turned white. I would happily live alone, reminisce about when I was a mother, and negotiate the bitter fact of not being able to see any grandchildren my daughter Non might bring into the world.

While I was in Paris congratulating myself on my various talents, I was in reality still bound to the past that would determine my future.

Life depends on the mercy of fate and is in the hands of time. As far as we mortal beings are concerned, we maintain ourselves in order to delay death, which is inevitable. I would negotiate with life by using my attributes of a whore and chameleon.

> *Who was I in my illusion?*
> *No answer came to mind,*
> *Yet life is real.*

Chapter Ninety-six

To realize my ambition of returning to Java, I worked hard to balance reason and feeling, performing, providing sexual favors, and spying. I travelled extensively to various cities in Europe for my work. I met and became acquainted with the respective countries' officials and generals. I was so good at being a chameleon that I was able to move freely from city to city as an exotic dancer while around me cannons and guns fired.

Month after month I continued my activities. The information I obtained through sleeping with officials and generals, I passed on to the interested parties. I gave information from Germany to France, and from France to Germany. Meanwhile I earned money and occasionally even enjoyed physical pleasure.

Two years into the war, the Germans began doubting my dedication. I heard this from von Bayerling, and Ladoux warned me to be careful because the British did not trust me.

As the ground under my feet became shaky, I met Vadim Maslov, a young Russian officer who worked for the French. Of all the men who shared my bed, with Maslov I found the power of love that had no ulterior motive. He was different from the other men I knew. Physically there was no comparison to his superiors, the generals, who also slept with me. They were much older, with characteristics idiosyncratic to men of that age. Maslov was twenty-one, so his outlook on life was very different from his superiors who had experienced life's highs and lows.

One of the advantages Maslov had over the generals was his eagerness to make love. He had a raging erection as soon as I started peeling off my clothes. This was very pleasing and I truly loved Maslov for his avidity. I was experienced enough not to be deluded about the physical side to love.

There was a type of limerick in Malay, often sung in community gatherings, which contained the truism that love began with sighting.

Dari mana datangnja lintah,
Dari sawa toeroen ka kali
Dari mana datangnja tjinta
Dari mata toeroen ka hati.

Where does the leech live?
He moves from the rice paddies to the river.
Where does love come from?
It moves from the eye to the heart.

And then there was a Javanese proverb, *witing tresna, djalaran koelina*, or love grows from frequent meetings. There was nothing secretive about making love. When an activity was carried out regularly, it naturally becomes a necessary habit. Having sex with a chosen partner will eventually make the partner the loved one. I felt this acutely with Maslov. I longed to have a lasting relationship with him, for a hundred, a thousand, even ten thousand years. In him I saw the most beautiful love poetry. He never failed to arouse my desire to have him and nurture his love until the end of my life.

I said, "Please stop fighting in the war so my love can grow with my heartbeat."

"My love is equal to my own breath, dearest," Maslov replied.

"My love is more powerful than death," I said.

"And I," Maslov said, "will write 'I love you' on the white stone of Uspensky Cathedral, the roof of Arkhangelsky Cathedral, and the wall of Blagoveshchensky Cathedral, so all of Moscow will remember our love to the end of time."

"I'd rather you took me to Bolshoi than to the cathedrals. I'd certainly like to include Moscow in my list of conquests. Performing at the Bolshoi would have my name etched into the collective memory of the Russian people."

"The war must stop. I'm tired of fighting."

"Do you believe this will end soon?"

"All wars will come to an end somehow."

"And then we'll have peace?"

"That's how things go. We have war in order to have peace. Not the other way around."

"I long for peace like in our love."

"When we make love, my dearest, we make war."

"No, making love is making peace."

"Love also contains war, dearest."

"I refuse to make war."

"Whether you like it or not, there's always war, even in love, and that's what keeps us alive."

"Maybe," I said. "But why?"

"Because when we make love, we compete with time, and we either have to defend ourselves or concede defeat."

"Fine. I'll concede defeat because I love you with all my heart, my body and my soul."

He laughed. And we made love. We made love in my house. Maslov was the only man who I allowed to sleep with me in my house. While we made love, Anna stood guard outside the bedroom.

Chapter Ninety-seven

Maslov flew north and I went southeast. I was scheduled to perform in Rome. By that time Italy had withdrawn its support to Germany. Anna and I arrived in Rome toward the evening.

The following day we went to the theatre for a rehearsal, followed by shopping on via Condotti and via Frattina. I wanted an Italian silk blouse as part of my costume for that night. The errand became increasingly urgent when after looking in a number of shops I still hadn't found the blouse.

I started to lose my patience and became irritated with the lack of courtesy of the sales personnel. In the last shop we visited, the saleslady was patently rude. She made us wait for an inordinate time before offering assistance.

"Can I help you?" she asked in Italian.

I answered in Italian, "Show me some blouses."

"What size?" she asked, haughtily.

"Medium," I answered.

"What color?"

"I prefer strong colors."

The saleslady looked as if she had swallowed vinegar, and took a number of blouses in various colors from a cabinet to place before me.

Baffled at the prices she quoted, I asked, "There's no discount?"

"I'm sorry," she scowled. "We only sell fixed-priced goods."

"A pity," I said, and walked out.

"What's the matter?" she called to me.

Without turning, I answered, "You are rude."

As we left the store, I noticed a man following us. I whispered to Anna, "Did you see the man wearing a grey hat?"

Anna looked in the direction I indicated, and couldn't find the man. "Which one? There are so many with grey hats."

"The one at the shop window, who looks like a mouse," I said.

Anna found him. "Do you think he's suspicious?"

"He scares me."

"I never thought I'd hear you admit to being afraid of any man."

"I'm not, but this one frightens me."

We stepped into a nearby restaurant festooned with Christmas decorations. It was December the eighth and Italy celebrated the Feast of the Immaculate Conception. We chose a table for four in the right corner of the room that was largely vacant. We waited some time before a waitress came to take our order. Since she didn't have any menus with her, I asked her to bring us one.

After I read the pages, I decided to only have coffee. Before I had time to place our order, a man startled me. He stood by our table and asked if the empty chair with us was occupied.

Caught unaware, I said, "No, go ahead."

After he sat down and I could look closely at his face, I recognized our stalker. I was no longer as fearless as when I accepted the German offer to be their agent H-21.

"Signorina Mata Hari, take note of the voice of the angels. If anything happens, do not admit to being H-21, but say instead you are Clara Benedix."

I was disconcerted. "Who are you?" I asked.

"It doesn't matter who I am," he replied. "Remember, your name is Clara Benedix."

"No, it certainly is not," I said. "I am Mata Hari. Who is this Clara?"

"It's a name to replace the H-21 code. The British have their suspicions about H-21, but they have no proof."

"Then why Clara Benedix?"

"That will confuse both sides, France-Britain-Russia on one side and Germany-Austria-Hungary on the other. That's all I wanted to tell you. Good day." With this he rose and started to leave.

I managed one last question. "Who are you?"

"The voice of the angels," he replied, and walked away.

I never found out who he was.

> *Buffeted by the wind I want to see*
> *Myself standing upright*
> *In the middle of Rome*
> *Taking a defiant stance.*
> *For courage is my weapon*
> *And I never concede defeat.*

Chapter Ninety-eight

Upon arriving in Paris, Ladoux immediately sent me to Brussels. I was to see Herr Wurfbein, a Belgian entrepreneur I knew, and ask for an introduction to General Moritz Ferdinand von Bissing. My brief was to lure von Bissing into bed and extract German military secrets from him.

Ladoux believed I could obtain the secrets from von Bissing using my usual feminine wiles.

"Do you trust me?" I asked.

"I trust your ability to do this job," he replied.

"What I meant was, do you still trust me?"

"I trust you as the Mata Hari I know."

"Very good. I trust you too. But you once told me that the British suspected me."

"Yes, and this is a good opportunity for you to prove yourself. Don't disappoint me."

I went to Brussels. However, the plan that occupied my mind was to use von Bissing to resume my fling of years earlier with the German crown prince. I never included the details of the affair in this account because I think it is irrelevant. In fact, my dalliances with the crown prince hadn't yielded anything useful, which frustrated Ladoux.

Chapter Ninety-nine

As it turned out, the British did doubt my loyalty to the alliance of France, Britain, and Russia. On my return to France, agents from Scotland Yard arrested me.

The challenge for me was how to dispel their doubts.

Accompanied by the two agents, Anna and I were taken from Calais across the channel to Great Britain. There we were driven to their headquarters, a red brick building on the Thames Embankment, for questioning by the Criminal Investigation Department of the London County Metropolitan Police Force.

They asked me who I was. Apparently my identity bothered them. I recalled the Italian man, "the voice of the angels." If I followed his suggestion and claimed to be Clara Benedix, the problem might be solved, but the consequences would be detrimental for me. I stuck to my pledge that once Mata Hari, I remained Mata Hari.

An ugly Scotland Yard officer whose name eluded me and was inconsequential anyhow, asked in an irritating tone, "How come Clara Benedix doesn't know Clara Benedix?"

"I was once married to a Scot, whose name was MacLeod. As far as I'm concerned, he's gone to hell. Before I married him, my name was Margaretha Geertruida Zelle. When I was still married to MacLeod, people called me Lady MacLeod. Now my name is Mata Hari, and only Mata Hari."

"You've changed your names three times, Margaretha Geertruida Zelle, Lady MacLeod, and Mata Hari. When did you start using your fourth name, Clara Benedix?"

I had enough. He was absolutely stupid. "I never used the name Clara Benedix," I said, my voice shaking from exasperation.

This did not reduce the man's obtuseness. Anything I told him, he promptly distorted. Yet he couldn't break me. Besides, whatever he said, I was not Clara Benedix.

He tried different strategies to make me confess that I was Clara Benedix. He said, "Maybe you were tired of Mata Hari and wanted to start fresh with Clara Benedix."

"I am not, and will never, ever be tired of Mata Hari. Do you know what the name means? It means 'the sun' or 'eye of the day.' It means 'one that gives life to humans.'"

"Isn't it the same with Clara Benedix? Clara, as in clarification, the act of clarifying, and Benedix, benediction, a blessing."

"Your inference is stupid. There's no correlation between Mata Hari and Clara Benedix. To hell with Clara. Mata Hari is my current and only name. Now excuse me. Or am I still suspected of being Clara Benedix? Forcing me to admit to be someone other than myself is absolutely insane."

The Scotland Yard officer shrugged. When he turned his lips down, his entire facial expression became more ugly.

"Good God," he scowled.

"Clara Benedix is a figment of someone's imagination. You'll never find her in real life."

The ugly one sat upright in his seat. "Are you saying we're dumb?"

"No such person lives in England, France, or Germany."

The ugly one looked sideways at his colleague sitting next to him, who agreed with what I said and took over the interrogation.

"What about Vadim Maslov?" he asked.

"What about him? Am I a suspect because I love a Russian man?"

He laughed and shook his head. "No, Russia is our ally and Germany is our enemy."

"So what's the issue here?"

"There's no issue when you love a man who is an ally, but it's our business to watch you if you love a man from an adversary nation."

"I love the Russian because of his humanity, not nationality."

This incited the two officers.

The ugly one rubbed his chin. "You seem to be keen on preferring humanity over nationality. Nationality is positive, part of God's grand plan."

"Excuse me. While matters are still within the human ability to solve, let's not use God to win an argument."

"But that's the core of Western civilization," he said.

"Maybe you should read the Bible more carefully. In the story about the chaos around the Tower of Babel, there is a fading sense of humanity, so much that the human population was broken into different nations. War is a manifestation of the failure to recognize our common humanity."

They were confused.

The ugly one spoke. "You love Maslov as a fellow human?"

"That's correct."

"Is that how you love the others?"

"Nobody is comparable to Vadim. I plan to marry him. He wants to take me to Russia. But while I still love him, I want to spend my old age in Boroboedoer. It is a peaceful, richly blessed place, and praised by your Sir Thomas Stamford Raffles during the brief time England occupied the country. I want to be buried there."

I hoped to infect them with some of my romantic ideas. I told them that Sir Thomas discovered Boroboedoer and was the first Western man who had it restored.

"So you intend to go back there to live."

"Exactly. Yes."

The ugly one whispered to his colleague. "I believe she's telling the truth."

"Maybe," his colleague replied.

And I thought, "Fuck you."

Chapter One Hundred

Scotland Yard established I was not Clara Benedix and I should have been released. However, having discovered that I was once married to a Scot, the officers turned their attention into that direction. The ugly one insisted on referring to Rudolph MacLeod as Campbell MacLeod.

I had to correct him repeatedly, "His name is Rudolph."

"He is Campbell," he would reply.

What exactly did the ugly one want to know about MacLeod? He asked me what my problems were with Ruud. I loathed talking about my marriage. It was like disinterring a coffin covered with layers of soil. But I didn't have a choice.

I told them about MacLeod's violent behavior and irrational jealousy throughout our married life, during the times we lived in Ambarawa and Batavia.

The ugly one was interested, so was the other. They listened without passing comment. It seemed my stories entertained them.

I told them how Ruud abused the servants and me. "He even took one servant as his concubine during my pregnancy. He was a heavy drinker. When he was drunk he terrorized the whole household, including our children."

When they remained quiet, I continued. "He wouldn't let me have beautiful clothes because he was afraid I'd look too attractive."

They had no further questions. Apparently they began to understand how I became Mata Hari.

The officers were also keen on hearing about my choice to have exotic dances from Java be the inspiration of my creative soul and the center of my performances. I took advantage of the opportunity to promote my artistic pursuit. I told them about Eastern mysticism and its traditional arts. I told them that dances in Eastern traditions, specifically in Indonesia, were integral to the people's spiritual lives.

"My dances are sacred poems in which each movement is a word. Each word is underlined by the *gending*, the entity of music."

"And the temple?"

"The temple is Boroboedoer. But my temple is in my heart. The temple in my dance can be faithfully reproduced here today, for I am the temple. All true temple dances are religious in nature, and each dance explains the sacred texts in gestures and poses."

They were breathless.

I was in my element as I explained that at its deepest core, art is religious.

Chapter One Hundred and One

Just as I thought I was crawling out of the tight corner I had been placed, a message came from Brussels and the ugly one resumed his questioning.

"You are not Clara Benedix, but you are H-21. We have just received information that you were trained at the German school of espionage in Antwerp, Belgium."

This nearly made me laugh. What poppycock.

"That's not true. All lies."

The ugly one looked straight into my eyes. Since I wasn't lying, I didn't flinch.

"But you know Fräulein Dr. Elsbeth Schragmüller?"

"Of course I do," I responded without hesitation. "Ladoux also knows her, because he is friends with von Bayerling, who introduced me to Dr. Elsbeth when I was performing in Berlin before the war."

"And where you performed was not a prestigious venue, not in the same class of La Scala in Milan, or the Grosser Saal in Vienna's concert hall. But that's not the issue here."

"So what is the issue?"

"Schragmüller teaches at the school of espionage in Antwerp. When you were in Berlin, she arranged for you to train at her school."

I burst out laughing.

"What good would that do for a dancer? If I were to train or study, I'd go to the Bolshoi Ballet Academy in Moscow, or study Stanislavsky's teachings at the Moscow Theater. I'm going to ask Vadim to take me to Moscow and learn from the excellent dancers."

Most people shunned talking about arts in the best of times. The ugly one was exasperated.

"Bloody hell. Talking to you is like putting up with the gibberish of provocateurs in Hyde Park."

"But I am not a provocateur. I am a dancer. Ladoux knows everything about what I did in Germany. Why don't you ask him?"

The ugly one said nothing. I had a quiet optimism that the end of this tiresome and irksome interrogation was drawing near.

Chapter One Hundred and Two

Poor Anna became increasingly concerned about me. She reminded me of the risks I took in my work. We were set free to walk around London, window-shopping at the antique shops that lined Portobello Road.

She said, "Aren't you worried?"

I was touched. "Now or tomorrow, what's the difference? Each day has its own worry."

"Your life is never safe. We're always followed."

"No place is safe in this world." I said, turning around to see who followed us this time. "Let them."

"Who is he?"

"The ugly one," I replied. "He will release us to return to Paris. I have my ways."

"We've been here for a whole week," said Anna.

"When I've finished with my *pas de boudoir* with him, there won't be any more problems."

Anna understood.

During my assignation with the ugly one, I made mental notes of the information he inadvertently revealed about military operations by the Triple Entente of Britain, France, and Russia. I learned that Germany had attacked Britain in February in Verdun, and in June seized Fort de Vaux. The following month Britain and France attacked the Somme and took Mametz Wood.

According to Britain's records, the campaign in the Somme caused 650,000 German casualties, 420,000 for Britain, and 195,000 for France.

In December 1916 General Nivelle became France's commander-in-chief, followed by another assault on Verdun, where 550,000 French soldiers and 450,000 Germans soldiers were killed.

What would happen in 1917?

The Allies planned to attack Noyon, and in April the United States would join the Allies.

This information was priceless. I knew how to use it when we returned to the continent. No doubt both Germany and France would appreciate the information.

Chapter One Hundred and Three

Anna and I were finally free to go back to Paris. The French military believed I was working whole-heartedly for France and its allies. They were unaware that I despised their naivety. I thought how I, a woman, beguiled men using my weapons of wiliness and nimbleness.

Since the beginning of time this always happened. Starting with Adam and Eve, and Samson and Delilah, men had been beguiled by women who were regarded as weak.

Women could defeat men without being like them. I didn't use any manly behavior or strength to get the better of men, yet there was no question about my numerous conquests.

The only man who eluded me was the bastard MacLeod.

I felt the acute pain of missing my daughter, Non. I wanted to go to Holland to see her. I wanted to know how she was during this time of war.

I asked the French officers via Ladoux for permission to go see Non. I had to know if she was safe, whether she had a beau, and was happy.

Ladoux said, "Yes, but don't stay very long. France wants you in Madrid to extract important information from the German military attaché, Major Arnold von Kalle. Under the cover of a performance, of course."

"Of course," I said, giving a chameleon-like promise, "because of France I won't stay long in Holland. I just want to see about my daughter."

Chapter One Hundred and Four

Anna and I traveled to Holland, and went straight for the house of Ruud's sister in Amsterdam, to find out where I could see Non.

Ruud's sister was cordial this time. She said, "Ruud has been sent back to the Dutch East Indies, and taken Non with him."

Disappointed, I asked her what had been on my mind for some time. "Does Non have a beau?"

Her response threw me. "She's just given birth in Banda."

"What?"

"Yes," my former sister-in-law said proudly. "I received a letter from her last week. Non married a KNIL officer, a man of Minahasa descent by the name of van der Een who is stationed in Banda."

I was dumbfounded.

Ruud's sister rushed to her bedroom, and returned with the letter.

"There, she says, a baby girl, and they named her Banda Gertrude."

"Banda Gertrude?" I repeated.

"You obviously know the name. I've never been to the Dutch Indies, so I wouldn't know. Just read the letter. She says Banda is part of the Moluccas. Since the baby was born there, she named her after the island."

I felt heady. The distance between Indonesia and myself shrank even further.

Good heavens, Non, I thought, I haven't heard from you for so long. And now with the first news, you made me a grandmother.

283

Chapter One Hundred and Five

I should have returned to Paris and prepared for the assignment in Madrid as I promised Ladoux. However while in Holland—a nation not involved in the war—a committee asked me to perform in Monte Carlo, Monaco. From there I was to perform in a number of other smaller cities.

I sent news to Paris notifying them of the delay in my return because of a busy performance schedule. I sent the same message to Berlin. Throughout the past year or so, I had performed successfully in many different cities despite the war. The Madrid assignment simply had to be postponed.

I didn't only perform in Western countries where crosses were displayed on fences, front doors, park benches, lampposts, stables, and even dog collars, but also in countries where the majority of the population was Muslim with unwavering nationalism. For instance, I had also danced in Istanbul and Cairo.

While I performed in Egypt, I learned several words and sentences in Arabic from the employees of the hotel where I stayed. Arabic didn't feel like a foreign language. A fair amount of the vocabulary had been assimilated into Malay. Those words were in dictionaries collated by Dutch linguists like the dictionary by H.C. Klinkert, *Maleisch-Nederlandsch Woordenboek*, published in Leiden 1902, which I used to learn Malay-Arabic script. I was not surprised when in Cairo, the hotel receptionist wrote my name in Malay-Arabic script on a piece of paper. I kept the paper with me.

In Cairo, I took the opportunity to go to Sakara, the oldest pyramid. Abd el Aziz, a hotel employee who I often chatted with, accompanied me. Sakara was only an hour's drive from the hotel.

Abd el Aziz had the same name as the road crossing at El Gumhuriya Road and was pleasantly handsome. I fancied taking him to bed. I had yet to experience a sexual encounter with an Arab, and wanted to verify rumors about their oversized private parts. But the possibility of having to go to a hospital because of an embarrassing "accident" didn't appeal to me.

So throughout my stay in Cairo, I only danced. I really enjoyed performing there. The Egyptians had a traditional belly dance, which was exotic to Westerners.

I loved Cairo. From my hotel on El Kornish Road, I had a view of the Nile River and its tributaries in the Sudan and Ethiopia. Gazing at the Nile, my mind went back to the era before Christ. I thought of Cleopatra, the powerful Egyptian queen as portrayed in Shakespeare's *Julius Caesar*. I remembered the dialogue between Cleopatra and Marc Anthony, in Act III Scene 13, and tried to put myself in her role:

> Ah, dear, if I be so,
> From my cold heart let heaven engender hail,
> And poison it in the source; and the first stone
> Drop in my neck: as it determines, so
> Dissolve my life! The next Caesarion smite!
> Till by degrees the memory of my womb,
> Together with my brave Egyptians all,
> By the discandying of this pelleted storm,
> Lie graveless, till the flies and gnats of Nile
> Have buried them for prey!

In the end, though I had admiration for the story, I could not be Cleopatra. I needed a bigger ego and more self-confidence.

Chapter One Hundred and Six

The tour took over a year. Anna and I went to many countries, including those not involved in the war.

I sent news to Ladoux I was stopping in Holland before my return to Paris, to see Ruud's sister for Non's address in Banda. Unfortunately my former sister-in-law did not have the full address, apart from "Non, Banda" written on the back of an envelope.

I left Holland no more informed than the last time. I had never been to Banda, a small island that is part of the Moluccas. I thought about the cruelty of life. Here I was a grandmother and didn't know the whereabouts of my daughter and granddaughter.

Chapter One Hundred and Seven

I departed for Paris with heaviness in my heart, accompanied by Anna. The French officers who made arrangements for my performances in Madrid wanted to meet.

During the journey, I pondered my situation. I was a grandmother, yet my sexual drive was nowhere near slowing down. I thought about Maslov and dreamt about our harmonious life together, not in Europe but in a rural village near Boroboedoer.

I closed my eyes to fall asleep without success. Luckily I had a book I hadn't finished reading, Herman Hesse's latest novel, *Knulp*, published the previous year. I preferred his earlier book, *Rosshalde*. Hesse was adept at communicating the psychological and mystical elements of a story. Readers of his novels in the original German language especially felt this.

While I read and pondered, the train rolled into Paris.

That evening I dined with the French officers in the Latin Quarter. Ladoux was missing. I had no time to ask about his whereabouts, because the conversation opened immediately with the officers briefing me on the assignment.

Madrid was my next destination, ostensibly for a series of performances but the real reason was to approach Major von Kalle. Luring von Kalle to my bed would not be a daunting task. With my exotic dances full of erotic promise, I had yet to fail in drawing military officers as well as state officials to my boudoir.

I was very much aware of men's obsession with a woman's body, which narrowed to conquering the vagina. I knew how to exploit that obsession. From what I learned from Nyai Kidhal in Ambarawa, I'd made men of enormous influence cry for more without fail.

That was how I extracted state secrets, and obtained information for France and Germany for pecuniary purposes.

I departed for Madrid to perform in two venues.

Juan, a Spanish driver who worked for the French, met Anna and me. He knew who I was.

"Señorita Mata Hari," he said. "I will take you to your hotel."

He started the car and told me that our rooms were booked at a hotel in Gran Via, but I was free to choose any other hotel on a main street in the city.

The main streets in Madrid were known by different attributes: *avenida*, like the Grand Via, *paseo*, or *calle*.

"From what I learned, you love staying near to a fine arts museum or a library," said Juan. "That's why I booked rooms at the Gran Via. Close by is the Plaza de la Cibeles, the road toward the National Library, and the Prado Museum. In the Prado you'll find paintings by Velázquez, El Greco, Goya, and many others."

"That's excellent," I said.

My mind was on the task assigned to me by France, and I confess to thinking about my monetary profit. To multiply this I had to be the chameleon again in relation to how I'd use the information I would elicit from von Kalle.

For some unknown reason, however, I had misgivings about the assignment, though it didn't seem difficult. I was not as sure of myself as I usually was.

Why was I plagued by doubts? I had no clear answer.

Did it have something to do with my beloved Maslov, who was risking his life at the frontier at this moment? Was this inherently my problem?

Suddenly I was a stranger to myself.

Until then I had never taken notice of intuition, which many regard as signals from the subconscious. I believed in intuition and the subconscious, but I put it in an agnostic context, separate from any religious overtones.

The Grand Via was located in the new central business district, where everything was modern and sophisticated. The surroundings encouraged me to be more skeptical about the Western traditions that were closely linked with the Church. To me, the concept of modernity embodied basic opposition to the hegemony of the Church that developed in the Middle Ages and ran into problems during the Reformation.

I had a spacious room on the third floor of the hotel. Anna had her own room.

My first performance was two nights away. I'd ask to be moved to a quieter hotel on the outskirts of the city after I completed the engagement. I needed to do some thinking.

I was amazed at wanting time to mull over things. Had I aged to that extent? While waiting for sleep to come and take me away, I saw Maslov in my mind's eye and was more convinced I was truly in love with him.

> *I confess to the Milky Way*
> *Nothing can stop true love.*
> *I am edelweiss on the mountaintop.*

Chapter One Hundred and Eight

When I fell asleep, I had a beautiful dream. Maslov took my hand and invited me to climb to the top of the Boroboedoer Temple. He said,

> *My love, Mata Hari, my dear heart,*
> *There is not a sun brighter than your name*
> *More eagerly expected in winter*
> *Adding more light to summer.*
> *Don't waste our hopes with words*
> *Because words are easily uttered at night,*
> *Then corrected the next day.*
> *Come and visit my satisfaction*
> *Fill my hunger with love and rapture.*
> *We unite in hearts fitted with doors*
> *In purity of love beyond utterance.*

Hand in hand, we walked to the top of the temple. And I said,

> *I am a dove listening to the song.*
> *With you I follow my heart's bidding*
> *Forgetting all inherited lies already said,*
> *Because I must relive the past scenes*
> *That shaped my essence as a snake*

Loneliness invoking evil thoughts.
I must fight to death for the sake of love.
The world where I'm a wanderer
Following the rational map
Will ebb too late to regret
But I hope to be a thug there,
Because my love for you told me to stop
At any port at any depot.
Though the moon promising hope
Refuses to appear to account
I swear on my mother's grave, Maslov my love
An oath on a clear conscience:
I will stop flying.

He held me tight and whispered in my ear,

I will live with you,
Ready to be the slave of your spirit.
Because love must be willing to be bound.

I returned his embrace, whispering in his ear,

If love is not free, my dear heart,
Our love will fail to be strong enough
To turn war into peace.

He released me, stretched his arms open, and invited me to hold him.
And he said,

We are merely images, dear heart.
Why allow logic to sway
Quibbling the essence of self?
Fate has brought you and me
To journey together to the end of heart
In this earth the verandah of heaven.

Yes, the eternal love in our blood
Is the vessel for our voyage in this world.
Understand that the edge may spell death
But there the seedling quickly grows
Into solid evergreen trees
Ever-promising perennial green.
I have been flying for hours.
I see the earth through the light of your body.

Pulling him toward me, I said,

My image was painted by the masters.
It dried quickly on the canvas.
Not needing a mantra
I praise the heavens with a strident voice.
The echo penetrates the Milky Way.
O talent that gives birth to beauty,
Listen to my eloquent song.
For my love is true from the heart
Freed from the gloom of fear.
Look at the sun when you long to see Mata Hari.
In the break of dawn I color the earth orange
Turning it bright red at dusk
Glaring white at noon.
But alas Maslov, sweetheart,
Always remember my name is Mata Hari.

He took me in his arms again, kissed me, and said,

From the sky I landed on this coast
Gazing at your face, reassuring your heart.
How could I doubt the echo of my soul
So tangible in my flesh and blood?

To which I responded, lovingly,

> *I am ready to be the airport*
> *Where you land your craft,*
> *Returning from the frontier of war.*
> *I will always wait for your homecoming*
> *In the land without borders or fences.*
> *I know our time will come.*
> *Kiss me long, dearest heart,*
> *So that I am free from the threats of fear.*

He let go of me, held my face, and kissed me for a long time.
Peace descended on us.

I woke disoriented. The sky outside was very bright. It was ten o'clock. I was not at the temple, but in Madrid. My soul had traveled to Boroboedoer in a dream of beauty, peace, and hope.

Chapter One Hundred and Nine

As usual during the day before a performance, I went to the theatre to familiarize myself with the stage, and see that everything was in order for the particular dances on the program.

I asked the stage manager, who spoke Spanish with a Galician accent, whether the evening's event was sold out. I always worried about the attendance of my performances.

The stage manager told me not to be concerned. All of the city's officials and foreign mission representatives were invited to the opening night.

Among those individuals, I had to find Major von Kalle.

When I came onstage, I glanced at the audience and immediately found von Kalle. I promised myself to enchant him with my dance.

At the end of the show I walked among the audience, something I usually refrained from doing. I carried a red carnation and offered it to von Kalle. I knew Juan and other French-Russian-British agents were watching. I said to von Kalle, "I'd be honored if you would come again tomorrow night."

"A pleasure, H-21," von Kalle whispered.

I recognized in him the demeanor of a military man inclined to stray from his matrimonial arrangements. I waited for him to say something and sure enough, after some social small talk, he asked where I was lodging. I gave him the name of the Gran Via.

Von Kalle made sure his aide-de-camp knew where it was. The man claimed to be a longtime Madrid resident, and I gave him my room number. Von Kalle nodded. Before I walked away, he reached for my hand, and kissed it.

"See you tomorrow," he said.

I replied, "Until tomorrow."

Later that evening, I was trying to fall asleep when there was a knock on my door.

"Who is it?" I asked, annoyed for being disturbed at two o'clock in the morning.

"Pardon me, Señorita Mata Hari," said a man with a Catalonian accent. "It is I."

"What's the matter?"

"I'm sorry to disturb you."

"I can hardly hear you," I got out of bed and opened the door. "It is two o'clock. What do you want?"

The bellboy bowed his head. "I am very sorry to disturb you, but a gentleman is here. A military officer."

That jolted me awake. I dressed and rushed down stairs. As expected, the officer was von Kalle. Despite the available plush chairs, he stood waiting. As soon as I reached him, he said, "I wish to take H-21 away. I had to come at this late hour to avoid undesired attention."

"Where are you taking me?" I asked.

"To a quiet place near the river."

"And without Anna," I said.

"Only H-21 herself."

His aide-de-camp, who was also his chauffeur, drove us westward from Gran Via, along Calle de Toledo to the Manzanares River. After he parked the car on the southeast bank, von Kalle asked him to leave us alone. "I brought you here this late so there are no walls with eyes and ears to see and hear us."

I smiled without comment.

Von Kalle looked curious. "Why do you smile?"

"You are right. There are no walls with eyes and ears on the bank of this river," I said, looking around at the surrounding darkness. "But the wind can carry our voices to ears a fair distance."

"That's only in folk songs, not in reality."

I laughed and he laughed too.

All this happened in the backseat of the car. "I have an important question from Berlin. They want to know how H-21 is doing."

I promptly put on my chameleon skin. "H-21 is doing very well, thanks to Germany and for Germany."

"That's excellent news," he said. "We received information that you were interrogated by Scotland Yard."

"Indeed. They thought I was Clara Benedix."

"Did they get what they wanted from you?"

"They did. Hot wind."

Von Kalle laughed. "And you? Did you also receive hot wind?"

"I wore a scarf for protection."

"Scotland Yard had information for you, of course."

"I'd rather not talk here. What about tomorrow? I'm very tired. The important thing is, the Triple Alliance of Austria-Hungary, Italy, and Germany will win. You may tell Berlin."

"Berlin is very concerned for your safety."

"As you see, thanks to the Triple Alliance, H-21 is well and as strong as the rock of Gibraltar."

"I will send a telegram to Berlin that you are doing well, still committed to our cause, and never to doubt you."

"Thank you."

I was pleased he trusted his chameleon. Privately I laughed at his naivety. After all, naivety was only one step away from stupidity.

Chapter One Hundred and Ten

Early the next morning Juan came to my door and said I was to move. They had another sumptuous hotel in an elite district along the Paseo del Prado.

I recalled that Juan had told me the hotel on Gran Via was chosen because of its proximity to the National Library and the Prado Museum.

Why move to Paseo? I wondered.

I suspected it had something to do with spying on von Kalle.

I told Anna to pack. I didn't voice the sense of foreboding that suddenly surfaced. Suspicion was necessary for my activities but this time I couldn't find the source.

Juan believed that at the new address I'd be away from German surveillance, and better situated to pry information from von Kalle. Maybe the French had briefed Juan. If the hotel turned out to be a trap, I'd have to wait until it was sprung.

At the hotel, I told Juan I didn't want to stay on the third floor. I asked the receptionist, a beautiful young Spanish woman with long wavy hair, in Spanish, "Do you have a room on the first floor?"

"Certainly, madam." The receptionist handed a key to the bellboy.

My room was in the center, right at the opening of the corridor, where guests passed each other to and from the ballroom.

The bellboy opened the door. I entered the room and immediately walked out. "I don't like this. There's too much noise. I'd need more quiet."

Finally I took a room at the end of the corridor. I liked this location because I needed a relaxed atmosphere if I were to extract information from von Kalle during pillow talk.

Chapter One Hundred and Eleven

After the performance, von Kalle offered to drive me to my hotel. I suggested we stop first at Puerta del Sol, an ornate gate at the entrance of Plaza Mayor.

Von Kalle took my hand to help me out of his car. After I stepped onto the ground, he didn't let go and I allowed him to hold my hand.

As we walked around the Puerta del Sol, von Kalle squeezed my hand. "You have beautiful hands and they're soft like a baby's." He sounded like a teenager who didn't know how to manage his sexual desire.

At the hotel, we sat in the lobby to chat and von Kalle reached for my hand again. I sensed he wanted to go to bed with me but he didn't know how to ask. He was very different from other military officers who kissed me as a start. I was at a loss at how to react to this unusual overture.

I decided to take the initiative. "Wouldn't we be more comfortable in my room?"

He jumped at the suggestion. "Of course," he said, with barely veiled eagerness.

Within no time we were having sex.

I closed my eyes and imagined I was making love to Maslov. I wondered if having sex with one man while fantasizing to be making love to another could be called transference. This was part of my job. I ensured my clients enjoyed themselves regardless of my own feelings.

And while pleasing them, I restrained myself from reaching orgasm. I did not allow myself to like my clients; I could not become attached to them.

The job, especially the pillow talk, benefited me financially and would enable me to realize my dreams. I was accumulating funds to build a house near Boroboedoer and live there with the love of my life, Vadim Maslov. I wanted the war to end soon so that Maslov and I could be together.

Lying in bed with von Kalle I told him what I had learned from the ugly one, and obtained information from him to tell the French when I returned to Paris.

"The British are sending their tanks eastward in September," I said, "via the Somme."

"We know. But what they don't know is that in January Germany is launching a submarine attack to defy American President Woodrow Wilson's ultimatum that he declared last April in relation to our submarine campaign. Mark my words, those Yanks will learn a thing or two."

"John Pershing, the American general, commander of the American Expeditionary Force, is planning to come to France in June."

Von Kalle seemed very pleased with the information I had given him, and paid me 3,500 pesetas that night.

When he radioed Berlin he emphasized H-21's loyalty to Germany. And I didn't think about the information he had sent, still confident in my skills as a chameleon. I thanked von Kalle for praising me in his message.

When I discovered that I had manifested myself in a different color than my surroundings, I realized too late that I had been over-confident to my detriment.

Chapter One Hundred and Twelve

I had another dream about being on top of the Boroboedoer Temple. I was with Maslov and my mother, Antje van der Meulen. Maslov was dressed like a groom, while I wore a suit of armor from the Middle Ages. My mother was neither dressed nor completely naked. This time, Maslov and I didn't climb the temple like in the earlier dream. We descended.

When we reached the ground, I said to Maslov,

> *At the foot of this temple,*
> *I want to continue my pilgrimage*
> *To the nirvana that is only in your heart.*
> *Bringing jasmine flowers*
> *I picked from the green valley,*
> *My wealth is an unchanging love*
> *In a solemn oath in my mother's name.*

Suddenly my mother slid down from the top of a pine tree. Announced by gamelan music, her voice carried by the wind, she called out to Maslov and me,

> *If the flowers spread beneath the pine tree*
> *Go well with the tune of my blessings*
> *No snails will come and devour the leaves.*

Riding the love which brought you to the world,
My spirit will last to the day without era.
Let me welcome you with the message
That the heart must fight for the truth.

Maslov was going to greet my mother, but she was lifted back to the top of the tree. Maslov was undecided for a while, and then he said tearfully,

I want to seize the compelling truth
And turn my face from any horizon
So my conscience will be the judge.
Not all tears represent sadness.
My tears show my hope for heaven.
I must go so I may return tomorrow
And build a pillar of heaven in a mortal body.

My mother didn't hear Maslov's promise, because she had closed her eyes and fallen asleep. I was so disturbed I called out to her,

Mother, why do you close your eyes?
I am abandoned in the time of happiness.
Standing uncertainly on awkward feet
I came to the temple intentionally.
I labored to take control of time,
Free, how all heroes tried to find it
While I amassed the crumbs
Under a long forgotten presence.

Maslov stretched out his arm for my hand and with a soothing voice he said,

Arise, my beloved, arise.
Even in a dark night smelling of death,
I am here carrying my love verses

302

Without fear of Beelzebub's threats.
For one-two-three highly cultured names
I am ready to become pious in your body and soul.

My mother, who sat with closed eyes on top of the pine tree, opened her eyes and shouted,

Amen!

A rat bit the tip of my big toe. I slipped off the bed and fell. Then I woke up. I lay deep in thought, unable to decode the significance of the dream.

The following morning I discussed my dream with Anna. Though neither of us understood its significance, we discussed it enthusiastically, acting as if we were seasoned dream readers.

"Impossible that the dream was meaningless," said Anna.

"I can't decipher it," I said.

"I have an idea, though I don't think it would do good because you trust your heart."

"Say it anyway."

"If I were you, I'd turn myself in, love."

"But I'm not you, Anna."

"See what I mean?"

With that arrogance, I maintained my strength, or pretended to maintain it. An hour later I began to waver and recalled the misgivings I had when I went to Madrid for my assignment.

I had felt something weighing inside me. But what did it have to do with my dream of the previous night?

Anna's suggestion to surrender sounded ludicrous to the freethinker in me. I realized that I had to address the arrogance that I began to suspect clouded my judgment.

"Never mind," I said to Anna. "Everyone has to make peace with his or her ego."

Chapter One Hundred and Thirteen

We were talking in the hotel dining room when Juan appeared and glumly informed me that I was being sent back to Paris.

"How is that possible?" I said crossly. I hated being treated in such a disrespectful manner. "I have a performance tonight."

Juan was aloof. I was disappointed because I hoped to have him on my side.

"Trust the crazy French," I said bitterly.

"If you knew the problem," he said, "you wouldn't be upset about leaving your admiring audience."

"No," I protested. "For a performer, this is betraying one's audience. Performance is part of life. It is the stage that has brought importance to the name Mata Hari. And Mata Hari is important only because of her appreciative audience. Without the audience, Mata Hari is nothing."

"Excuse me, señorita," said Juan. "Once again, when you've learned what the problem is, you may, and ought to, modify your opinion."

I was curious as to why Juan was so obtuse. His expression did not reveal anything. Finally I asked him what he meant by the problem. "If you don't reveal the problem, nobody can understand what it is."

"You are asked to return to Paris because Flight Captain Vadim Maslov has been shot."

"What?"

"You heard me, Señorita Mata Hari." Juan hung his head. "You are expected in Paris."

"My God. I must go." I was amazed at my own words. It was the first time after so many years that I mentioned God's name, especially in an utterance from the heart. I realized how difficult life could be for a freethinker.

All energy left me. The bones in my body turned into soft cheese. I had no control over my faculties, no control over the tears streaming down my cheeks.

Two things competed for priority. I either stayed loyal to the stage, a part of my life, or abandon the stage to rush to the side of my lover, who was also a part of my life.

This was a difficult challenge. There was no way I could do both at the same time.

I chose Maslov over the stage, and became acutely aware of my limitations. I was no longer able to only love. I also needed to be loved, and Maslov fulfilled the latter.

I loved Maslov, and Maslov loved me.

I didn't experience the same fulfillment with the stage. I loved the stage, but as an inanimate object, it never told me it loved me. I learned from the history of performance that a prima donna was merely a stage display and she had to be young and good-looking in order to be admired and loved. When she grew old, her skin wrinkled and her middle spreading, her days as a prima donna were behind her. She could only dream about her past glory in utter loneliness.

That was why I had to find the one I loved and loved me, so that I wouldn't fear growing old, being Banda's grandmother and a mere old woman for others.

This unexpected event made me think far ahead into the future. The all-powerful time played havoc with people's lives, and they had to dance to its tune.

Anna packed hurriedly and we took the next train for Paris.

I was tense throughout the journey from Spain to France. Unanswered questions filled my mind. I was worried sick about Maslov.

I pulled my *velo*, a Spanish scarf, over my head and face, probing my memory for any omen I missed that preceded this tragedy.

I tried to deny I was fearful that my last dream, where I descended from the top of the temple, was such an omen. I rallied the courage to admit that such was the case. I said to Anna, "You were right, Anna, my dream had significance."

Anna nodded, pleased that her opinion was acknowledged. She said, "I've always thought so, love."

> *Oh, if you only knew these tears*
> *Flowing together with the blood.*
> *Be aware, oh soul, my love is only one.*
> *I no longer utter words of desire*
> *In the grips of sudden fear.*
> *I sing the psalms in place of vows*
> *Praising love as pure as the lily*
> *That grows on the slopes among the rocks.*
> *Maslov, dear heart, listen*
> *I am coming to you wrapped in belief*
> *Of the mystery held by the mind*
> *And body and soul of the lamb.*

Chapter One Hundred and Fourteen

The train slowly entered Paris on the thirteenth of February 1917. Before it came to a complete stop, a squadron of French soldiers rushed into the train car. I thought it had something to do with an emergency associated with the war until I was ordered to stand. I yelled out the names of generals whom I knew intimately, but without avail.

None of the soldiers showed me any deference or courtesy. I was dragged out of the train in the roughest and most indecent manner. A very ugly soldier used his moment of power to grab and squeeze my breasts.

"Stupid bastard," I cursed him.

He snickered.

When we walked off the train, he pushed me on the platform and told me to move along to see his commander.

I soon stood face to face with Pierre Bouchardon. The expression on his face was as cold as the snow falling outside. Bouchardon was not a man who could be lured to bed. He looked like a clay statue, except that he breathed. I wondered if his heart was made of the same material.

I assumed a business-like approach. "This is a mistake," I said.

He threw me a haughty and dismissive look. "To whom are you speaking?"

I wanted to slap his face, but I gathered my strength and said, "I'm talking to you."

He raised his head and squinted at me. "Pardon me," he said, and ordered his subordinates to take me to Élysées Palace Hotel.

From there I was taken to the prison of Faubourg Saint-Denis. After a brief stay I traded that cell for another at Saint-Lazare.

It was still winter, and in the northern parts of Europe, people only sponged themselves, since it was too cold to bathe. However, not being able to bathe caused me extreme discomfort.

In Java I had learned to wash twice a day. Adhering to the native fashion, I used a scoop to ladle water from a large trough, which I poured over myself again and again until I was completely clean and refreshed. In Java, I reminisced longingly, there was plenty of water. Inhabitants of the archipelago refer to their country as *tanah air*, meaning land and water. I believed it should be referred to as *air tanah*, or water and land, because the sea dominated the land.

In the prison of Saint-Lazare I often yelled angrily about the lack of water. But no one in the prison, especially that son of a bitch Bouchardon, paid any attention to me.

Bouchardon's interrogations were a sustained attempt to destroy my spirit. Père and Soeur, and also Anna, heard leaked information about my case that suggested the French were doing this deliberately to strike fear into the German authorities. They made sure Germany knew their agent H-21 had been captured, was under heavy interrogation, and certain to be executed after a farcical court hearing.

From the beginning, Père always made me feel better and his words made me hang on to what was left of hope in my heart.

Whenever he came with Soeur, they asked me to pray with them, read verses from the Bible, usually from the Song of Solomon, or verses of David from the Psalms.

Gradually they brought me back to memories of my childhood days in Leeuwarden.

I had more to contend with than the reality of life in prison. I still didn't know what had happened to Maslov.

Chapter One Hundred and Fifteen

I kept asking, "Where is Maslov?"

Bouchardon finally told me that Maslov was being treated in one of the hospitals, because one of his eyes had been destroyed by the poison gas sprayed by the Germans at his capture.

"He wasn't shot?" I asked.

"It makes no difference," said Bouchardon.

"In that case, let me see him."

"There are no concessions for a traitor."

"I am not a traitor."

"So what are you?"

"Call me a dancer-concubine, or a concubine-dancer, but not traitor."

"Why not admit that you are H-21?"

"Everything has been revealed. What's the use of talking?"

"Not all has been revealed. For that reason, you need to tell us everything you're holding back."

"I'm not holding back anything. And please, there's no use torturing me. I'm only an ordinary woman. I beg you, please let me see Maslov."

"There is no such concession. What did you get from von Kalle, and what did you give him?"

"Very well," I said, spreading my legs apart and lifting my skirt. "What he got from me was my cunt, and what I got from him was his cock."

Bouchardon turned crimson.

"Liar!" he exclaimed angrily.

I hurled abuse at him in Javanese: *"Kirik!"* Bastard! *"Asu!"* Mangy dog!

As he disappeared behind the door of my cell, I screamed, "Let me go, you son of Satan. Bring Maslov to me." But he was gone.

> *Maslov, Maslov,*
> *Am I a butterfly*
> *Who flies in the time*
> *Of catastrophe?*

Chapter One Hundred and Sixteen

It wasn't Maslov who came to me in the prison of Saint-Lazare, but Edouard Clunet, now in his seventies.

When I first came to Paris and my agent introduced him, he was going to help me win back custody over my daughter, Non. Even in his sixties, he was quite a sensation in bed.

"I will be your defense counsel, my love," Clunet said when Bouchardon brought him to see me.

It was a surprise to see him after so many years. I hadn't expected him in that infernal place. Père and Soer visited to pray with and for me, but since we were all together, we chatted like old friends. We talked about various things accompanied by some laughter, just like people chatting in a café in normal life, not in wartime, let alone in captivity.

Clunet enjoyed himself, and said to Père, "I am the defense counsel who will defend Mata Hari. I owe her. For that reason, I will win the case for her. The charges are driven by a political motive. First, France wants to inflame the population to hate Germany. Second, France wants to divert attention from the rumors of the scandal involving officials who had intimate relationships with Mata Hari. Sorry, Mata Hari."

"Don't apologize," I said. "Go on."

"Yes, yes," Clunet continued. "Third, in order to manipulate nationalist sentiment, Mata Hari has been depicted as a traitor of France.

Fourth, a link is forged to the realm of religion. Treason to one's nation and nationality is made into a big sin, a big, unforgiveable sin."

I was miserable and angry. "What bad luck," I said.

Père attempted to raise my low spirits. "Don't let your heart and mind be destroyed by politics," he said. "Politics don't take care of love and its truth, because love and truth are used by politics in its ambition for power. Sins defined by politics are tools to corner opponents in an effort to legitimize worldly ambitions. Don't believe what the politicians call sins. There is only one big sin, the sin of denying the omnipresence of God as our savior. That is the only unforgiveable sin. All other sins are forgiven."

Père took his Bible out of the pocket of his black robe. Flipping through the pages he stopped at the chapter of Isaiah and asked me to read it.

I was shaken. I had heard this part read in English in Batavia when Perkins took me to an Anglican church: "Come now, let us settle the matter, says the Lord. Though your sins are like scarlet, they shall be as white as snow; though they are red as crimson, they shall be like wool."

Yes, I'd remember it to maintain my hopes.

Despite being a freethinker, I had called out God's name when I was told of Maslov being injured. I was that devastated. I now hoped that God really existed and was omnipresent. And if that were true, I was prepared to call His name for Maslov's sake, provided He performed a miracle and released me from this foul prison to reunite with Maslov.

Chapter One Hundred and Seventeen

In the afternoon Bouchardon appeared outside the grill of my cell door. He stood there scowling without saying a single word. The expression on his face was as sour as vinegar.

One of his subordinates brought a chair. He positioned it to face me, but sat with his back turned.

"Once again I'm asking what information you gave von Kalle," he said.

"None. I'm amazed you never asked the reverse. France sent me to Madrid to spy on von Kalle."

"Spare me your lies," Bouchardon said. "We're not interested. What we want to know is what you said to von Kalle. There's no need to lie and obfuscate, because we have proof."

I had to smile. He was bluffing and I had to think fast.

"You may be smart, Captain Bouchardon, but you aren't that clever. You insist that I confess to being H-21, saying you have proof. You know damned well that's irresponsible fiction."

Bouchardon shifted uncomfortably. I knew then that he had no proof.

When he recovered, Bouchardon smirked and I began to worry.

"Do you think we live in the Stone Age?" He rose to put a foot on the seat while holding on to the back of the chair. "Don't you know that we have sophisticated radio communication?"

I tensed as soon as I heard the word "radio." Von Kalle told me in Madrid that he had to inform Berlin that H-21 was still loyal to Germany. I was dumbfounded, and my concentration was broken. Bouchardon looked like a ghoul.

"Obviously you thought we were stupid," he said. "Listen, Mademoiselle Mata Hari. In his radio cipher communication with Berlin, which we intercepted, von Kalle told of a submarine blockade to France complete with an elaborate map of France's camps on the northern Belgium borders which he obtained from German's agent H-21."

It was Bouchardon's turn to take center stage.

"You can't escape the trap you set yourself. You deserve the punishment that fits your crime." Bouchardon spoke as if he were telling a story. "You have committed a war crime. You will be tried in court. Your *avocat* lover, Maître Edouard Clunet, will try to defend you. But believe me, your betrayal of France will make it impossible for you to avoid suitable punishment."

I could not find anything to say in my defense. "Please," I begged.

Bouchardon gloated with a strange expression on his face. "What do you want?" he asked, sitting down.

For a few moments I wasn't sure how to put my request to him. Finally I said, "I want Maslov."

"Why do you keep asking about Maslov?"

"Maslov is my reason for living."

Bouchardon laughed. "Right now, you should ask about prosecutors and judges. They will determine your fate. France has appointed the prosecutor and the judge who will decide what happens to you. Unlike your defense counsel, these are not men who are interested in having a dalliance with a dancer."

I cursed him in Malay for his insults. "Kirik! Asu!" Bastard! Mangy dog!

Chapter One Hundred and Eighteen

Ten days later Bouchardon returned, still gloating over the significant power he had over my fate.

"I could bring Maslov here," he said.

Immediately turning ecstatic, I said something which suggested I had abandoned my freethinking self. I gave thanks to God with humble sincerity.

Bouchardon was making a fool of me.

He said, "Wait a minute. Bringing Maslov here is not easy. How would you feel if I brought you Maslov's statue instead?"

"Damn you, Bouchardon."

He laughed and whistled. A guard brought a chair for him. Taking his seat, Bouchardon said, "I see that you're very fickle. I'm convinced Maslov will be disappointed in you."

"Never," I said. "Never. Impossible."

"Look, Madamoiselle Mata Hari. Before the opening of your trial, I will ask for the last time about the role of H-21 played in regards to Marie Bonaparte. We know that H-21 was instrumental in staging an affair between Marie Bonaparte and Prime Minister Aristide Briand to get French support for her husband's claim to the Greece throne."

"What else do you expect of me?" I asked, unable to control my emotions. "I'm exhausted."

He pretended to be dismayed. "We apologize that our hospitality does not live up to the Versailles standard and traditions."

If the grates did not separate us I would have punched his nose.

"Mademoiselle Mata Hari," Bouchardon crossed his legs, "We received information that you said Briand would eventually defeat his opponents in the war. Is that true?"

I didn't answer.

"Very well," he said. "Silence can be interpreted in many ways. Now answer me, did you, as H-21, say that France is under British political control? And that France is too scared to do anything? Tell me what you meant by these allegations."

"Why should I bother? You've already established them as fact."

"You admit to making those claims?"

"I did not. I am innocent."

"Then who is guilty?"

"Your job is to find the answer to that question. Look for an opportunist operating in the shadows. He must be a French counter-espionage agent, someone who has known me since I was recruited by France."

Bouchardon seemed to think about what I'd just said. He fixed his gaze on me for a moment.

"Could Ladoux be this mysterious agent?" he asked.

"I don't know. That's your suggestion."

"If it were up to you, who should I suspect to be the agent?"

"I don't know. I carried out whatever instructions Ladoux gave me. If you are suspicious, you have the power to investigate."

"I never said I was suspicious."

"You are correct, but I don't have a particular man to name as the source."

Bouchardon rose. "You can present your theory to the court. That is if the court wants to believe anything you have to say."

Chapter One Hundred and Nineteen

The months passed as I sat in my cell at Saint-Lazare prison. In June I was still held captive, not knowing what would happen next.

Bouchardon remained his annoying self.

Père and Soeur put the name of God in my vocabulary, yet if the grate were not there to protect him, I'd have destroyed Bouchardon's ugly face, or at least made him uglier.

I asked Bouchardon again to let me see Maslov. His response made me more angry and hateful.

"Expel Maslov from your heart and mind," he said coldly. "You will never see him again. Even if you were allowed to see him in his present deformed state, you wouldn't love him."

"That's a lie," I screamed. "If it's true that he's injured and there's no money for necessary medical treatments, I will find the money. I will use all of my money to pay any costs."

"A futile exercise. Your bank accounts have been confiscated. You and Maslov will never see each other. You may even die on the same day."

I screamed until my lungs hurt.

"It's not you who decides when we'll die. It's in the hands of God."

Bouchardon laughed.

"You believe in God now?"

"Yes, and I also believe in Satan."

Bouchardon walked away.

Chapter One Hundred and Twenty

"Who cares about me?" I said to Anna. She had come to see me before Père and Soeur's regular visit. I wiped my tears, and denied that I had been crying over my miserable lot.

Still slightly sobbing, I said, "Why was I born such an unfortunate woman? I thought people deemed their humanity more important than nationality. Now I realize that we put nationality above our humanity. What do you think, Anna?"

"You're growing, love, maturing," she replied.

"So you think I've changed?"

"Yes," says Anna. "You have changed. Outwardly you're the same, but your heart has undergone changes."

"But what does that mean? Why doesn't God grow and change with me? Where is God when I'm in this wretched state?"

Anna slips her hands between the grates and takes my fingers.

"Love, don't direct your anger at God in your misery. You never asked where God was when you were happy."

It is as if she slapped my face. I tried to defend myself, except that I couldn't find the right words. My mind was a blur.

I wanted to do some thinking. But the more I thought, the more pessimistic I became. Giving up did not come naturally for me.

Père and Soeur found me in that contemplative state with Anna.

"Thank you for coming." I was comforted by their presence. They brought peace to my soul, like they were my spiritual father and mother.

Before they said anything, I started to pour out my woes.

"I am very sad."

Père calmly responded, "As long as humans live in this world, there's always sadness. We're only rid of our sadness in heaven. Now what makes you sad?"

"I feel like I'm damned. I no longer hope to see those I love most, my daughter and my lover."

"Love itself has the power to maintain hope. Even in misery and dire situations, a heart filled with love has the strength to fight misery and dire situations, to find hope from the only source of love, God."

"But Père, love makes me cry and I hate tears."

"Don't do anything unnatural. If you want to cry, go ahead and cry. Cry as much as you need to. Howl aloud if you want to. It will release your mental burden."

"I find myself at a dead-end, Père."

"Accept the situation. Regard all paths as middle paths. Maintain love and forgive yourself for past mistakes. Then the past mistakes will be forgiven and forgotten."

"To tell you the truth, I don't know if I will see tomorrow."

"Every tomorrow in human life has its own problems. The only certainty is death. But for those who believe that beyond death there is life, it is important to take the middle path."

I quietly pondered what Père said and tried to accept the tempting possibility. I was touched by his concern, but still restless.

"Père, I don't know how to accept the situation."

"As I said, take the middle path. There is no need for hesitation."

"That's right, love," Anna said.

I looked at Anna. While uttering her encouraging words, the shadow of an omen crossed her face. Her eyes clouded with tears and she had difficulty hiding her sadness over my desperate situation. Anna knew me well. She even knew the identities of the men I slept with. She also knew about my love for Maslov.

319

I told Père and Soeur of my restlessness, "Bouchardon said I'd never see Maslov again. Can you imagine what that means to me? It is the end of the world." I burst into tears and howled until my lungs hurt.

Chapter One Hundred and Twenty-one

I had another dream about being with Maslov, the last one.

I didn't recognize the location of the dream. It was no longer Boroboedoer, nor my childhood home in Leeuwarden. In that dream I walked into a sitting room on a cloud. Around me everything was red: red chairs, red table, red walls, even Maslov and I were red.

In some Eastern traditions, the color red symbolized courage and bravery, while in the West it signified blood, murder, massacre, or sacrifice. When I awoke, I fell into meditative thinking. Was I close to my death? A shiver ran the length of my spine.

In the morning when Soeur, another nun, and Père came to see me, she asked, "What did you dream of?"

I told her of my dream. "It was brief. Very brief. In the red chamber, Maslov took me in his arms, and we made passionate love, so passionate that at reaching orgasm, which was excessively noisy, I found myself drenched in Maslov's semen.

"Then I recited for Maslov a poem by Arthur Rimbaud I had read in Ambarawa in real life, which belonged to René the hermit who lived on the slope of Mount Oengaran. It was an assemblage of two poems, 'Song of the Highest Tower' and 'Morning of Drunkenness.'

O may it come, the time of love,
The time we'd be enamored of.
Now is the time of the *Assassins*.

"That was my dream," I said to the threesome on the other side of the grate. "When I woke up, I fell out of bed."

They were silent.

"Don't tell me it was a bad dream. I can make my own conclusion. I know France will make me a sacrificial lamb. France will kill me."

Bouchardon appeared. At seeing him, I screamed hysterically. "France will kill me. France will kill me. I know."

Bouchardon retreated from the door.

Père tried to calm me. "Take heart, my child. We still have the court to administer justice for you."

Shortly after, Clunet joined us. He said, "I will win your case in court."

I was pessimistic and said to all of them, including Anna, "I read a quotation that said, when people seek justice in court, they will find injustice."

"Seek God's way in prayer," said Père.

Chapter One Hundred and Twenty-two

Bouchardon submitted my case to Prosecutor André Mornet, a lieutenant in the French military, and on June 24, 1917, I was taken to the Palais de Justice.

A large crowd gathered outside the building. They wanted to see me, who the press labeled a World War I sex symbol.

I wore a blue outfit, complete with a wide brimmed hat that complemented my complexion. Since it was summer, I wore light cotton gloves. Flanked by two guards, I walked toward the defendant's seat.

From there I noticed two people study me, trying to look unconcerned from their respective spots. One was Clunet, the first man I went to bed with in France, and the other was Henri "Robert" de Marguérie, an official in France's Ministry of Foreign Affairs, who was my lover on several occasions.

Then I saw Père and Soeur, as well as Anna who gave me a look filled with concern and sadness.

The judge opened the session, which was conducted *in camera* to avoid a breach in security. The judge was Albert-Ernest Somprou, a lieutenant colonel who nervously tugged at his trousers before taking a seat.

Even after a glance, I knew Bouchardon was lying when he said that the judge and the prosecutor were men of strong faith. The way Somprou pulled at his trousers suggested he was a man unfaithful to his wife. I had no doubt that he liked other amusements. The solemn appearance aided by the garb could not fool me. In fact, it nauseated me. I always said, "They look formidable like prophets, but behave like pigs."

Somprou was serene, unlike the forbidding chief prosecuting attorney, Lieutenant André Mornet, who resembled an orangutan the way his thick moustache and beard hid his mouth.

It was Somprou who proposed the court be conducted *in camera* and Mornet accepted the suggestion.

Pointing his finger at me, Mornet presented his case. "The case of this prostitute has already been made clear. During interrogation in Saint-Lazare, the defendant was unable to deny the evidence of the radio communication that implicates her and proves her treason to France for the benefit of Germany. She therefore deserves the death penalty. I put it to the court that the defendant has used her body and her sexuality, which fits the category of nymphomania, to elicit France's secrets from her admirers and hand them over to France's enemy. For that reason, I move that this prostitute be sentenced to death."

I was frightened into silence.

Mornet stood and strutted like a champion. He derided witnesses for the defense and dismissed them as undignified. He questioned Marguérie, who appeared as a defense witness. "Is it true that you have known this prostitute, Mata Hari, for over ten years, and did you have sexual relationships with her during those years?"

Marguérie answered firmly, "I refuse to answer questions if this court is made into a stage to taint people's characters."

The judge asked Mornet to moderate his language.

After Mornet rephrased his question, Marguérie answered, "That is correct. I respect this lady."

"When was your last encounter with Mata Hari?"

Marguérie replied with another question, "In what manner?"

"Do not pretend to be innocent," Mornet said. "I repeat my question. When was your last encounter with Mata Hari?"

Marguérie stood his ground. "And I ask, what do you mean by encounter?"

"I refer to an encounter during which military conflict was discussed in bed."

"That did not happen."

"Please tell us, what you discussed when you both were in bed."

"As someone who is not an expert on artistic matters, I found her discourse on art very pleasant indeed."

"Are you trying to tell the court that your conversation with Mata Hari in bed was only about art?"

"Yes, that's correct."

The judge silenced the laughter that ensued and said to Marguérie, "Please continue."

"Very well, your honor. I am a very busy man, who doesn't understand much about art. What I've found very refreshing about my friendship with Mata Hari is her broad knowledge about the subject. She also has an incredible mastery of the philosophy of beauty, aesthetics, and the exotic culture of the Dutch East Indies, to which she always refers as Indonesia. And of course I've enjoyed her mastery of the art of the boudoir."

Laughter again filled the room.

Then Mornet said, "You want to convince the court that Mata Hari has been righteous in her profession?"

"I believe she has," replies Marguérie.

That answer caused Mornet's face to shrivel.

I had a quiet respect for Marguérie, especially when, at the end of his cross-examination with Mornet, Marguérie rose and nodded at me. His gesture gave me such comfort.

I prayed that the judge had the wisdom to listen carefully to the witness. Maybe I still had reasons to hope.

What would the verdict be?

I waited.

Chapter One Hundred and Twenty-three

Hoping for my acquittal was a futile exercise. In fact, I suspected there was an unsaid agreement between the prosecutor and the judge to convict me.

In the Military Court where I was tried, a narrative infused with legal power was prepared, and said that I had committed treason and deserved to be sentenced to death.

"I cannot accept that," I screamed. "I admit to being a prostitute. I admit to being a performer of exotic dances. I admit to being a spy. But I deny being a traitor. There is no basis for that accusation."

No one could help me.

The judge read his verdict. I was sentenced to death. Still to be decided was the execution date. The court also agreed that I must pay all the costs of the trial.

When would the execution be?

I didn't know.

Not knowing made day-to-day life increasingly unbearable. I fell into a deep depression.

When a photographer came to take my picture, my intuition told me that it wouldn't be much longer. I had no doubt that on those photographs I looked much older than I actually was. Père and Soeur still faithfully came to my cell. Exhorting me to pray, they comforted me. After the verdict, Anna visited almost every day. But she didn't say much any more. She just took notes of everything I wanted her to do after my death. When I asked Anna to look after my things, her answer heartened me. "Your things, even the smallest items, will remain the possessions of the famous Mata Hari. I will take care of them and make sure the name Mata Hari continues to shine, love. As long as *matahari* shines, Mata Hari will be remembered."

Epilogue

Mata Hari was taken to Bois de Vincennes, on the outskirts of Paris, for execution by a firing squad.

Even those who had misgivings about her showed their sympathy.

That morning, Père, Soeur, Anna, and Clunet, went with her to the forest to witness the execution.

Before they left, Père Arbaux asked Mata Hari to pray together, and on arrival at the execution site he again asked her to pray so that Mata Hari's soul would unite with those of the saints residing in God's house.

In his prayers Père uttered, "And I will dwell in the house of the Lord forever."

An officer of the firing squad stepped forward to tie a piece of black cloth around Mata Hari's head to cover her eyes, as was done to those sentenced to death, but she refused.

"I want to see how I am shot to death. I will not have any parts of me covered. I want to take off my clothes so my body will be free of all burdens of Western civilization, which is entirely false and artificial." Without hesitation or embarrassment, Mata Hari removed her clothes and stood completely naked.

The firing squad was visibly tense and awkward. Mata Hari said, "Naked I came from my mother's womb, and naked I will depart."

The squad commander asked, "Are you ready?"

"Yes," Mata Hari replied. "Oh, but I nearly forgot. If I may, I have one request."

"Go ahead and ask."

"I want to kiss Père."

Père was disconcerted and unsure at the request. Fear flitted across his face. But when the commander instructed him to comply, Père obliged. He approached Mata Hari and halted in front of her. Trembling, he closed his eyes.

Mata Hari held him in a tight embrace and gave him a long, passionate kiss.

When she finally pulled herself away, Mata Hari said, "I don't understand why you chose a celibate life, wasting your sexual ability. Isn't sexuality also a gift of God? By kissing you I wanted to tell you, being created a man and a woman is a beautiful gift. We can enjoy sex as a natural heavenly process. Don't you agree, Père?"

Père did not respond. He made a sign of the cross and mumbled a prayer.

"Remember me, Père," Mata Hari said, "I am the woman who kissed you with all sincerity. Remember me as a human being who believes that love and sexual passion are gifts from God."

Mata Hari raised her right hand to signal the firing squad. "All done, gentlemen," she said. "Please fire. I have chosen to die as a woman. Thank you, God."

Mata Hari died on October 15, 1917, with God's name on her lips.

Notes

All Bible quotations from the New International Version ©1984

Prologue
Aufklärung: Age of Enlightenment.

Chapter One
Indonesien: Oder die Inseln des Malayischen archipel: Indonesia: Or the Islands of the Malay Archipelago, Volumes 1–5, first published in 1884.
Natya: Dance.
Boroboedoer: New spelling, Borobudur.
Vadim Maslov: Also known as Vladimir de Masloff.

Chapter Two
's Gravenhage: Also known as Den Haag, or in English, The Hague.
Batavia: Now known as Jakarta.
"But I want you to realize…": 1 Corinthians 11:3
"Nevertheless, in the Lord…": 1 Corinthians 11:11–12

Chapter Three
Shiva, King of the Dancers: Now displayed in Hall 1 Rijksmuseum.
Celebes: Now known as Sulawesi.

Speculaas: a traditional short-crust cookie baked for St Nicholas' feast day on December 5.

"I studied music several years ago…": Marius Hendrik van 't Kruys, composer, conductor, working in Rotterdam, Groningen, graduate of Koninklijk Haagsche Muziekschool, 1897.

Chapter Four
Atjeh: New spelling, Aceh.
Kebenaran bisa direka melalui pembenaran: You can justify anything and turn it into the truth.
Joost van den Vondel: Dutch poet and playwright, who wrote in Sophocles style and known as Holland's answer to Shakespeare.
Schouwburg: A theater building.

Chapter Five
Zeedijk: District in Amsterdam where prostitutes walked the curbs wearing next to nothing.

Chapter Six
"What he meant…": In Dutch, "the walled sea" is Walletje, another name for Zeedijk, which means sea walls, or popularly known as "Rode Lamp" meaning red light, the area in Amsterdam where prostitutes sell their services.

Chapter Seven
Mount Soembing: New spelling, Mount Sumbing.
Mount Merbaboe-Merapi: New spelling, Mount Merbabu-Merapi.

Chapter Eight
Beierlaan: Now Jalan Kesatriaan, in the suburb of Matraman.
Meester Cornelis: Now Jatinegara.
Oengaran: New spelling, Ungaran.
Willem I Railway Station: Now a railway museum, called Museum Kereta api Ambarawa.
Biefstuk: Beefsteak.
Kakoes: New spelling, kakus.

Chapter Nine
Bodjong: Now Jalan Pemuda.
Ars longa vita brevis: Art is long, life is short.
"Nightwatch": Known in Dutch as "De Nachtwacht," the painting's real
    name is "Het korporaalschap van kapitein Frans Banning Cocq en
    luitenant Willem van Ruytenburch."
"The Jewish Bride": Known in Dutch as "Het Joodse bruidje."

Chapter Ten
"Bathsheba at Her Bath": Known in Dutch as "Het toilet van Bathseba,"
    now in Rijksmuseum Hall 207.
Soerakarta: New spelling, Surakarta.

Chapter Twelve
…Protestant church in Heerenstraat: Now Jalan Letjen Soeprapto, once
    also called Jalan Mpu Tantular.
Meester Cornelis Pijnacker Hordijk: Governor General from 1888–
    1893.

Chapter Fourteen
Jogjakarta: Also known as Yogyakarta.
Mbah Koeng: New spelling, Mbah Kung.
Sri Sultan Hamengkoeboewono: New spelling, Sri Sultan
    Hamengkubuwono

Chapter Fifteen
Mendoet: New spelling, Mendut.
Kesoeroepan: New spelling, *kesurupan.*

Chapter Sixteen
Jogja: Diminutive form of Jogjakarta.
The Dutch East India Company: Known in Dutch as *Vereenigde Oost-*
    Indische Compagnie.

Chapter Eighteen
Rimbaud: Arthur Rimbaud, exponent of Symbolism in French literature, 1854–1891. His books are *Le Bateau Ivre* (The Drunken Boat, 1873) and *Les Illuminations* (Illuminations, 1895).

Chapter Twenty-two
"Devotions": From *Illuminations and Other Prose Poems* by Arthur Rimbaud, translated by Louise Varèse (NY: New Directions Publishing, 1946, 1957).

Chapter Twenty-three
Djoernatan: New spelling, Jurnatan.
Bodjong: New spelling, Bojong.
Benedenstad: In Javanese, "grejo Blenduk." Now known as *Gereja Protestan di Indonesia bagian Barat* (GPIB), or the Protestant Church in Western Indonesia.

Chapter Twenty-seven
"Song of the Highest Tower": From *A Season in Hell* and *The Drunken Boat* by Arthur Rimbaud, translated by Louise Varèse (NY: New Directions Publishing, 1961).
"Morning of Drunkenness": From *Illuminations*.

Chapter Twenty-eight
Njo: New spelling, Nyo.

Chapter Thirty
Tjiliwoeng: New spelling, Ciliwung.
Waterlooplein: Now Lapangan Banteng.
De Ster van het Oosten: Now the Kimia Farma Building.
Lady Chapel: A chapel attached to a cathedral devoted to the Virgin Mary.
Snouck Hurgronje: A twenty-three-year-old scholar of Muslim literature, who also had the Muslim name, Abdul Gaffar.
Protestant Pastor Hoëvell: Minister for Secretary of the State.

House of Representatives: The lower chamber in Dutch Parliament.

Sociëteit de Harmonie: Formerly on the corner of Rijswijk (now Jalan Veteran) and Rijswijkstraat (now Jalan Majapahit).

Batavia's 280th anniversary: According to Dutch documents, the date of the fall of Iacatra into the hands of the Dutch.

Chapter Thirty-one

Hotel des Indes: On the corner of Gang Chaulan (now Jalan Hasyim Asyari) and Molenvliet (now Jalan Gajah Mada). Demolished in 1971 and in its place stands the Duta Merlin building.

Kramat Boender: New spelling, Kramat Bunder.

Chapter Thirty-three

Buitenzorg: Now known as Bogor.

Chapter Thirty-four

…hold them fast: Proverbs 5:22.

…lion statue: Monument commemorating Dutch victory over Napoleon in Waterloo, Belgium in 1815, demolished by the Japanese during WW II.

Chapter Thirty-five

St. Louisa de Marillac: A noblewoman (1591–1660) who left her sumptuous home to serve the poor. Co-founder with St. Vincent de Paul of the Daughters of Charity.

Chapter Thirty-six

Rooseboom: Major General Willem Rooseboom (1842–1920), appointed the sixty-first governor general in 1899.

Willemskerk: Now *Gereja Protestan di Indonesia bagian Barat Immanuel*, opposite Gambir Station.

All Saints Church: Anglican Church near Taman Tugu Tani.

St. Hovhanneskerk: Now part of BI courtyard on the corner of Mohammad Husni Thamrin and Budi Kemuliaan streets, after the demolition in 1964.

Schouwburg: Now Gedung Kesenian Jakarta.

Chapter Thirty-seven
...last two hundred years: The building was demolished in 1985 during the New Order era.

Menado: New spelling, Manado.

Chapter Thirty-eight
Pasar Baroe: New spelling, Pasar Baru.

Gioeng: New spelling, *giung*.

Chapter Thirty-nine
Madame Bovary: A novel by Gustave Flaubert, published in 1857.

Chapter Forty-one
Bandoeng: New spelling, Bandung.

Soekabumi: New spelling, Sukabumi.

Tjiandjoer: New spelling, Cianjur.

Stamboel: New spelling, *stambul*.

Grand National Hotel: Now the head office of Perusahaan Jawatan Kereta Api, or Indonesian State Railways, Java.

Sociëteit Concordia: Now Gedung Merdeka.

Bragaweg: Now Jalan Braga.

Kedoe: New spelling, Kedu.

Kebon Radja: New spelling, Kebon Raja.

Chapter Forty-three
Koelanter: New spelling, *kulanter*.

Beboeka: New spelling, *bebuka*.

Ketoek tiloe: New spelling, *ketuk tilu*.

Chapter Forty-nine
Ida Sang Hyang Widhi Wasa: The One Supreme God of Hindu Dharma, with His three manifestations known as Brahma the Creator, Wisnu the Preserver, and Shiwa the Transformer.

Chapter Fifty-three
Koealasimpang: New spelling, Kualasimpang.

Chapter Fifty-four
Katjang merah: New spelling, *kacang merah*.
Tjokelat: New spelling, *cokolat*.
STOVIA: *School tot Opleiding van Indische Artsen*, then a well-known school of medicine. Now Gedung Kebangkitan Nasional.
Pakoe Alam: New spelling, Paku Alam
Fort de Kock: Now Bukittinggi.

Chapter Fifty-five
Koningsplein: Now Lapangan Merdeka.
Passar Baroe: New spelling, Passar Baru.
Nawawi Gafar Soetan Ma'amur: New spelling, Nawawi Gafar Sutan Ma'amur.

Chapter Fifty-seven
...along the roads in Weltevreden: Now the area between Lapangan Merdeka dan Lapangan Banteng.
... nos et mutamur in illis: The times change, and we change with them.

Chapter Sixty
Ngawi: A small town near Madiun, where the Dutch had built the most feared military prison.
Bubakan: A civilian prison located in Bubakan, Semarang. In its place is a shopping complex.

Chapter Sixty-one
...suburb of Kota Tai: Now known as Kota, between the railway station and Pinangsia, formerly the location of a Dutch fort.
Sam Kauw It Kauw: A combination of three religions adhered to by the Chinese: Taoism, Buddhism, and Confucianism.
Pintoe: New spelling, Pintu.
Piéta: Depicting Mary holding Jesus' lifeless body across her knees.

Chapter Sixty-two
Groote Klooster: Now Santa Maria Convent.
Noordwijk: Now Jalan Juanda.

Chapter Sixty-six
...main public library: *Bibliotheek Bataviaasch Genootschap van Kunsten en Wetenschap*, now Perpustakaan Museum Nasional.

Chapter Sixty-seven
Kedoengdjati: New spelling, Kedungjati.

Chapter Sixty-eight
Hotel Toegoe: New spelling, Tugu. Now Jakarta Bank.
Toegoesche: New spelling, Tugusche.
Exhibition for Arts and Crafts building: Now Tugu Railway Station.
Kyai Widjojodaroe: New spelling. Kyai Wijoyodaru.
Oedik-oedik: New spelling, *udik-udik*.
Djedjak banon: New spelling, *jejak banon*.
Pakoe Alam: New spelling, Paku Alam.

Chapter Seventy-two
Soematera: Now known as Sumatra.
Celebes: Now known as Sulawesi.

Chapter Seventy-four
Lampoeng: New spelling, Lampung.

Chapter Seventy-six
Madoera: New spelling, Madura.

Chapter Eighty-one
Prime Minister Aristide Briand: Granted the Nobel Prize for Peace in 1926.

Chapter Eighty-seven
Soemba: New spelling, Sumba.

Chapter One Hundred and Four
Banda Gertrude: During World War II the name Banda Gertrude, with a number of aliases Banda MacLeod, Wilhelmina Vandereen, and Margarida Zelle among others, was known as an Indonesian spy under the Allies when the US and the Allies were fighting Japan.

Chapter One Hundred and Eleven
3,500 pesetas: Approximately US$700.